A TALENT
FOR MURDER

A TALENT FOR MURDER

A Novel

PETER SWANSON

WILLIAM MORROW
An Imprint of HarperCollinsPublishers

HarperCollins books may be purchased for educational, business, or sales promotional use. For information, please email the Special Markets Department at SPsales@harpercollins.com.

FIRST EDITION

Designed by Kyle O'Brien

Library of Congress Cataloging-in-Publication Data has been applied for.

ISBN 978-0-06-320503-1 (hardcover)
ISBN 978-0-06-335901-7 (international edition)

24 25 26 27 28 LBC 5 4 3 2 1

To the Steinback family,
So much talent, none for murder

Someone is dead.
Even the trees know it.

—Anne Sexton, "Lament"

A TALENT
FOR MURDER

JOSIE

Even though Josie Nixon had graduated from college and gotten married and knew how to hang curtains and had opened a retirement account, going to this conference still felt like the most grown-up thing she had ever done. Something about being sent somewhere for your work, about being paid to travel, about attending a professional event that had an acronym, just seemed so fucking adult.

After checking in at the long table in the student union building of Shepaug University, accidentally standing in the A–M line instead of the N–Z, Josie was given a cool tote bag with the AEC logo on it. It was white canvas, designed to look as though it were paint-splattered. She took the bag with her to one of the vinyl couches along the side wall and sat down. Inside the bag was her name badge, plus a lanyard to hang it on, and the program for the three-day-event. There was also a bottle of water, a bag of locally made potato chips, and a chocolate bar, also from a local company. She loved free stuff, and all her loot made her inexplicably happy. After snapping a picture on her phone of the other teachers checking in, she sent a text to Travis, even though he'd already told her that he didn't need a play-by-play of her weekend. He wanted her to feel independent, do whatever she wanted, but she did want him to know she'd arrived safe. She'd have felt that way if the roles were reversed. He texted her back right away, one red heart and one black.

She studied the program even though she'd already read it online, pre-picking the workshops and panels she hoped to attend. What was cool about the Art Educator Conference was that even though it had a pedagogical bent, many of the workshops were simply art instruction.

She was most excited for collage, and for the puppet-making workshop. Two teachers wandered over and asked if they could share the couch. She slid along and they plopped down next to her, a man and woman, the man with a gray ponytail and the woman tall and fairly ravishing. Together they looked at the program. They were clearly colleagues, they'd been to this conference before, and they were making lots of jokes about the content. When the man read the name of the puppet workshop out loud, the woman said, "Hard pass."

When Brian, her supervisor, had told her that she'd been approved to attend this conference, she'd let him know it was going to be her first work trip. "Be prepared," he'd said, "teachers are the worst at conferences, like poorly behaved children. They do things they'd never let their own students do."

Suddenly feeling awkward, Josie stood up from the couch and wandered through the student union. It seemed like the vast majority of attendees had come in pairs or small groups. And they were more conservatively dressed than she thought they'd be, for art teachers. Lots of tucked-in shirts on the men and denim skirts on the women. She was wearing her oldest jean jacket over a lace-up burgundy dress. She had on her oxblood lipstick and her black pendant necklace, and she suddenly felt a little bit out of place, like the new kid in school who wore the worst possible outfit on day one. Telling herself it didn't matter, she made her way across the campus, its lawns yellow from the dry summer, to the dormitory where all the attendees were going to be staying. It was an ugly concrete building that looked more like a chain hotel next to an Outback restaurant than a dormitory at a New England college. In the downstairs lobby there was another check-in desk. She gave her name and they handed her a piece of paper that listed her room number and the combination that would open the door. Her room was on the sixth floor. She took the elevator, crushed in by another group of teachers, who were talking about a restaurant in town that was supposed to be great, then found her room. It was about what she'd expected: a single bed; concrete walls that had been painted white; bathroom down the hall. What she hadn't expected was the sliding glass doors that led to a shallow balcony. She hated heights—just the existence of an open balcony made her head feel dizzy and her heart thud. At least the room seemed to have air-conditioning, a noisy vent pushing in stale cool air. She told herself it was going to be an amazing weekend, even if she didn't make friends, then unpacked her rolling suitcase, laying out possible outfits for the next three days.

The following day she reminded herself that things were still great, even though she continued to feel alienated from her fellow teachers. Not surprisingly, the puppet workshop was absolutely amazing. She'd created a witchy-looking puppet in about fifteen minutes, using swatches of fleece fabric and string, and she couldn't wait to try it out with her middle schoolers during the next year. She hadn't been a huge fan of the teaching-methods panel but loved the found-object printmaking class, where they'd all been ushered outside to look for things to make prints with. She'd found an old plastic spork, plus some gingko leaves, and made a print that was now pinned to her dormitory-room wall.

On the Saturday night of the conference Josie drank way too much wine at the cocktail hour and found herself explaining polyamory to a group of art teachers from Sudbury in Massachusetts.

"So, are there rules, or simply no rules at all?" one of the female teachers, a young woman in paint-splattered jeans and an oxford shirt, asked Josie.

"There might be with real-deal polyamories, like the ones who get together for meetings and stuff. For Travis and me it's more like, we know that we're in love and that we're going to be together forever, so why not have the occasional hookup? Why lose that exciting part of life, you know?"

"And you tell one another?"

"Yes," Josie said. "That actually *is* a rule. No hidden flings. It has to be all out in the open."

"And what would happen in one of you fell in love with someone else?" This was an older man with a white goatee who leaned in very close when he spoke to someone.

"But isn't falling in love with someone else a risk for everyone in a marriage?"

"Sure. But I'd say that you're increasing the risk by taking your clothes off with other people."

Josie took a sip of her wine, spilling some down her front because her glass was fuller than she had remembered. Had someone just bought her a new drink? "Sure, absolutely," she said. "It's a risk, but the way I see it is that I'm so in love with my husband that I'm just not worried about it. And if it did become an issue, then I guess we would deal with it. Together."

"How often do you guys have flings?" This was from the woman in the oxford, and now she was leaning forward as well.

"So that's the thing. This is all more of a theory right now than an actuality. We live in upstate New York—not exactly swinger central."

"I thought you lived in Woodstock."

"We do. It's more Birkenstocks and crystal deodorants than young polys."

"So you're only interested in other young people, which means I'm out of the running," the older guy said, then laughed like he'd made an outrageous joke.

"I don't know who I might be interested in. I guess I'll know it when I meet them."

"So, is this trip . . . ?"

"Travis gave me the go-ahead, and I'd be up for it, but like I said, it's not just with anyone. I mean, I want to be into it."

Afterward, when Josie was alone again, sitting on another stiff vinyl couch, looking at the program for the hundredth time, she went over the conversation with the three Massachusetts teachers and felt a weird sense of shame. It had been okay at the time, but now she felt dirty, remembering the way they looked at her, and imagining that they would trot out the conversation as a funny story from the convention. That weird-looking girl who was trying to fuck someone. She stared at the program without seeing the words and told herself that it didn't matter. It had been her truth and they could make fun of it if they wanted. And she *was* having a good time at this convention, even though it was now clear that she wasn't going to find someone to play with in quite the way she hoped. And now it was early in the evening and she was only thinking about the print she'd made that day and how excited she was about getting back to her dorm room and looking at it again. She hadn't felt that way about a piece of her own art for a long time.

"Do you mind if I sit next to you?" It was an older man, slender and tall, holding a bottle of beer.

"Oh sure," Josie said. "Sit down."

He sighed as he sat, as though his body hurt. Or maybe he was just happy to be away from the throng, like Josie was. For a moment she didn't think he was going to speak to her, but he turned and said, "Sorry if this sounds creepy, but I was happy to see you sitting alone. I spotted you yesterday and was hoping we'd meet."

"Just a little creepy," Josie said, but then she smiled to let him know she was only kidding.

Later, when they were naked in her dorm room, awkwardly entwined in the single bed, she had what felt like an out-of-body experience, the room shimmering with dark energy, her soul, or something that felt like her soul, floating a little above her body. The encounter with the man had started off kind of hot, him throwing her down on the bed, almost panting with sexual excitement. But then something had gone wrong. She'd climbed on top of him and felt him go instantly soft. Things had worked out in the end, her on her side, him behind her using his hands to make her come. Still floating a little above herself, she imagined her conversation with Travis, her telling him all about the encounter, about how she'd enjoyed herself, but maybe not quite as much as she'd been enjoying using the waffle maker at the breakfast buffet.

"Which was better?" he asked her in her mind.

"Waffle maker."

She laughed in her thoughts and she must have laughed out loud as well, because the man said, "What's funny?" and then she was back down inside her body.

"Nothing," she said.

"Sorry if I was . . ."

"No, it was great."

And then they were talking, and that part was actually interesting. She told him she thought he was afraid of sexually free women, and he laughed and said he probably was. And then he'd asked her what *she* was afraid of, and she told him how scared she was of heights.

"These rooms have balconies, you know," he said.

"Like that wasn't the absolutely first thing I fucking noticed when I walked in here."

She was still drunk, plus she'd eaten an edible an hour earlier, and somehow he talked her into stepping outside on the balcony in order to face her fears. They were both naked out there, the sky swarming with stars, their bodies drying in the cool night air. It was actually good—exciting, really—maybe only because it was dark and she couldn't actually see how high up they were, or maybe it was because she was now having the kind of experience that she thought she might have on this trip. Something new, and a little dangerous. She felt alive, but she also felt excited that the next day she would be returning home. It was time. And now she had new ideas for her classroom, plus she couldn't wait to see Travis, tell him all about her weekend. They hadn't spoken that day at all. Suddenly she realized just how much she missed him.

And that was when she was thrown off the balcony.

PART 1

HALF WINTER, HALF SPRING

CHAPTER 1

They'd met the way couples met nowadays, online, paired up because they were both self-proclaimed book nerds, both seeking a stable monogamous relationship without kids. He'd been married before, just after college, for three years. It had been an amicable divorce (according to Alan) and there hadn't been any children. He said he had no idea what his ex-wife was even doing with her life now—they'd lost touch completely.

Alan and Martha, after a few introductory texts, had met for dinner, Alan driving to Portsmouth from his home outside of Scarborough in Maine. The best part about dinner that night—besides the truffle fries—was that there were no awkward silences. Alan was chatty, and funny, and unselfconscious. Martha didn't exactly feel romantic stirrings, but she did have fun. And later that night she told herself that having fun while eating in a restaurant with a strange man was no small thing. She hadn't dated anyone in more than ten years. And she hadn't had sex for five years, not since a brief and awkward coupling at her fifteen-year college reunion. So she told herself to say yes to Alan Peralta, yes to further dinner dates, yes to sex if that was something he was interested in, yes to being in a relationship with him.

And that was what she did. She kept saying yes. It wasn't hard to do. Alan was very sweet, easy to be with. Yeah, he made a lot of dumb jokes, but he knew they were dumb. And when they eventually got around to having sex, that part was nice, too. She wasn't exactly attracted to Alan, who was raw and bony with deep-set eyes, but he had a grace about him, and at least he didn't want to do anything strange in bed, except for some occasional dirty talk whispered into her ear.

Martha would have been happy to simply stay in a committed relationship, but Alan's mother was a strict Catholic, *and* the most important person in Alan's life, so during a weekend away to Kennewick on the southern shore of Maine, Alan lowered himself to a knee while they were on a cliffside walk and asked Martha to marry him. It was a moment that Martha had long believed would never happen to her, any kind of proposal, let alone such an old-fashioned one, and she had been filled with a surge of gratitude and love that propelled her to tell him yes right away. Toward the end of the trip, however, Alan said that he'd noticed she'd been quieter since the proposal, and she'd had to admit that he was right.

"Maybe it feels too sudden," she said. "Give me one week."

As it happened, Alan was traveling for the next week and Martha spent that time thinking about her decision. She did love him, she believed, although she wondered if she was truly *in* love with him. He had never really raised her pulse. And she had never yearned for him when he was away. But she realized that those two negatives, even the phrasing of them, were clichés about romantic love, and not necessarily based in reality. She loved his company. They could talk to one another. He smelled nice. And one thing she kept coming back to was a moment when they had first been casually dating, an evening in Portsmouth, when they were taking a stroll after dinner out. They'd been walking side by side along a dark sidewalk. It wasn't raining, but it had rained all day and there were still puddles on the streets, and the occasional drip of water from gutters and trees. At one point during the walk they approached a section of the sidewalk where water was still falling in a steady flow from a large hotel awning. Without slowing down Alan had slid his hand around Martha's waist and guided her smoothly away from the dripping water. Gallantry, but with the grace of a dance move, and Martha still remembered the tiny shiver that had coursed through her body when he'd touched her.

And maybe that was more important than yearning, just having someone looking out for you in small ways. Yearning never lasted anyway. Kindness did.

Martha said yes to Alan when he returned from his trip. She told herself she wouldn't be completely giving up her independent life. Alan traveled so much for work that she'd have plenty of time alone.

They honeymooned in London, Alan making a list of pubs he wanted to visit (he had a passion for beer), and Martha was happy to go along. Toward the end of that trip they'd visited an elegant Victorian pub during a rainy afternoon, Martha studying her Fodor's travel guide while Alan leaned against the elaborate bar chatting with the bartender. She watched him, his loud American voice at odds with the quiet man behind the bar, noting the way that Alan won over the reluctant Brit, who was now smiling and giving Alan tastes of the different beers they had on cask. It was at this moment that Martha had two competing thoughts. One, that she'd married a nice man. And, two, that he was a complete and utter stranger to her. She realized she didn't really know him any better now than she had after that first date, when she'd returned home to her two-bedroom house in Portsmouth and decided that if Alan wanted to see her again, she'd agree.

A year later, and there were some days Martha never thought of her husband. And some days he was all she seemed to think about.

It was natural, she supposed. Even though she was thirty-nine she was still a newlywed, married less than a year. She actually hated the word "newlywed," or hated other people saying it, like Donna from the library, who called her "the newlywed" in a wink-wink kind of way for about six months after she and Alan were married. Martha preferred the phrase "newly married," but however you said it, that was what she was, a newly wedded person, with all that that implied.

On the days she didn't think much about him it was because of how seamlessly he'd slid into her life. Alan was a careful and predictable man, and Martha had a careful and predictable life. On the days she thought about him, it was because there was something inexplicable about his presence, something that nagged at her. Back in high school and all through college Martha had kept a journal that was entirely made up of passages from books she loved, and poems that she would copy out in her tight cursive handwriting. She spent hours transcribing in her journal, and every once in a while she would come across a word, a word she knew well, that would suddenly not make any sense. She'd be convinced it was spelled wrong, or completely made-up by the poet or author. This never happened with a word like "crepuscular," but always with a simple word like "apron." Suddenly she'd be staring at it and the word would make absolutely no sense. That was what Alan was like, a plain even-tempered man who sometimes made no sense.

He was away right now, on a business trip to Denver. She thought of them as business trips, but that implied breakfast meetings and decision-making and men and women in suits. Alan was really a traveling salesman, maybe the last traveling salesman in the modern world, Martha sometimes thought. He did wear suits when he went to conventions, but that was so he could wear one of his ties that were for sale. He sold novelty clothing items at teachers' conferences. Not just ties, but also buttons, and silk scarves for the female teachers. He sold T-shirts as well, and vests. Most of what he sold was math- and science-related. Ties decorated with the periodic table, buttons that celebrated Pi Day. Even though he never brought his merchandise home—he owned a storage unit in Newington—she'd seen a bunch of it just a month ago when she'd gone to visit him at a local high school math teachers' conference. He'd been wearing his uniform—the dark pants, the white shirt—

but he'd also been wearing suspenders filled up with funny buttons, and a red tie with the times table on it. Before they'd gone to lunch, she watched him sell a young female teacher a T-shirt that read MATH TEACHERS AREN'T MEAN. THEY'RE ABOVE AVERAGE.

Maybe she thought more about him when he was away. No, she definitely did. Jean, one of the library regulars, was talking to her about *Downton Abbey*, and Martha, who had been thinking of Alan, was suddenly aware that she'd been asked a question and couldn't remember what it was.

"Sorry, Jean, what?" Martha was behind the desk, slowly working her way through a pile of returned books, and Jean's head bobbed on the other side of the desktop computer.

"Do you think that someone will write a *Downton Abbey* novel?"

Jean had asked Martha that before. "If there's money in it, then I suspect someone will do it."

"*You* should do it, Martha." Jean was apparently under the impression that because Martha read so much, she would also be able to write a publishable book.

"I should, shouldn't I?" she said to Jean. "Make a fortune. Leave this library for good."

"Oh, Martha." Jean smiled. She wore no makeup except for lipstick and some of it was on her right canine. Martha decided not to tell her.

Alan was coming home from Denver that night, a flight that was getting in around midnight. Maybe that was why she was thinking about him so much today. When he was around, he was simply there, blending into the well-worn furniture of their cozy house. But during his trips away, and immediately upon his return, he loomed large in her mind.

She wondered why that was, and suspected it had something to do with what had happened when—a few trips ago—he'd returned from Connecticut. She'd been standing at the bedroom window after hearing his car pull onto their pebble drive. It was a little before dusk, the light with that magical glow that clarifies everything it touches, and she could see Alan's face as he got out of the driver's side and went around to the back of his Hyundai to retrieve his luggage. He was tall and angular but moved with a languid elegance—it was what most attracted Martha to him initially. There was a grace about him that didn't fit his rather studious face, gaunt almost, with large eyes. But that night, watching from her window, it was like she'd never seen him before. His face had an almost cold, ruthless look to it. She told herself she was seeing him from a distance, and that he was tired, but still, it was alarming to witness an expression on his face that she felt she'd never seen before. After gathering his luggage and locking his car, he then stood for a moment looking toward the sunset, his jaw slack, his eyes empty and uncaring. Then she watched him take a deep breath, swelling his chest. He shook his head and his expression changed, back to the vacuous sweetness of the Alan she knew. He even smiled, as though he were willfully transforming himself. Then he headed indoors.

She came down the stairs to meet him, and he greeted her the way he always did. A huge grin, some corny joke such as, "Honey, I'm home," or "Was that your boyfriend I saw going out the back?" and then they hugged. Sometimes upon his return he'd used the phrase, "Hello, family." It struck her as overly sentimental, although a part of her was moved by the sentiment.

But that moment from the summer, that view of his unguarded self outside of their house, had stayed with her. She forgot it when he was around, but often thought of it when he was on a trip, and almost always thought of it on the days he returned.

The last hour at the library went fast. One of her favorite patrons, Mr. MacNeice, who came in at least twice a week, had asked her for recommendations of woman authors he hadn't read yet. She'd mentioned a few of her favorites—Edith Wharton, George Eliot, Joan Didion—but he told her he wanted young, contemporary writers. Mr. MacNeice (Martha thought his first name might be Alec, but she wasn't sure) was at least eighty years old, if not older. They browsed the stacks together and he ended up leaving with Zadie Smith's *On Beauty* and *Station Eleven* by Emily St. John Mandel. Martha knew he'd return in less than a week having read both books.

She left the library in Kittery at about a quarter after five and got back to her house in Portsmouth ten minutes later. Even though she worked in Maine and lived in New Hampshire, on more than one occasion she'd actually walked to the library, just two miles away, over the Piscataqua River.

The house she shared with Alan was a cottage-style two-bedroom, its top floor a recent addition by the previous owners. The front of the house had a large living area that led into a small dining room and smaller kitchen. Upstairs were the two bedrooms, and a strangely large bathroom dominated by a hot-tub bath in black tile. Alan had let her decorate the house, and she'd filled it with bookshelves and overstuffed furniture. Before taking off her coat, Martha fed Gilbert his dry food. He meowed at her, his standard complaint, then consented to try it. She then made herself her own dinner. When Alan was away she rarely cooked. Instead, she would put cheese and deli meat and crackers and some fruit and sometimes some carrots on a cutting board and bring it with her to living room. She put on one of the home renovation shows that she liked and Alan didn't, and slowly picked away at the food on the board. She didn't particularly care for the couple who were having their very beige house redone into another beige house, and she found herself thinking about Alan again. After he'd returned from that trip to Shepaug University in Connecticut, after she'd watched him from the bedroom window, she'd decided to look up the conference he'd just been to. It was a strange whim. Well, maybe not strange. Alan always let her know where he was going and she often took a look at the conference sites. It was curiosity.

When she'd typed in the words "Shepaug" and "teachers' conference," the first thing that came up was a news story. One of the participants, a middle school art teacher from Woodstock, New York, named Josie Nixon, had committed suicide over the weekend. It was a short news article from a local paper. She'd apparently jumped from the sixth-floor balcony of the dormitory that she had been staying in. There was a mention that the police had concluded there had been no foul play, and then there were two paragraphs about how this latest death had reignited an argument about the dormitory building itself. Apparently, since it had been built, there had been more than one jumping death from the open balconies.

The day after Alan had returned from that trip she'd asked him about Josie Nixon, and he'd given her a blank look before saying, "Oh, I heard about that. Terrible."

"Did you know her?"

"I don't understand the question," Alan said. It was a minor annoying habit of his, that instead of simply asking Martha what she meant, he always said how he didn't understand her question.

"I mean, did you have any contact with her during the conference? Did she buy anything from you?"

"I guess she might have, but if she did, I don't remember. My customers are like one big blur to me, honestly."

Martha thought that was the end of the conversation, but about five minutes later, after talking about something else, Alan said, "It did cast a major pall over the conference when word got around."

"What do you mean?" Martha said.

"The young woman who killed herself. After word got around, the conference turned kind of grim. The weather didn't help, either."

That had been the end of their conversation on the suicide. But she'd thought about it—the way he looked on his return, those few words—repeatedly. She'd read somewhere once that our memories are never reliable, that what we are actually remembering is not the event itself, but a replay of the last time we remembered the event. Our minds play videotapes, and those videotapes degrade over time. Martha wondered about that now as she pictured Alan in the driveway, the setting sun burnishing him, his face empty of any kind of humanness. And then she pictured him gathering himself, taking a breath, and smiling. In the beginning she'd read this action as him trying to change his mood, shake off the road, and prepare to enter back into his real life. But now she saw it differently. The smile wasn't for him. It was a smile that would be for her. He was practicing, the way an actor might alter their face or posture while waiting in the wings for their cue. He was practicing his smile.

CHAPTER 2

She was dozing when he finally returned. Moving bars of light from his headlights swept across the wallpaper of their bedroom as he parked in the driveway. And then she heard the faint sound of the trunk being opened and closed, followed by the less-faint sound of him coming in through the front door. She could tell he was being quiet, trying not to wake her. Gilbert jumped heavily off the bed to go and investigate, but Martha decided to stay put. He'd be upstairs soon, probably take a shower, get into some clean pajamas, then slide under the covers and up against her body. She curled onto her left side and waited, but she was asleep by the time he came to bed.

In the morning, Alan was up before her.

"Oh no," Martha said from the tangle of sheets. "You're up already."

"Shh," he said. "Stay in bed. I have that breakfast meeting with Saul, remember?"

"Oh yeah," she said, pulling a second pillow underneath her shoulders. "I remember," she lied. "How was Denver?"

"Was I in Denver? When was that?" He chuckled at his own joke. "It was good, actually. Decent sales."

"Oh, I'm happy for you."

Before he left, Alan unpacked his carry-on bag in the bedroom while they talked some more about the convention he'd been at for the last three days. Then she told him about having to fire one of the volunteers at the library because she was talking too much to the patrons.

"Can you fire a volunteer?"

"You can tell them that their services aren't needed anymore. Jill was going to do it, but at the last minute she panicked and asked me to talk to her. It was awful."

"I'm sure you were as nice as possible."

"She asked me if it was something she'd done, and I lied and said that the board wanted to reduce the number of volunteers. I don't think she believed me."

When Alan had gone downstairs, Martha got up, brushed her teeth, and combed her hair, but stayed in the cotton nightgown she'd slept in, pulling a cardigan on over it because she was cold. She got down just as Alan was at the front door, wearing his wool winter coat. It was early April, but as she often thought, and sometimes said, in New Hampshire April is really just March Part Two. "Let me at least get a hug before you go," she said, sliding into his arms. Alan had large strong hands and he ran them up along her rib cage, grazing her left breast.

"Maybe we could take a little nap this afternoon," he said. "I'll be home around three."

"I'd like that," Martha said.

"What are your plans today?"

"Nothing," she said. It was Monday, but since she'd begun working from Tuesday through Saturday, Mondays were now her Sundays. "I can wash your clothes from the trip this morning. I was going to do laundry anyway."

"That would be a big help."

After he was gone, she took a long shower, then made herself tea and toast. Since having that little talk with herself the night before, she suddenly felt stupid about her suspicions. What had her suspicions even been, exactly? That Alan was grumpy when he returned from work? That Alan had something to do with a young teacher committing suicide?

It had begun to rain outside, a cold spring rain, and she was actually happy about it. Her mom had always reminded her that when she was a seven-year-old she had declared rain to be the best weather because it was reading weather. And she had never really shed that opinion. After starting a load of laundry she was looking forward to getting back into her novel, *Less Than Angels* by Barbara Pym. She'd never heard of Pym until one of her friends on Facebook posted something about her, and now she was steadily working her way through all of her books.

Alan's clothes from his trip were in the laundry basket and his bag was stowed away in his closet. Considering how much he traveled, she wouldn't have blamed him for never really unpacking. But he was fastidious about putting things away. "When I'm home," he liked to say, "I'm truly home."

She made two piles on the bed, one of colors and one of whites, then took a close look at Alan's two white shirts, making sure they were in good shape, no underarm stains or frayed collars. They both seemed fine, but flipping one of the white shirts around she spotted a reddish brown stain on the lower left-hand side of the back of the shirt. She touched it with a fingertip, a stain that looked as though a finger had left it. A finger dipped in something—chocolate, maybe? She looked closer, even sniffing at it, and there was the slightest smell of something elemental, earthy. Could it be blood? She tried to imagine Alan getting a paper cut or something on his finger, then wiping at his back. She made the move herself, twisting her arm around to see if it made any kind of sense. It didn't really.

Something moved inside of her, her organs shifting. Was there really blood on her husband's shirt?

She should just ask him about it. "Oh, honey. Did you cut yourself on your trip? I think I found some blood on one of your shirts." That's what an unsuspecting wife would do, right? And he would tell her about pricking his finger on some brooch he sold and then it would be over. But instead she found herself sitting in front of her laptop about to see if anything strange had happened during Alan's recent trip. All she knew about the conference he had just come back from was that it had been held in Denver, Colorado, and that it had been a conference for high school English teachers.

"I thought those were busts for you," she'd said before he'd left.

"They used to be. Old-school English teachers definitely did *not* go in for novelty mugs, but I think it's changing. I sell a ton of grammar T-shirts."

"What's a grammar T-shirt?"

"Oh, you know, LET'S EAT KIDS. Then, LET'S EAT (comma) KIDS"—he ran his finger across his chest to demonstrate—"and then it says something like PUNCTUATION SAVES LIVES."

"Oh, funny," Martha said. She really did think that most of Alan's humorous T-shirts were actually quite clever.

"Well, it's a break from math teachers, and for that I'll be thankful."

Martha punched in "English teacher" and "conference" and "Denver" and came up with something called Southwest English Teachers Symposium, or SWETS, that had been held this weekend. She read a little bit about it—it had been held at a downtown hotel, and the keynote speaker was a novelist Martha had heard of but hadn't read, giving a talk on diversity in curriculum choice. There was one small article about the conference in a local Denver paper, more of a mention, really, that said how the city of Denver would be inundated with English teachers over the weekend, so be sure to "watch your grammar" to avoid a scolding. It felt like something that might have been written fifty years ago, but Martha was a librarian and was used to stereotypes.

She put in a new search: "Denver" and "crime." She scanned the list of hits and nothing jumped out at her. She changed the search to simply: "Denver assault." Why assault? she thought as she hit the return button. She then switched the findings so that they were restricted to news stories, the most recent of which had the headline: "DPD Investigating Assault of Woman Found in Parking Lot." The article was dated yesterday, the incident occurring fairly close to where Alan had been staying. She clicked on it.

> Police are investigating an alleged incident of assault in the Five Points neighborhood on Friday night. The victim was found unresponsive at the 25th Street Parking Lot just after 2 A.M.
>
> The 21-year-old woman had suffered a head injury and is currently in stable condition. A spokesperson for the Denver Police Department said that they are looking for anyone who might have witnessed the attack to come forward.

After reading the brief article twice, Martha stood and walked from the kitchen back to the bedroom. Once there, she was confused for a moment, couldn't even remember climbing the stairs, or why she'd come to her bedroom. But then a familiar series of beeps alerted her that the washing machine had just completed a cycle. She looked on the bed, where Gilbert was now happily sleeping on a pile of colored laundry, and she remembered that she'd thrown the whites into the wash. It was a vague memory, though, even if it had happened less than an hour ago. Alan's white shirt with the bloodstain was now just a freshly laundered shirt. Maybe she'd done it on purpose, or maybe it was simply that the whole thing was ludicrous, the idea that her husband, the traveling salesman, was some kind of homicidal maniac. It would have been markedly stranger if there had been no crimes committed in Denver over the weekend.

She went to the washer and transferred the whites to the dryer, then went to get the remaining pile, but Gilbert lashed out with a paw when she tried to gather them up. She decided she wasn't in a rush and left Gilbert on his pile of Alan's clothes.

"What do you smell there?" she asked her cat. "What's Alan been up to?"

He stared back at her as though he knew but would never, ever tell.

• • •

That night, over dinner, Martha asked Alan about the shirt. He'd looked flustered at first, eventually claiming that he had no idea how the stain had gotten there.

"You think I'm some kind of serial killer, Martha?" he'd said, raising one brow.

It was an obvious joke, but something in his tone made Martha's flesh crawl a little bit. "Why would you say that?"

"I don't know. Because I had blood on my shirt?"

"I mean, wouldn't I think that maybe you'd cut yourself first? Why go straight to serial killer?"

"I was just making a joke." He put his hands up in a gesture of surrender.

That night they watched two episodes of the current season of *Outlander*. Alan fell asleep halfway through the second episode, the way he always fell asleep, his eyes simply closing while he remained in his normal seated position. Martha turned the volume down and flipped over to HGTV, not because she felt like watching it, but because she wanted something mindless on while she thought. She decided to calmly appraise her situation because she kept going over the odd discussion with her husband at dinner. She told herself that if she'd married a bad man, a man who (maybe) assaulted people, he'd have had some ready-made excuse for the evidence on his shirt. As it was, he'd seemed genuinely baffled by it. Or had he? She couldn't figure it out, and she thought, once again, that she just didn't know him that well, despite the fact that they were married. She knew everything external about him—the way he moved and spoke and made love and ate his food—but his internal world was a complete mystery. When he lay in bed at night she had no idea what he was thinking about, and she didn't know if that was unusual or not. Maybe everyone was the same as her, going through life surrounded by people who amounted to being little more than strangers?

Still, it bothered her. That sort of thing—not knowing—had always bothered her. Maybe it was why she'd become a librarian. When she was twelve years old, she'd given a class presentation on her favorite novel, *The Westing Game*, by Ellen Raskin. Afterward the teacher, Ms. Myrvoll, had asked a few questions. One of them, and Martha remembered this like it was yesterday, was whether Martha sought out other books by Ellen Raskin. She hadn't, really. In fact, she'd hardly thought of it at all. It was the book she loved, not necessarily the author, but that night she lay in bed and thought about the question. Suddenly she not only wanted to know everything that the author had ever written, she was now determined to read it all. The next day had been a Saturday and she'd talked her mother into driving her to the library.

"That was the day you became obsessed with libraries," her mother had said, on more than one occasion. The other thing she liked to say, used to like to say, was how Martha always had her nose in a book. It was mostly true, what her mother said, but Martha wasn't just obsessed with books. She was obsessed with getting the whole story. How many books had this author written? What was their life like? Did they have a secret pseudonym?

A week later Alan went to another conference, this one for community college educators down in Chapel Hill, North Carolina. The weather had finally turned nice, and on Alan's first day away, Martha walked into downtown Portsmouth to do some shopping and eat lunch at a Mexican restaurant she liked. While she was there Alan texted her a picture of himself, the hotel swimming pool sparkling in the sun behind him. He was wearing a Hawaiian shirt and wire-rimmed sunglasses. "Water's lovely," he wrote.

Something about that picture—since when did Alan send selfies?—made Martha feel as though a spider were skittering across the nape of her neck. Had he suddenly decided to send her updates from his trip, something he'd never done before? And if that was the case, then why? That night, after cheese and crackers for dinner, she went to her computer and decided to do the thing that she had been postponing doing since finding the shirt with the stain on it. First things first, she did a search of every email she'd gotten from Alan since they'd been in a serious relationship. He had a habit of always sending her his itinerary when he went away on a trip. It was always very formal, the subject reading "Wichita Trip" or "Chattanooga Conference" and then he'd provide details: the dates of travel; his flights, complete with links; the hotel he was staying at. It was actually a very helpful thing that he did, since Martha often found herself wondering where in the country he was at any given moment. She found a spiral notebook in one of the drawers of her desk and opened it up to a blank page, writing down a chrono-logical history of her husband's trips. Since shortly before they'd gotten married he'd been on twenty-three trips.

After making her list she opened up a browser window and be-gan to search news stories. It took her three hours, but when she was done, she had written down five separate incidents.

On February 4, 2018, about two months before she and Alan were married, a twenty-four-year-old prostitute named Kelli Bald-win was found bludgeoned to death in Atlanta, Georgia. That same weekend Alan was at an Atlanta trade show of high school curric-ulum materials.

Three months later, Bianca Muranos, a single mother and a receptionist in the Chicago area, was found dead in the alleyway behind a downtown conference hotel. Cause of death was listed as blunt-force trauma to the head. This was in May, the same weekend that a national conference on STEM education was being held at the same downtown conference hotel.

In July of that same year was the incident at Shepaug University that she knew about already. Josie Nixon, pronounced a suicide.

The fourth incident had happened at the Making Math Fun

Conference, an annual event held every October in Fort Myers, Florida. That conference had actually been mentioned in the article Martha found about Nora Johnson, the victim. She had been a bartender at the hotel where the conference was taking place and had been found strangled in her car in the hotel parking lot. One of the parking attendants at the hotel had been arrested and subsequently released.

The final incident that Martha recorded, not including the recent assault on the unnamed woman in Denver, involved another young woman, Mikaela Sager, identified as a massage therapist, in San Diego on the second weekend of February, when Alan had been attending a conference for English teachers. Her body had been discovered on Mission Beach, and the earliest stories had referred to the death as being an accidental drowning while later stories referred to it as a suspicious death.

Martha read through all her notes, then, barely conscious that she was doing it, she said all the names out loud. "Kelli Baldwin, Bianca Muranos, Josie Nixon, Nora Johnson, Mikaela Sager." She said their names again, adding, "and the woman whose name I don't know in Denver."

CHAPTER 3

Martha stood and paced around the downstairs of her house, at one point scooping up Gilbert and carrying him with her. He liked to be held as long as the human doing the holding kept moving. When Martha found herself back at her desk in the living room, she stared at the list again, tempted to cross out the jumping death of Josie Nixon in Connecticut. It was an outlier, the victim being an attendee of the conference, and the death being ruled a suicide. But she decided to not cross it out in the end. That was the trip Alan was returning from when she'd watched him in the driveway, practicing his smile. That phrase echoed in her head. *Practicing his smile.* Why else would he have smiled that way in their driveway? Humans—real humans—don't practice their emotions. Or maybe they do, she thought, remembering being a middle schooler and practicing biting her lower lip in the mirror because a friend had told her it was how to look sexy. Gilbert was squirming and she let him down, one of his nails snagging on her sweater as she did so. She plucked at the loose strand of wool, annoyed that she'd let her cat wreck another of her sweaters, but then she was thinking of Alan again. Maybe he was *always* pretending with her. Every action and every word simply a way to hide the inhuman thing that he really was. The radiator clicked on and she jumped. Telling herself to calm down, she returned to her computer.

There was another reason Martha had decided to keep Josie Nixon on the list of her husband's possible crimes, and that was the fact that Josie's death had occurred at Shepaug University. Shepaug made Martha think of Lily Kintner. Lily was a friend from graduate school, and if Martha remembered correctly, she had grown up in Shepaug.

She put Lily Kintner's name into her browser. There wasn't much, but there was a rather strange story. Lily had been involved in a dispute with a Boston Police Department detective who had apparently been stalking her. It had led to an incident where she had stabbed the police officer in self-defense. He hadn't died, but he had been removed from the force, while Lily had dropped all charges.

None of this surprised Martha, who knew that Lily wasn't really like other people. Maybe I should find her, she thought. And as soon as that thought entered her mind, Martha felt an almost physical sensation of relief, her back loosening, her lungs working better. Because, after reading the news articles that she'd found that morning, she did know that she had to do something. She either needed to confront Alan, or else bring the evidence to the police, and both of those possibilities were impossible to even comprehend. If she was wrong about her suspicions, and she most likely was, then her marriage would be over. What she really needed was a friend, someone to talk with about what she'd found, someone to look at the evidence through objective eyes. But she didn't have friends, not really. No, that wasn't true. She had friends, but not friends whom she could talk to about her husband. Not currently, anyway.

But Lily might just be perfect. When they'd been at grad school together Lily had helped Martha out of a scary relationship. Martha often wondered what might have happened to her if Lily hadn't stepped in and coached her through that particular breakup. And what she remembered of that time was that Lily had been utterly practical, almost coldhearted, about the whole thing. She hadn't been emotional or judgmental. And that was exactly what Martha was looking for now. She didn't want to tell Donna from the library, who would probably just keep exclaiming, "Oh my God," again and again before telling her that she needed to flee the country. She could call her sister, currently living in Alaska, but she knew how that conversation would go. Her sister would accuse her of reading too many books and watching too many movies and that the whole idea was ridiculous. But Lily . . . Lily would actually listen.

Wondering about how to find her, Martha remembered Lily's semi-famous father, David Kintner, an English author who lived somewhere in New England. Back in grad school Martha had read a few of his books, for no other reason than that she'd become good friends with his daughter. She remembered, in particular, a book called *Slightest Folly*, a very dark comedy about a fictional boarding school in England called Scoldingham. It was sort of an *Upstairs, Downstairs* type of book, focusing on both the pupils and the staff members. Martha had loved it, and she'd been surprised when she found out that Lily had never read it.

"Aren't you curious?" Martha had asked.

"I've read some of his stuff, but I'm saving that one for when he's dead." She'd said it with a straight face, as though it weren't a morbid thing to say at all. But that straightforwardness was what Martha had liked about Lily.

Wondering if David Kintner was still alive, Martha put his name into a new tab in her browser, and discovered that he was, although nothing indicated that he was still living in Connecticut. The last major news story about him had been a car accident he'd been in with his second wife, Gemma Daniels. He'd survived and she hadn't, and, judging from the number of articles written about it, it had been a big story in Britain, where it happened.

She did find an old profile of David Kintner, done long before the car accident, in which there was a picture of him and his then-wife Sharon Henderson, a local artist, standing in front of a dilapidated farmhouse. The caption referred to the place as Monk's House, David's name for the farm. The town was Shepaug. On a whim, Martha searched the name "Sharon Henderson" and "Shepaug," and among several hits was a White Pages listing that included a phone number. She wrote the number down in her notebook. She wasn't ready to make a call yet.

Before going to bed that night, Martha got into bed with both her Barbara Pym book and her wedding album. She flipped through the album, the images so familiar to her. It had been a small affair, just thirty-five guests, most from Alan's side of the family. Martha had only invited her mother and her sister, her sister's second husband and three stepchildren, two unmarried aunts, and one friend, Bethany Hart, whom Martha had known since elementary school. Lucy, her sister, was maid of honor, and she'd made a really sweet toast that had turned very religious at its close, something that had made Martha cringe at the time. In fact, something about the whole wedding, and about looking at the pictures now, was making her cringe inside. Why do humans want to celebrate their relationships? There was something almost unbearable about it.

There was one picture that Martha looked at more than the others. It was a candid shot during the cocktail reception, the small group assembled under a tent at the vineyard where they were married, a field of grapes in the background. Martha, in her wedding dress, and Alan, in his suit, were talking with a group of Alan's college friends. Everyone was laughing, but Alan's eyes were looking a little to the side, at another small group of talkers, which included her sister's stepdaughter, a strikingly pretty teenage girl who had worn a very small dress that day—Alan's mother had referred to it as "four handkerchiefs and a piece of string." Was Alan looking at her, ogling her, on his wedding day? Was that the man she married?

Early the next morning, after a night of brief snatches of sleep and forgotten dreams, Martha got up a few hours before she needed to be at the library. She showered and dressed and made herself breakfast. Then she sat down at her desk, the phone number for Lily's mother in front of her, and prepared to make the call. She was thinking about what she might say when the cell phone in her hand vibrated with an incoming call. It was Alan.

"Morning," she said.

"Morning, sunshine," he said back, sounding chipper.

"Everything okay?"

"Yeah, why? Because I'm calling? I was just going to text you, then decided I'd rather hear your voice instead. I knew you'd be up."

"How's Chapel Hill?"

"It feels like summer here already. My booth is actually outside on the main quad under a tent and I've sweated through all of my shirts."

They talked for a while about the weather and then Alan said, "I've been thinking. You and I should take a trip."

"Oh yeah? Where to?"

"I've been thinking about that, as well. You know how we both hate the heat in August. Maybe we could go to the North of England for a week. Haven't you always wanted to visit Haworth?"

It took Martha a moment to realize he was talking about Brontë Country, but once she figured it out it made perfect sense. On their first date they'd had a long conversation about *Wuthering Heights*, her favorite book.

"I'd like that," Martha said.

"Would you?" He sounded genuinely happy, as though he'd just asked her to marry him again and she said yes.

"Of course."

"Great. I have to go and open my booth, but when I get back let's pick a week and start to plan."

"Okay," Martha said, meaning it.

"One last thing before I let you go. I've been thinking of changing my walk."

"Changing your what?"

"My walk. I was thinking about it, how my feet point in and I lean forward a little, and I think I should have a much cooler walk. That's all."

"What did you have in mind?"

"I don't know, something smooth and iconic. Maybe Sean Connery's walk, the one he had in *Goldfinger*."

"Well, you should work on that, honey," she said.

He laughed and said, "I will."

After the call Martha sat unmoving for about five minutes, realizing that she had a faint smile on her face. Alan had two comic sensibilities—corny jokes, and then a kind of dry absurdist humor like that bit about his walk. She loved his dry humor and Alan knew that. It was like he was trying to win her back, being funny, promising vacations. A part of her—the part that believed in love curses and fate and the presence of ghosts—felt as though Alan had sensed that she was about to make a phone call that would alter their lives forever and that he'd called to intervene. Not that he knew what was happening, just that he felt it. And then she thought of his words—offering a vacation to a place she wanted to visit, making the kind of joke she liked—and she wondered if he'd practiced his call before making it. Like a sales pitch. Had he also reminded himself to sound like a regular human being? To smile on the phone because she'd hear it in his voice? An image of a frozen smile on her husband's face flared into her mind. She shivered, just as Gilbert rubbed his face against her ankle.

After feeding her cat she thought more about Alan's phone call. Maybe he was simply being thoughtful in suggesting a trip to see Heathcliff and Cathy's moors. Of course, she knew that he was thinking about all the English beer he'd be able to drink while they were there, but that didn't mean it wasn't a sweet thing to do. She thought about the tone of his voice when he'd said, "Would you?" as though he were genuinely happily surprised that she was interested in the possibility of the trip. It was one of his better traits, that he didn't take her for granted and that he felt grateful for her love. And now she didn't know what to think. He felt unknowable to her, but so was Gilbert, in the way that cats were unknowable, and she loved him fiercely despite it.

About twenty minutes before it was time for her to leave for her job in Kittery she had a different thought. What if Alan knew she was on to him, and he'd invited her to England to murder her in the moors? Was he going to do it there because it would be easier to get away with it, or did he want her to die in a place she loved? The thought of it made her almost laugh out loud at how ridiculous her life had become. But then she thought: Just talk to someone else about it. Call Lily. What harm could it do?

CHAPTER 4

It was gently raining as I left the coffee shop holding my paper bag of savory scones. They have scallions and cheddar cheese baked into them and my father had decided that they were the perfect accompaniment to his morning egg. I did try to reverse-engineer them once in our own kitchen, but I am not a particularly good baker and my scones came out with the consistency of clumps of sand.

I looked up at the sky, a mix of dark rain clouds and thin wisps and decided that the rain would be short-lived. It's a two-mile walk back to Monk's House, but it was a warmish morning for April. I've never really known why humans are averse to walking through rainstorms. Why is getting wet on a walk less pleasant then getting wet on a swim? I suppose it has to do with clothes, of course, but, really, it's not so bad. The rain picked up as I turned onto the walking path that brought me across disused tracts of farmland. I spotted two crows, having their morning conversation, and wondered if they were complaining about the rain.

I was soaked when I got home, and my mother, walking gingerly since her fall, stepped out onto the front stoop as I came down the driveway. She was wearing a shirt I recognized as her favorite of her many paint-flecked shirts, and I remembered that her friend Brenda was coming over for lunch later. "Lily, you're soaked," she said as I came up the steps.

"It's a soft day," I said, not immediately remembering where I got that expression from, only that it annoys my mother.

"Are you quoting your father?"

"No, he wouldn't say that. I think it's some kind of Irish expression."

"Go and get out of those clothes and take a hot shower. Did you remember that I'm having a lunch guest today?"

"I did remember. Brenda the mosaic artist."

"And you got a phone call," Sharon said as I was halfway up the stairs.

I turned. "From who?"

"Let me get it. I wrote it down." Sharon walked lopsidedly back into the kitchen as I dripped on the stairs. I was trying to remember the last time I got a phone call from anyone. Of course, it helps that I'm not listed on the landline that reaches the house I am living in, and that even though I now own a cell phone, no one knows my number. A few names went through my head: Inez Garrett, my old boss at Winslow; Henry Kimball, although he usually just shows up announced.

"Martha Ratliff," Sharon said. "She told me she was hoping I had your phone number, so I told her you live here with us. Is that okay?"

"Sure," I said, my mind attaching an image to a name I hadn't heard in well over a decade. Martha's rather foxlike face, all thin features, and hair the color of a cardboard box.

"What else did she say?"

"Just for you to call her. I wrote down her phone number."

"Okay, thanks," I said, and continued up the stairs.

Martha Ratliff, when I'd known her, had been the closest I'd ever come to having a genuine female friend. We'd done the same Archival Studies Program at Birkbeck College in Maryland more than fifteen years ago. It had been a happy time in my life. I was relieved to have left my college years behind, along with my doomed relationship with Eric Washburn, and I was pleased to have identified a career that interested me. I'd always loved libraries but saw them as places that favored the new over the old. There was always that

New Arrivals shelf situated front and center, while older books with cracked spines and beautiful cover art wound up in piles at library book sales going for three for five dollars. Why did people want new art? I understood why people created it, but why did other people want it? Why does someone read a brand-new romance novel if they haven't read all of Austen yet? So, when I discovered that the field of library science included archival studies, at its simplest the preservation of historical documents, I knew instantly that I had found my career.

We were a small group at Birkbeck for the two-year graduate program. Six women, one man. During orientation the other female students seemed giddy with the idea that we'd all be spending so much time together. They were all bookish and a little awkward, the type of girls who were told during high school that they would blossom in college, then told during college that they would be happiest in graduate school. The one man of the group—Larry Childs—was the true outlier. Not only was he a man, but he was Black, and slightly older than the rest of us, maybe late twenties. Like me, he was quiet during orientation, watching through the thick lenses of his glasses. The head of our department, a woman named Deirdre Jones who reminded me of my mother, led us in several activities during a welcome dinner, including an icebreaker activity called "Two Truths and a Lie." I remember that I went last and it gave me time to think about what I wanted to say. I made jokes to myself about what I *might* include as one of my truths: *I murdered my college boyfriend with cashews*, for example. In the end I said that I'd grown up on a farm named after Thelonious Monk, that I'd once kept a raccoon as a pet, and that I was an avid quilter. It was only Larry Childs who guessed I wasn't a quilter. I wish I remembered what he had said during that silly icebreaker, but I do remember his lie. He'd said that he was a direct descendant of Frederick Douglass. Most of us believed it.

I do remember what Martha Ratliff said during that orientation, only because it struck me as a strange thing to admit to people she'd just met. Her lie had been something silly like she'd once gone over Niagara Falls in a barrel, but one of her truths was that she believed she'd been cursed by a high school friend who practiced witchcraft, and that it was a love curse. Deirdre Jones had said, "Oooh, I can't wait to hear more about that," and then moved on to the next person.

It did make me curious about Martha. She was from Missouri, awkwardly tall, with long brown hair. Her eyes were always blinking rapidly and you could tell that she had a bad habit of chewing on the inside of her cheek. I decided after the icebreaker that she was the only woman in our group that I was interested in getting to know, and it turned out that I was right about that. A week into our first semester, the most social member of our class, Cecily Makouns, had a dinner party at her apartment just off the Birkbeck campus. I was living a few miles away, having found a room for rent in a two-hundred-year-old house on the edge of a salt marsh. The room had been listed at the Student Housing Department, and when I'd asked the student worker there about it, she'd made a face and said that it was a very good deal but that the woman who rented the room was a little bit strange. I went to look at it anyway. It was a wooden house that hadn't been painted for years and had faded to the color of an oyster shell. There was a wide porch that fronted three sides of the house, and my room came with a small portable stove and its own bathroom.

The woman who lived there was named Ethel Watkins. She was a foul-tempered eighty-year-old who had been born in the house and never lived anywhere else. During our interview she asked me if I had a boyfriend and I told her I was done with all that. She must not have believed me, because she scrunched up her face into a scowl. I stared back at her, purposefully not saying anything, and she moved her head back like a dog that had just been batted on the nose by a cat. I told her I'd take the room and she reluctantly agreed.

At the dinner party at Cecily's house I told them all about my living situation while we ate vegetarian enchiladas that were served with plain yogurt instead of sour cream. After dinner we drank wine in the living room and I found myself chatting with Martha Ratliff, who asked me multiple questions about my new landlady. "She sounds like a witch," Martha said.

"She looks like one," I said. "Her hair, anyway."

"Could I visit sometime? I made the mistake of getting a room in the graduate dorm and it's like a prison cell."

"Of course," I said. "Unless you're scared of witches. You've already been cursed, right?"

She laughed, and I decided that she was pretty when she showed her teeth. "I have. I had a love curse put on me by my high school nemesis, Eve Dexter. I actually caught her doing it to me. It was Halloween night, but she wasn't dressed in a costume or anything. I was in my bedroom at about midnight and something made me look out the window. She was standing on my lawn in the moonlight staring up at my window."

"Why did she curse you?"

"Because I kissed her boyfriend. Not even while he was her boyfriend, but after he broke up with her. I didn't even particularly like him, but I hadn't kissed anyone yet, so I didn't feel like I could turn it down."

"You weren't one of those girls who wanted a perfect first kiss?"

She rolled her eyes. "God, no. I didn't care."

"So, she found out."

"Exactly. Eve found out. We'd sort of been friends, but that was the end of that. She got her posse to shun me at school and call me a slut in the hallways. I thought that would be the worst of it, but she must have looked up how to perform a love curse on me. It actually made me respect her a little more, except that the curse worked."

"How do you know that's what she did to you?"

"I didn't know at the time. But my senior year at college I went to a friend's home for the weekend, and her mother, who was a part-time psychic, I guess, took one look at me and said that I'd had a love curse put on me. I immediately remembered that night—it just flashed through my mind. And it all made sense. Every guy I hooked up with in college turned out to be awful in some way."

I was nodding, listening to her story, and she said, "I know what you're thinking, that every guy everyone hooked up with in college was awful—"

"No," I said. "I believe you. You're probably cursed. What are you going to do about it?"

"Avoid men," she said.

But Martha Ratliff didn't avoid all men that first year at Birkbeck. First, she became friends with Larry, both of us did, but it was clear to anyone with half a brain that Larry was smitten with Martha. We all thought something was going to happen between them, but then, at the beginning of our second semester, some of us were having drinks out at a bar that primarily catered to college students called the Hideout. Larry was there, I remember that, and so was Martha, and Cecily brought along someone none of us had met. His name was Ethan Saltz and he was a visiting writer in creative nonfiction. Cecily made the introductions as Ethan loomed over the table. He looked like an Ivy League quarterback. Blond hair and a lantern jaw, and one of those bodies that formed a V, wide shoulders and a tiny waist. I watched his eyes scan the table, resting on each of us and putting us in categories (same as I was doing to him, to be honest), and then his eyes landed on Martha. Her pale midwestern skin reddened considerably. Ethan asked us what we were all drinking, then bounded off to the bar like a dog playing fetch. I looked over at Larry, sitting next to Martha, and saw that he had seen the same thing I had, that Martha had fallen in love at first sight, or something like it, with this handsome stranger.

CHAPTER 5

During the whole Ethan Saltz affair, once I'd realized what he really was, I kept going back in my mind to that night at the Hideout, when he'd been brought up to our table and introduced to our small group of library science grad students. I remembered his eyes scanning the group, then landing on Martha and lingering there. When he'd returned with drinks it was as though we all cleared a space for him exactly where he wanted to sit, right next to Martha.

At the time I wondered why he'd picked her so suddenly and decisively. And I also wondered why he hadn't picked me. That sounds vain, I know, and I had no interest in the Ethan Saltzes of the world, or any men, for that matter. But I did know that I was attractive, in the same way that a rabbit knows it looks appetizing to a fox. I'd grown up in a house that served as a revolving guest retreat for drunken artists and writers my whole life. I'd been stared at long before I'd ever hit puberty. But that wasn't the reason I had sworn off both men and love. Eric Washburn was the reason. I'd fallen in love with him and he'd betrayed me. Familiar story, I know, but it had taught me not just what men would do to women, but also what I would do to the men who betrayed me. That was a part of me I didn't particularly want to meet again.

I was happy that I didn't need to fend off Ethan Saltz on the night we all met him, but I was also a little worried, even at the time, that he'd focused all his attention on Martha. I didn't believe in love curses, but I definitely believed in asshole guys, and Martha had just attracted one. It occurred to me at the time that he was separating her from our herd not because he was attracted but because he sensed weakness in her.

The night ended with all of us going our separate ways outside the bar, our goodbyes plucked away by a frigid winter wind. None of us were surprised that Ethan Saltz happened to be going in Martha's direction.

On the following Monday, each of us drinking our tea in the student union, I asked Martha what had happened. "Not details," I said. "Just the big picture."

She thought for a moment, then said: "I have a boyfriend, I guess."

"What about the love curse?"

She'd laughed, although her eyes looked sad to me. "Oh, that hasn't gone anywhere. I already know that Ethan is going to break my heart, but I guess I don't care. He's so beautiful, isn't he?"

"He *is* beautiful," I said.

After that conversation Martha disappeared for a while, deep into her burgeoning love affair. All of us in our small program disappeared a little, as well. It was a cold winter for Maryland, and the second semester course load was much harder than it had been in the fall. We saw each other in classes, but there was less socializing. On the rare occasion that Cecily hosted a party, or we all got together at the Hideout, Martha would either not come, or she would show up for one drink with Ethan, clinging to his arm like a castaway clinging to a piece of raft. When Ethan spoke, usually telling some amusing anecdote about the undergrad writing class he was teaching, Martha stared at him with an intensity that made us all uncomfortable. On paper, Ethan was a catch, and it wasn't just his looks; he was smart and witty, and a surprisingly good listener. When someone else was talking, he would fix those blue eyes on them as though it were the best story he'd ever heard. It was a trick, of course, the ability to do that. I recognized it, but I only recognized it as a seducer's trick. At the time, I thought that Ethan was some kind of serial monogamist, a man who traveled frequently and who quickly found a willing sex partner wherever he ended up.

I was sure that there was a long line of bereaved young women in his wake, but there was no real crime in that.

But sometime in March, just as Maryland began to thaw, I saw something different in Martha. She was thinner, if that was even possible, her skin not just pale, but somehow chalky, as though if you touched her the pasty color would come off on your fingers. She seemed beat down, and one of our professors confided in me that she was in danger of flunking out.

I knew that there could be multiple reasons for why she might have changed, but somehow I thought it had to do with Ethan. I considered confronting her, but I knew that she would deny there was anything amiss. I told myself to leave it alone.

And I would have, I think, had I not driven up along the Chesapeake on one particularly nice Saturday in early April. I'd stopped at a crab place, then decided that I didn't want to wait in the long line that snaked out of the door. I got back into my car and was getting ready to pull out of the parking lot when I saw Martha and Ethan leaving the restaurant and making their way to Ethan's Jeep. There was something unnerving about seeing them from afar. Martha walked a step behind him, her eyes on his back, and then she waited at the passenger-side door until Ethan gave her the go-ahead to get in—at least that was what it looked like from where I watched. I stayed in my car, engine running, and watched them pull out onto the road and head south. I followed them, expecting them to return to Birkbeck, but instead they headed inland, ending up in a town called Port Tobacco, where they parked in front of a divy-looking bar called the Three-Legged Dog. The sun was beginning to set as they entered the bar.

Since I hadn't eaten, I drove for a while and found a burger joint that had either been designed to look like a 1950s diner or was a place that was genuinely unchanged for the last sixty years. By the time I had finished the dried-out burger I had decided to take a look in the Three-Legged Dog. I don't know why, exactly, but I wanted to see them in the wild; Ethan Saltz was slowly, and maybe intentionally, changing Martha Ratliff, and I wanted to know more. If they saw me right away, then I could have a drink with them and depart, but maybe I could find a spot to keep an eye on them.

I parked a couple of blocks down from Ethan's Jeep, donned a winter wool cap, pushing my hair up under it, and walked to the bar carrying my copy of *The Bloody Chamber* by Angela Carter. I pushed through the pneumatic front door of the bar and spotted an empty two-person booth to my right and went directly there. I took off my jacket but left my hat on. A waitress came by and I ordered a gin and tonic. After it had arrived, I finally looked around the place. It was larger than it had seemed from the outside, with both booths and tables, and was anchored by a large oval bar at the center of the room. Toward the back was a pool table and a jukebox, currently churning out a country song about drinking tequila. Ethan and Martha were on the far side of the bar, sitting shoulder to shoulder, and I could just make them out over the array of bottles and the fast-moving bartenders, three women all wearing the same pink T-shirts emblazoned with the logo of the bar. It was possible that either Ethan or Martha would look up and see me across the blue cigarette smoke of the room in my cramped booth, but I doubted it. I decided to stay put and observe.

I was there for three hours, nursed three drinks, discouraged four men (one of whom claimed to be an Angela Carter fan), and watched as Ethan and Martha played some sort of game, the rules of which I couldn't quite figure out.

From what I could tell, they would each have a drink at the bar— his looked like a whiskey and soda, and hers was a glass of white wine—then one or the other would wander away, only to come back with a third party. If Martha was the one to go patrol the teeming bar, then she usually came back with a man, but once she came back with a woman. Introductions were made, and at some point it seemed as though Ethan would say something that would cause the person to leave.

When Ethan left the bar, he'd come back very fast, always with a woman, and he'd make a big deal out of introducing her to Martha. Once I saw him pointing out the features of a particularly drunk participant, as though he were trying to sell her to the highest bidder. He was laughing. I kept worrying that he'd come over to the other side of the bar, where I was sitting, but he never did. There seemed to be a natural split that took place in the Three-Legged Dog that put the quiet couples and the loners on the right side of the bar, while the left side had turned into a freewheeling Saturday night party, soundtracked with classic country sing-alongs.

I decided that I'd seen enough, and also that I was lucky I hadn't been noticed. As I was looking for my waitress to pay my bill, I watched Martha and Ethan talking to a girl who wasn't possibly drinking age. She had long black hair and wore a cropped top and low-rise jeans. She was staring at Ethan as though she'd met a movie star. Before I paid my bill, the three of them left together.

I returned to my house on the salt marsh and thought about what I had seen. It was apparent that Ethan and Martha liked to go out to bars and find someone to have a threesome with. And if that was how they spent Saturday nights it was certainly no business of mine. But something about Martha's complacency in the situation, and Ethan's casual glee, made me wonder if what was happening was less than consensual.

The next time I saw Martha was in the Archival Appraisal class that we were taking together. Afterward, we walked across campus together.

"I saw you the other night," I said.

"Oh yeah?"

"Saturday night. I drove down to Port Tobacco and had a quick drink at a bar there. I saw you with Ethan."

We were walking side by side and I glanced at her and saw the look of alarm and fear on her face. "You should have said hi," she said, her voice fairly normal.

"Honestly, I was just in there for a quick drink, and you two were obviously on a date and I thought it might have been awkward. It's silly, though, I *should* have said hello."

A Frisbee floated past, nearly clipping me on the shoulder, and the guy who caught it yelled out an apology. "Things good with Ethan?" I said, trying to make the words sound as casual as possible.

"Um . . . good?" she paused, and then said, "Things are very interesting with Ethan."

"Okay," I said.

We walked in silence for a moment, birdsong in the air, and I willed myself to wait her out.

"He's sexually adventurous and I'm not, and that's not a bad thing. I mean, it's fun. He's fun."

We reached the student union, and instead of going in I steered Martha to a wooden bench that faced the main quad of the campus. We both sat. She began to speak, almost manically, as though she'd been dying to share with anybody the details of her relationship.

"I know that he's going to Vermont for the summer for some writing retreat and that that will be the end of our relationship. It's probably for the best. I mean, I never thought for a moment that I would wind up married to someone like Ethan Saltz. I just keep telling myself that being with him is an experience. I mean, he's into threesomes, and we've done that and it's okay, and he's very into weird role-play stuff, and some of that has been a little scary, so I told him that maybe I'd passed my comfort line, or whatever you want to call it."

"What did he say?"

"Oh, he laughed. He laughs at everything. And then he said the thing that's really been bothering me. He called me a project. He said, and I'm pretty sure these are the exact words: 'You're my project, Martha. That's why I picked you, you know, to see how far I could get you to go.' "

"Ugh," I said.

"I think he was just kidding, honestly. But, yeah, it's icky."

"Has he hurt you?"

She hesitated long enough for me to know that he had, then she said, "Nothing extreme. But . . . okay, now I'm actually going to tell you this . . ." She took a deep breath. "So, on Saturday night when you saw us at that bar, we were there to pick up someone to have a threesome with, which we'd done before. And we did end up going home with this kind of fucked-up local girl. I'm saying *fucked-up* because she was really drunk, and things got very strange very fast, and . . . I won't go into details, but Ethan was trying to get *me* to hurt *her.*"

Martha pressed the heel of one hand to an eye, and I put my hand on her back and left it there. After a while I said, "You have to leave him, you know. That's why you told me about it."

"I know," she said.

We formed a plan that evening, the two of us sitting on her single bed in her tiny concrete-block dormitory room. She'd decorated the room with framed *New Yorker* covers, most of them depicting a cat, although one of the covers, a watercolor of the New York skyline, was an issue I recognized from 1986, one that contained a story written by my father called "The Final Days of Martin Tobey."

"Ethan won't mind," Martha said. "I mean, he won't mind emotionally, or whatever. But he really does see me as a project, and I'm not sure that he's finished with it . . . with me."

We rehearsed some breakup lines together, and Martha made a plan to meet Ethan the following night at the Hideout. The plan was that I'd walk in around ten thirty. We established some easy signals. For example, if Martha took a sip of her drink after I walked over and said hello, then it meant that I shouldn't stick around. If she pushed her hair back behind an ear, that meant I should join them. That way, if it turned ugly, I'd be there as support.

The next night I walked into the Hideout at ten fifteen, and immediately spotted Martha and Ethan at one of the back booths. I went to the bar and got a club soda with lime, tilting my stool so that I could keep an eye on them. From where I was sitting, I could see the back of Ethan's head, his golden hair, and I could see Martha, her face anxious, explaining herself. When there was a lull in the conversation, I slid off my stool and walked over to them.

"Oh hey," I said.

Martha tucked a strand of hair behind her left ear as Ethan looked up at me and said, "Hey, Lily."

"Join us," Martha said, sliding out of the booth. "I've just got to run to the bathroom."

I slid onto the wooden seat of the booth vacated by Martha and looked at Ethan across the narrow table. He seemed amused. "How are you?" I said.

"It was like watching a puppet," he said, still smiling. "Martha's lips were moving, but your words were coming out of them."

"Excuse me?" I said.

"Whatever. It's no big deal to me." He was leaning on the table and I could smell him. Masculine soap, the way he always smelled.

"I still don't know what you're talking about."

"You do, actually, but I'll play along. Martha just broke up with me, and since you're here to shepherd her home safely I'll say this to you: If I wanted to get her back it would be the easiest thing in the world. But, honestly, I just don't care enough to go through the effort. Also, since you're here now, I realize you're probably just pissed off at me because I wasn't attracted to you, but you would have been too easy. You're already a monster, Lily. It takes one to spot one."

"Hey, Ethan," I said, lowering my voice. "I *am* a monster. Remember that, okay?"

Martha was coming back to the booth, a little unsteady on her feet, either from too many drinks or from the stress of telling Ethan it was over. I stood up quickly and said, "Martha, I don't feel too good. I hate to do this to you, but could you walk me home?"

"Of course," she said, and after getting her coat we left together, Ethan laughing in his booth.

Martha came back with me to my rented room. We had to pass Ethel Watkins, my landlady, who liked to sit in the front room watching reruns of sitcoms on her old flickering television set. I thought she'd make a comment about my visitor, but she just glared at us both as we headed upstairs. Martha spent the night. She was full of adrenaline, telling me again and again exactly how the conversation had gone, then explaining how she really was going to give up men going forward. She fell asleep in her clothes on top of the covers and I curled up next to her.

That following week we were inseparable, Martha alternately giddy and bereaved because of the end of her relationship with Ethan, while I was wary of a counterattack. But it didn't come. I only saw Ethan once, crossing the quad in a rugby shirt and cargo shorts. Our eyes briefly met, but there was no expression on his face.

Sometimes I wonder if Martha and I would have stayed friends after graduate school, or if I blew it by what I'd said to her on the final night before our summer break began.

"What are your plans?" she'd asked. We were sitting on the front porch of Ethel's house, drinking wine and trying to ignore the blackflies.

"I'll probably spend time with my mom, do some reading. And I might go up to Vermont and kill Ethan Saltz."

She'd laughed her toothy laugh, and said, "Yes, make the world a better place."

I should have left it there, but I was young then, and maybe I thought that Martha could handle hearing about my transgressions.

"I'm serious," I said. "I'm a firm believer in ridding the world of people like Ethan Saltz. It wouldn't be hard to get away with it."

A look of genuine shock crossed Martha's face as she realized that I really was serious.

"Or not," I said, and laughed.

That summer I kept the rented room and bounced back and forth between Maryland and Monk's House in Connecticut. I spent August in London with my father. I didn't visit Vermont and I didn't kill Ethan Saltz. Martha and I stayed friendly for the next year of school, but, honestly, it was never the same, and I wasn't surprised that Martha and I lost touch after school. All of which made me curious as to why she was contacting me now.

CHAPTER 6

s this Martha?"

"It is. Hi, Lily. Long time." Martha could tell that her voice was shaky. She was in her office at the library and got up to close her door.

"It *is* a long time. But it's nice to hear your voice," Lily said, and Martha felt that she was being genuine.

"It's nice to hear yours, too. You're back living with your parents?"

"I am. It's a long story, but the short version of it is that they got divorced but my father can't be alone, and my mother doesn't have enough money to support herself, so they need to live together. I'm there to keep them from killing one another."

"Sounds like a lot," Martha said, settling into the conversation, realizing that she'd missed Lily over the years.

"It's not too bad," Lily said.

"Are you working?"

"Do you know Winslow College in Massachusetts? I got a job there about a year after we both finished school. It was good, but I left a couple of years ago to come back here, and now I am mostly unemployed, although I'm busy working on my father's archives."

"Oh, how's that?" Martha said, happy to keep the focus on Lily for a while.

"He keeps threatening to burn them in the fireplace, but he's all bark and no bite. He kept *everything*, including some pretty scandalous journals. How about you? Working?"

"I'm the director of a public library in Kittery right now. Before that I was doing archival work at Boston University, but I don't mind being back in a classic library setting."

"No, of course not."

Martha didn't say anything right away. Part of her just wanted to keep talking about what they'd been doing since they'd known each other all those years earlier, but she also wanted to get to the point. Finally, she said, "So, I called you for a reason."

"Okay," Lily said. "I'm listening." The way she said it made Martha feel as though they were hanging out in her dormitory room in Maryland all over again.

"So, I got married."

"Oh yeah? When was this?"

"A little over a year ago. Alan is slightly older than me. He sells educational materials, so he's always traveling." Martha didn't really want to go into what he sold just yet because people always had a lot of questions.

"And has he broken your love curse?"

"Oh, you remember that?"

"Of course I do. In fact, I was pretty sure you were calling about something to do with Ethan Saltz."

"Ugh, that name. Just hearing it makes me shiver."

"You haven't heard from him?"

"No, thank God. I'm calling about my husband. I think I just need to tell someone what's going on with him."

"Is he hurting you?"

"No, no. Not at all. He's this totally sweet guy, at least I think he is. Hey, I wasn't going to ask this, but now that we're having this conversation . . . Do you think . . . Is there any possibility we could meet up and do this face-to-face?"

"Sure," Lily said. "You live in Maine?"

"I live in Portsmouth, New Hampshire, but I work in Maine. I could come to you, though. Alan's away on one of his trips. I'm at work, but we are well staffed and I could leave anytime." Suddenly, more than anything, Martha wanted to actually see Lily. She didn't want to have this conversation over the phone.

"I'm happy to meet halfway. I wouldn't mind taking a drive today."

Martha brought up a map on her desktop computer and they decided to meet for an early dinner in Worcester, Massachusetts. She picked an Irish pub called Tipsy McStaggers because it was located right off the interstate, and they agreed to meet at four in the afternoon.

After hanging up Martha felt so relieved that she burst into sudden unexpected tears. She hadn't known what to expect from the phone call, and part of her had wondered if Lily even remembered her. The fact that she had, and that she'd even remembered the love curse, was somehow a huge relief. And now they were going to meet in person and Martha could tell Lily what she suspected, and hopefully Lily would laugh the whole thing off, talk her down off the ledge. And that would be the end of that.

After the crying jag, Martha sat for a moment and composed herself. She sent a quick email to her staff saying that she would be leaving early that day, then tried to get some emails done that she'd been avoiding. Mary, the oldest librarian on staff, popped her head into Martha's office to ask a question, and then, after Martha had answered it, said, "Hon, are you okay?"

Martha reflexively swiped at an eye and said, "Yes, fine." When Mary didn't immediately leave the room, she added, "I just talked to a friend who's going through a very rough time in her marriage. That's why I'm leaving early, to go and meet her."

"Oh, that's too bad," Mary said, and frowned.

After Mary left the office, apparently satisfied with the half-truth, Martha decided it was time to leave. She stopped off at home to get her notebook, and decided to change. What was the right thing to wear when you were meeting an old friend to talk to her about your suspicious husband? She finally selected her best jeans, the slightly worn ones, and a printed top that one of the younger librarians had once referred to as "boho."

Tipsy McStaggers was an enormous restaurant on an acre of

parking lot, its front paneled in green-painted wood and festooned with flags and strung lights and Guinness signs. It was bright outside in the parking lot, and Martha's eyes took a moment to adjust as she stepped into the dark interior of the restaurant. It was like a Walt Disney version of an Irish pub, every nook and cranny plastered with a shamrock or a leprechaun or another Guinness ad. A hostess ambled over and asked if it was just her.

"I'm meeting someone but I'm early."

"You can sit wherever you want."

She wandered into the confusing restaurant, passing two alcoves that each had a small bar and seating area, then went up two steps to what seemed to her to be the main bar area. She climbed onto a padded stool, ordered a Guinness from the college-age bartender, and waited. From where she was, she could look back toward the front entrance of the restaurant, and she found herself alternating between tiny sips of her drink and glances at the door. Earlier in the day she'd been so relieved about this meeting, but now that it was about to happen, she felt both nervous and slightly embarrassed. Had she really just asked someone she hardly knew to drive two hours to hear a wild theory?

She finished her beer and asked for a water. It was close to four and a few single drinkers had come into the restaurant, plus one group of college boys, two of whom wore Holy Cross sweatshirts. Her phone vibrated; it was Alan, calling again from North Carolina. She rejected the call and sent a Can I call you later? message. He responded with a thumbs-up emoji.

She turned to look at the entrance again and found herself looking at Lily, standing two feet away. Martha had wondered if she'd changed, but she hadn't. Long red hair, pale skin, those intense green eyes. They hugged, and for a moment Martha thought she might cry again, but she controlled herself.

"Let's grab a table, or a booth," Martha said.

"Okay," Lily said, and they signaled a passing waitress to indicate they were moving to a booth in one of the alcoves. They sat across from each other.

"You look the same," Martha said.

"Do I? I don't feel the same. You look different."

Martha laughed. She remembered this about Lily, that she didn't say the things that everyone was supposed to say in social situations. "In what way?"

"You look more confident, like you've reached the age you were born to be."

"Ha. You're probably right, although I'm not feeling particularly confident."

A waitress showed up and Martha ordered another Guinness while Lily asked for the same. After she left with their order, Lily said, "So what is going on with your husband?"

Before going into the bloodstain and the time she spied on him in the driveway and the deaths she'd found online, Martha found herself just talking about Alan, about their courtship and his job, and what he was like. She even told Lily how, although they'd gotten married, she still felt as though she didn't know him at all. That he was a stranger to her. Lily was nodding.

"Do you know what I mean?"

"Do I know what you mean when you say someone's a stranger to you?"

"Not just someone. Sometimes I think everyone is a stranger to me, that I'm doomed to never really understand another living soul."

Lily took a sip of her beer, her eyes on the low ceiling. "I'd say that's a pretty universal emotion. People who think they know everything about someone are probably deceiving themselves."

Martha nodded. Lily said, "So what is it that you think your husband is doing behind your back? Do you think he's cheating on you?"

"No, it's not that." Martha took a breath. "I think he might be a whole lot worse."

CHAPTER 7

W"hy do you think that?" I said.

And Martha told me her story, how a few days earlier she'd discovered a bloodstain on the back of one of his shirts after he'd returned from a trip to Denver, and how she'd studied recent news stories and found a report about an unsolved assault that had happened during his trip. And then she talked for a time about spying on him from her bedroom window one night when he'd returned from a trip, and how she felt as though he were practicing his smile, transforming himself into a different person for his return home. She seemed embarrassed about that particular incident, as though she were imagining things, and I told her that it did seem at least a little suspicious. And finally she told me how she'd gone back and discovered a total of five unsolved homicides, all women, all youngish, and all occurring in cities that Alan had been in for work. "Am I crazy to think this?" Martha said.

"You're definitely not crazy to think this," I said, wondering if maybe she'd been crazy to marry this particular man. "But you're thinking it doesn't make it true. Why did you come to me?"

"I don't know. At first I figured I had two choices. I could go directly to Alan and tell him what I'd found out and see what he had to say. But if he actually is this kind of . . . monster or whatever . . . then it would probably be a stupid thing to do. And if it's all just a strange coincidence, then how would he feel about my accusing him? I mean, how could he ever trust me again, knowing what I suspected him of? I think it would ruin our marriage. And that's not what I want to do."

"Uh-huh," I said.

"The other option, I suppose," Martha said, "was going directly to the police. But it's the same problem. If they took me seriously, and if they questioned Alan, then he would know it was me that had brought it to them. Either way, it would be over. Our marriage, I mean."

"And you don't want to hurt your marriage?"

"Not if Alan's innocent, no. I know that I said all those things about him being a stranger, but it's not as though I don't love him. I do. And I think my life is better with him in it. Honestly, I think I'm here with you just hoping you'll say I'm being silly and that I should just forget the whole thing." She had finished her Guinness, and there was a little bit of beer foam at the corner of her mouth. "I've thought of you a lot over the years, Lily. That thing with Ethan Saltz was so horrible and I feel like you saved me. I sometimes wonder what would have happened to me if I'd stayed with him. I thought of you as someone who had helped me before in a bad situation, and then I also thought of you because one of the conferences that Alan attended was at Shepaug University. That's near where you live, right?"

"Same town. It's where my mother met my father."

"So, then you became my third option. I could tell you what I thought and get your opinion. And at this point whatever you tell me to do, I'll do. I don't feel like I can make this decision on my own right now."

"I get it," I said. "You did the right thing."

I watched her take the first real deep breath she'd taken since we'd sat across from each other.

"Tell me more about the conference at Shepaug," I said. "Was there a death there?"

Martha had a large tote bag next to her and she pulled a notebook from it and said, "I've catalogued what I found like a good librarian. I almost didn't include what happened at Shepaug because it was a little bit of an outlier."

"How come?" I said.

She was flipping through the notebook and came to the right place. "Out of the five incidents, and I'll tell you about all of them, this was the only one where the death was someone who was an actual attendee at the conference."

"What was the event?"

"It was a K-through-twelve art teachers' weekend conference, and Josie Nixon was a middle school art teacher from upstate New York. She jumped from one of the dormitory balconies."

"Oh, I remember that," I said. "It was just last summer." I'd heard about it from my mother, who tells me about every tragic event that happens locally. She often begins the story by saying something along the lines of, "Can you believe it?" while looking at her phone, possibly assuming that I'm looking at her phone as well.

"Right, and it was ruled a suicide, so, technically, it's not an unsolved homicide."

"But it could have been a homicide," I said.

"All I know is that it happened when my husband was there. Also, that was the conference he was coming from when I watched him from the window, when he . . ."

"Right," I said. "I can definitely check it out, if you want? Just don't get your hopes up. I know a few people at Shepaug, but I doubt they know anything that wasn't in the newspapers. But maybe I'll find out something. Is that what you want me to do? To help you?"

"I guess so. I don't know. One part of me just thought that I could tell you what I found out and that you could tell me what you thought I should do."

"I'm happy to do that, I guess, but I also think that you don't have enough information yet. Like you said, if you accuse your husband of this and he has nothing to do with it, then it'll probably wreck your marriage. And you said that's not something you want to do . . ."

Martha was nodding.

"Where is your husband now?"

"He's in North Carolina. Another math conference."

"Are you worried he might—"

"Of course I'm worried. I'm petrified. If he comes back and I discover that some woman has been assaulted or killed there, then this is on me. I could have done something about it."

"Well, there's nothing you can do about it now. He's already there. It's not like you can call the FBI and they'll arrest him because you found blood on his shirt."

"Okay," she said, nodding.

"When does he come back?"

"Tomorrow night, and then he's home for the whole week and the next weekend. Monday he's off to somewhere else, for a whole week, I think. Somewhere in New York State."

"Okay. This is what I think we should do. First of all, keep an eye on any news stories from North Carolina—where is he exactly?"

"Chapel Hill."

"If something happens there, then I think you need to go immediately to the police."

"You're right," Martha said, her eyes fixed on me. I could tell that she just wanted to be told what to do, and now that I was doing that, she was staring at me the way a drowning person stares at a life raft.

"If nothing comes up, then I'll do some of my own research, not just at Shepaug, but at the other places. And we'll make a decision together. We're not there yet, but maybe the accusation can come from me, or be anonymous."

"I hadn't thought of that."

"Your job is to note anything suspicious when he comes back and let me know right away if you find anything. Does that work for you?"

She wiped at an eye and said, "Yes. So, you don't think I'm crazy?"

"I don't know yet," I said, saying it in a way that I thought made it clear it was a joke. Her face fell, and I quickly added, "Just joking. No, I don't think you're crazy at all."

"Do you think my husband's a serial killer?"

Our waitress had returned, hovering around three feet from the table, and we both noticed her at the same time. I asked for the check.

"Oh my God," Martha said. "You think she heard me?"

"She probably thought we were talking about some TV show. *So You Think Your Husband's a Serial Killer.*"

Martha laughed. "Probably. So, do you?"

I weighed what I was going to say and finally decided to say the truth. "It's a lot of evidence, Martha, that many unsolved deaths. The bloodstain, I think, can be explained away, but all the similar assaults in cities he was in . . . I don't know, it seems like a lot of smoke."

"For there not to be a fire," Martha said.

"Right," I said. "Although, as you pointed out, these are major cities he travels to. It would be more suspicious if a weekend passed without there being some kind of unsolved killing."

"Shepaug's not a big city."

"It's not," I said. "Look, all I'm saying is stranger things have probably happened. The world is full of coincidences."

The check came, and Martha insisted on paying it. I let her. After putting down cash, she said, "Oh no. We were supposed to have dinner, weren't we? We can stay."

"That's okay," I said. "I'm not even hungry yet, and we talked about what you wanted to talk about. And now we have a plan."

Outside of Tipsy McStaggers I walked Martha back to her car. The sun was low in the sky, but it was still bright enough outside that my eyes were adjusting from the dim interior of the faux–Irish pub we'd just exited. At the car she said, "We didn't even talk about the other suspicious deaths I found."

"You have them written down in your notebook?"

"I do. I could send you a copy."

"Why don't I take a picture?"

That's what I did. She flipped through the notes she'd taken, not just the names and dates and places of potential victims, but also a list of every business trip Alan Peralta had gone on since they'd been together. I took pictures with my smartphone, the recent acquisition spurred on by my mother. Then we hugged, and I walked back to my own car, humming to myself. It took me a moment to realize what the song was, and then it came to me. "Martha My Dear" by the Beatles. The brain is a strange machine.

That night I sat with my father in the living room at Monk's House while he played records and sipped whiskey and water. I had just come down from my room, where I'd spent most of the evening looking into the death of Josie Nixon on the Shepaug campus. I'd also done some research into the other deaths that Martha had found. All young women, all unsolved crimes. When my eyes began to ache, I came downstairs to have a drink with my father.

"Oh, I have something for you," he said, after I sat down across from him. He got up and wandered off, returning a few minutes later with a full drink and a used copy of *The Complete Poems* by Anne Sexton.

"For you," he said.

"Yes, I know. I ordered it."

"And I opened it."

"Do you often open mail that's addressed to other people?"

"Well, it was book-shaped, and I'll admit I didn't look at the name on the label. My old friend Ian Peck has been threatening to send me his new book and I thought it might be that."

I picked the book up, smelling it. "I'll forgive you your trespass," I said.

"Thank you. Are you an Anne Sexton fan?"

"I don't know yet," I said. "It was a recommendation."

"Henry Kimball?"

"Good guess," I said. My father was right. It had been a year since I'd last seen Henry, a year since he'd asked for my opinion on a case he'd been working on, convinced that he'd been set up as a witness to a crime. He had been, and it nearly got him killed. The last time I'd seen him was when he'd come down to visit after being released from the hospital, lucky to be alive, and slightly brain-damaged. In the year since I'd seen him, we'd been writing letters back and forth, the ancient kind done with pen and paper. It was partly an affectation but mostly a necessity. Henry and I had a history together. Shortly after I'd first met him, I'd stabbed him in the stomach, worried that he was on the verge of discovering some of my secrets. That was back when he'd been a police officer and he'd suspected me of murder. Since then, he'd become a private investigator. No one besides my parents knew that we were friends.

"He's the Sexton fan, then?"

"In his last letter he said how much he'd been enjoying rereading her poems, and so I ordered this book."

I watched my father's face, the varying responses he might make flickering across it, until he landed on, "Back in my day, we just fucked the people we were in love with."

That night, I lay in bed and thought about Martha and her love curse, and a little bit about Anne Sexton, since her book of poems was open on my chest.

Before coming up to bed I'd read a random poem from the book aloud to my father. The first lines of the poem were, "It is half winter, half spring, and Barbara and I are standing confronting the ocean."

When I finished the poem, my father said, "It's kind of half winter, half spring right now."

"It is."

"Not my favorite time of year."

"No?"

"When I was younger I didn't mind things ending, and I liked the beginnings of things, but these days I prefer the middle of things. Maybe I'm just old."

"You liked the poem, then?"

"It kept my attention," he said.

The next morning I decided that I would spend the day finding out what I could about Josie Nixon and her suicide. Alan's next conference was about a week away. It gave us some time, but not much. As Martha had pointed out, if Alan attacked another woman on one of his trips while we were taking our time trying to figure out what to do, then we would be partly responsible. I had a sudden vision of the dead women that we were now responsible for—Josie Nixon, the sex worker from Atlanta, the bartender from Fort Myers, the receptionist in Chicago, the masseuse in San Diego. I could picture them standing in a line, watching me from some other place, no expressions on their faces, but with eyes that were telling me, telling Martha and me, not to let it happen again. I read their names from the photographs on my phone. Josie Nixon, Kelli Baldwin, Bianca Muranos, Nora Johnson, Mikaela Sager. They stared at me some more through eyes I was only imagining, asking the questions I suspect that the dead always ask: Why me? Why now?

CHAPTER 8

Alan was arriving at Manchester Airport at five, which meant that he'd be home not much later than six thirty. Martha texted to let him know that she'd be making dinner that night.

She was roasting a chicken, hoping that a familiar task would stop her mind from spinning. And it was one of their favorite meals, Martha loving the way it made the house smell. In the past she had found it a calming smell, a reminder that for the time being she was home safe and there was food in the oven and the world outside could wait. But now, with the oven timer ticking down, the house beginning to darken while clouds gathered outside, Martha felt a deep sense of fear, manifesting itself as a hard knot at the center of her chest. It was one thing to *believe* that your husband was some kind of monster who preyed on women, but she had spoken it out loud, told Lily about him, set the wheels in motion. And now all she could think was that when he came through the front door he'd take one look at her face and know exactly what had happened.

But when he finally did come through the door, wet with rain, he left his bag in the foyer, quickly crossed the living room to the open kitchen, kissed Martha, and asked if he had time for a hot shower.

"Of course," she said, waiting for him to really look at her and know what had happened. Waiting for him to see that pulsing knot at the center of her chest or her trembling hands.

But all he said was, "It smells amazing in here. I'll be right back."

While he showered, Martha drank a third glass of wine. It didn't relax her, but it made the room shimmer with unnatural light, so she made herself eat two pieces of the soft baguette she'd bought, spreading camembert on top. She wasn't hungry, but the act of chewing and swallowing did calm her a little bit. She took the chicken out of the oven, checked the small red potatoes—they still needed time—and added the sheet of asparagus where the chicken had been. Her glasses were steamed up and she took them off for a moment. Alan didn't know what she had done that morning. Even if he was a monster, he wasn't someone who could peer inside of people to read their innermost thoughts. Just as she couldn't read his thoughts. She took a sip of her wine and then went to their stereo system, flipping it on, pairing it with her phone, then picking a mix called "Dinnertime Jazz."

"Ooh, romantic," Alan said, sneaking up behind her in the kitchen. She jumped, making one of the strange sounds that came out of her when she was frightened. Alan laughed, one of his loud cocktail-party laughs, then apologized.

"Sorry, I'm jittery, for some reason," she said. "Maybe it's the weather."

"Flying in, we could see lightning out along the coast. The woman next to me was praying, I think."

"How was the conference?"

"I'll tell you all about it tomorrow. But it was fine. Can I help with dinner?"

Martha pulled the potatoes and asparagus out of the oven while Alan carved the chicken. Then they brought everything to the table and started to eat.

When he finished the food on his plate, Alan leaned back and said, "Have you thought some more about a trip to England this summer?"

"I have," Martha said. "It sounds perfect." An image went through Martha's mind: Alan and her at a country pub, the moors in the distance. She suddenly longed to be there, not because it would be a nice trip, but because if they were there together it would mean that her husband was innocent, that the nightmare she was in would have come to some kind of benign end.

"You okay?" Alan said.

"Oh, sorry. Daydreaming already about our trip. I think it would be great. You said you'd thought of a possible week already?"

"Sometime in August. Let's talk about it tomorrow. All I have energy for is maybe some television and then straight to bed."

A small ripple of relief went through her that he didn't want to have sex. He often did when he was back from one of his trips, but he usually let her know he was in the mood first. Sometimes he did it jokingly, saying something like, "Shall we make it an early night?" while raising and lowering his eyebrows, but sometimes he was a little more direct, pushing up against her while she was doing the dishes, sliding a hand down between her legs. And, just as he always let her know ahead of time if he wanted sex, he usually let her know if he didn't, saying something like what he had just said about being so tired, or that he could sleep for a week if given a chance.

After the dishes were done and they were watching *The Great British Baking Show* together, she began to wonder if there was some correlation between what had happened on a trip and whether he wanted sex or not when he came back. Maybe his exhaustion meant that he'd found and killed a woman down in Chapel Hill. The taste of roasted garlic hovered at the back of Martha's throat and for a moment she thought she might be sick. She took a deep and quiet breath. Maybe it was just the opposite. Maybe when her husband came home, his hands all over her, dying to get her into the bedroom and strip her clothing off, it was because he'd killed a woman just hours before. Maybe it was a celebration.

"You okay over there?" Alan said.

"Oh, fine," Martha said, wondering what had made him ask. "A little acid reflux, if I'm honest."

"Take something."

"Okay, I will." But she stayed seated while Paul Hollywood analyzed some under-baked biscuits. She wondered how she was going to get through the rest of the night, let alone the next week.

When the episode ended, Alan said he was heading up to bed, and Martha said that she might stay up and watch a little more television. Right before he left the room he turned and asked, "You sure you're okay? You seem a little tense tonight."

"Just my period, I think," she said, even though she'd had it less than two weeks ago.

"Lady troubles," Alan said, almost to himself, before leaving the TV room.

An hour later Martha stepped into their bedroom to hear Alan snoring into his pillow. She shut the bedroom door and went back downstairs into the dark living room, opening up her laptop, telling herself that she'd just do a quick check of North Carolina news to find out if anything had happened over the weekend. Perched on the edge of her office chair, she typed in "Chapel Hill," which brought her to the local paper, the *News & Observer*. She scanned the news section, relieved that the lead story seemed to be that a team of firefighters had rescued a kitten from the roof of an apartment building. As far as she could tell, there were no recent murders, or violent crimes. Still, she did a search using the words "Chapel Hill" and "unsolved." There were multiple hits, but nothing recent. She erased her browsing history, closed the laptop, and took the first deep breath she'd taken that night.

Martha worked the next day at the library, the hours passing in an almost dreamlike way, as though everything moved a little slower. She was working every day that week, and Alan was home on one of his staycations. He didn't have a conference over the next weekend, and they'd talked about going somewhere, maybe down to an inn they liked in Gloucester, on Cape Ann.

"You doing okay, hon?" Mary said to her as she was walking past the reference desk. Martha must have been staring into space.

"If one more person asks me that," she said, then saw the look of shame on Mary's face and immediately apologized. "Oh, sorry, Mary. I'm fine, honestly."

"I was just hoping you don't have that flu that's going around. Margie had it and said her throat felt like she'd swallowed thumbtacks."

"No, I'm fine. It's probably nothing."

But that night she told Alan that she thought she might be coming down with something, that she felt flushed and her throat hurt.

"And you're getting your period," he said, and it took her a moment to remember that she'd lied about that to him the day before.

"When it rains . . ." she said.

She set herself up in the guest room, reading her book and having saltine crackers and ginger ale for her dinner, deciding that even though she wasn't sick she could probably happily eat that particular meal on any given day. At ten o'clock Alan popped into the room to say good night, standing in the doorframe. "Hey, can I ask you something out of left field?" he said.

"Okay," she said, alarmed by the serious tone in his voice.

"Don't freak out on me for asking this, but are you having an affair?"

She looked at him for five seconds trying to process the words and saw that his face was bloodless, his jaw rigid with anxiety. "What?" she said. "No, of course not. Why are you asking?"

"It's just . . . a feeling, I guess. You've been a little distant lately, and I go away for long periods of time. And there's another thing, but I don't know if I want to say it. It'll make me sound crazy."

"What is it? Now you *are* freaking me out a little."

"So, you seemed so distant yesterday, and you were kind of vague about what you'd done over the weekend, so while you were in the shower . . . I went and checked your odometer. In your car."

"I'm sorry. You did what?"

"I checked your odometer. And I saw that you added about two hundred miles to it since the last time I looked."

"Since the last time you looked? Please explain that to me."

"I don't understand your question."

"Why do you know what my odometer is at?"

"I always know that, just like I know exactly how much money we have in our checking accounts, and how long it's been since we changed the water filter in the fridge, and the exact sales figures on all my merchandise. It's just how I think. Where did you go, Martha?"

His little speech had been long enough for Martha to decide what to say. "I had lunch with a friend in Worcester. Her name's Lily Kintner and she lives in Connecticut, so we met halfway there."

"You've never mentioned her before."

"Honestly, we're not that close. We went to grad school together, then lost touch, but she reached out to me and we talked on the phone and decided last-minute to meet up. We went to this awful Irish pub that you wouldn't believe—"

"I don't understand why you didn't tell me about it." He tugged at an earlobe.

"I would've, I guess. I mean, I didn't make a decision to not tell you. The thing is, we both drove all this way to get together, then we basically ran out of things to talk about halfway through our first drink. It was depressing. You know how I've talked to you before about not having any real close friends and about how that makes me feel bad?"

Alan nodded.

"Well, I suppose part of me hoped that maybe Lily and I would rekindle our friendship, but it just didn't happen. And it made me feel like it was *me*, that I was the one who's incapable of being close to someone. I think that's why I didn't bring it up."

Martha wiped at her eyes, surprised to find real tears there. She was lying, but she wasn't lying about how she felt about herself with regards to friends. Alan came across and sat on the edge of the bed, put a hand on her leg.

"I am not cheating on you, Alan, I promise. I would never do that in a million years." The tears kept coming.

"I know," he said. "I know that." The words sounded comforting, but his jaw was still rigid, and the earlobe that he'd been pulling on a moment ago was bright red.

"What about you?" Martha said. "You're always traveling. Are you ever tempted?"

"Tempted to what? To cheat on you?"

"Yeah. I mean, I don't think you do. I'm not accusing you, but . . ."

Alan's eyes were resting on the bare wall behind the bed. He finally said, "What possible reason would I have for cheating?"

CHAPTER 9

After my father took his seat at the breakfast table, and while my mother was still at the sink, I asked both of them who they still knew at Shepaug University.

David, who preferred not to talk before his morning egg, said, "No one."

"That's not true, David," Sharon said. "You know Gerry Severn."

"I know Gerry Severn," he said to me.

"Who's that?" I asked.

"Gerry's the head of the English Department," my mother said, "or was, a little while ago. He must be seventy years old now, at least. He was the man who invited your father to come and be a writer-in-residence. If it wasn't for him, Lily, you would never have been born."

"What about you, Mom, who do you still know?"

"At Shepaug? Carrie Michaelson, of course, and Mark Loomis. Why are you asking this?"

"Who do you know who's gossipy?" I said, realizing that most university people were naturally disposed to talk behind their colleagues' backs, but what I really wanted was someone who would have thoughts, and maybe even opinions, about Josie Nixon's death.

"Gossipy?" my mother said.

"I have a friend who's interested in applying for a job there, but she wants to get the full scoop about the place. You know the stuff: How much infighting is there? What departments to avoid?"

"Oh, let me think," Sharon said, as my father carefully removed the shell from his soft-boiled egg. "Well, the biggest gossip at Shepaug was Patty Riley—you remember her, don't you, Lil?—but that was an age ago."

"Try Libby Whatshername," my father said suddenly. "She taught in the English Department."

"She's long gone," Sharon said.

"What, dead?" David said. "I don't think so. I saw her two weeks ago at the bookstore. I mean, she might be, but she'd be freshly dead."

"No, I mean she's long gone from Shepaug. She's your age."

"All I know is that I ran into her at the bookstore and without even asking she started to tell me everything that had happened to everyone we ever knew at Shepaug. And now I'm going to stop talking for a while and concentrate on my breakfast."

Later, after my father went to his study for the morning, I followed him in and asked him about Libby. "She's not going to help your friend out any," David said. "The gossip she mostly had was about who had died and who was still alive. Old person's gossip."

"I actually want to find something else out," I said.

"Oh," David said, his unruly eyebrows raising a fraction.

"There was a suicide on campus last summer. It was during a teacher-training conference and one of the participants leapt from Milner Dorm."

"Yeah, I heard about that. Did you know that Arnold Milner, who donated the money for that atrocity, was a pedophile?"

"I did not know that."

"He was."

"You think that has anything to do with that conference participant jumping out of his building?"

I'd said it as a joke, but my father thought for a moment and said, "There are more things in heaven and earth, Lil."

"Yeah, I suppose. Look, all I'm trying to find out is if it was a clear suicide or if there was something suspicious going on."

"Well, Libby will probably be your woman for the job. I think her last name is Frost."

"I don't suppose you have contact information for her?" I said, not really sure why I was asking. My father didn't own a phone and probably didn't know what "contact information" even meant.

But he thought for a moment, then said, "She's down at Stone's Throw probably every morning. They have a coffee shop there now, you know."

Stone's Throw was the name of our town's independent bookstore, run by a longtime Shepaug resident named Stanley Perrini. It was one of the few places where my father agreed to go, partly because he liked Stanley, and partly because there was a whole shelf devoted to David Kintner books in the store.

"When were you there that you saw Libby?"

"I *see* her whenever I'm there, but I *talked* to her a couple of weeks ago. It was some morning you weren't around and your mother dropped me off there on her way to rehab her hip."

Our town center was about two miles from Monk's House by road, and about a mile and a half if you walked through Brigham Woods and then cut across the old Keene Farmstead. I put on my boots and set out through the woods, reaching the bookstore about five minutes after the morning rain had really turned torrential. I stood just inside the entranceway and dripped for a few moments. The coffee shop area was to the right, a counter offering hot drinks and baked goods, plus about five small tables, three of which were occupied. I barely remembered what Libby Frost looked like, although she'd been one of my father's coworkers during the years he was at the university, but from where I stood I could hear a woman's slightly cracked voice and knew immediately that it was Libby. She was diminutive, her hair back in a gray ponytail, her mouth circled with the tiny wrinkles that longtime smokers had—but the voice was unforgettable.

I went to the free table closest to her and draped my wet coat over the chair, then got myself a hot tea from the teenager behind the counter and took my seat. Libby was still talking. She was seated at her table, a picked-at croissant in front of her, but the woman she was talking with was standing up, in her coat, a Stone's Throw plastic bag in her hand. I recognized the woman's posture as belonging to someone looking for an opportunity to interject a few words to indicate she had to get going. Sure enough, after Libby finished a story about her neighbor turning her garage into some sort of Airbnb rental, the woman in the coat said, "Lib, I've got to run. Scruffy's at the vet."

"Go, go," Libby said.

I pried the plastic lid off my tea and blew on it. I'd been thinking about how to introduce myself to Libby Frost when she suddenly said, "I know you. You're David Kintner's daughter."

I turned. "Guilty, I suppose."

"You won't remember me," she said, brushing croissant crumbs from the front of her purple sweater, "but David and I taught in the same department back in the caveman days."

"You're Libby Frost," I said, and her eyes lit up.

"Oh, smart girl. I am. How's your father? You know, I saw him here not too long ago, and he told me that he was late for his hormone replacement session . . ." She looked at me questioningly.

"He was kidding you."

"Yes, I figured that. He was always a naughty man, your father."

I asked her if I could join her at her table, wanting to get closer to her just so she'd speak a little more quietly. She was thrilled for the company, she said, and spent twenty minutes recalling some of the stuff my father got up to during the years he was an adjunct professor. Most of what she told me was harmless—the department meetings he slept through, the time he drunkenly gave a reading from a new book all while impersonating the then–department head's voice perfectly. "No one would get away today with what he got away with, I'll tell you," Libby said, with a faraway look in her eye, and I wondered if she'd slept with my father. It was hard to imagine, looking at her now, but my father, and my mother, as well, had made quite a sport of infidelity back when they were married.

"You know, I was thinking of you the other day," I said.

"Oh yeah?"

"I met this guy—he's the husband of one of my dearest friends— and he said he'd spent a week at Shepaug last summer for some teacher-training conference. Didn't you used to arrange the summer programs?"

"No, you're thinking of Diane Hodder, probably. Back when I was at Shepaug my husband and I rented the same house in Tuscany each summer. They couldn't have paid me to stay here in Connecticut during the summer months."

"Right, Diane Hodder. Haven't thought of her in years."

"Was your friend's husband at the art teachers' conference?"

"Probably," I said.

"You must have heard about it, but that was the conference where one of the participants jumped from Milner."

"Yeah, I know. That's why we were talking about it. It was awful, he said."

"Oh, I'm sure. Poor girl."

"What do you know about it?" I said, leaning in close, hoping to invite her to tell me any salacious details she might have up her sleeve.

"Do you know who found her . . . found the girl's body, I mean? It was Jim Prescott, out for an early run. I heard she was naked. Can you imagine?"

I didn't know who Jim Prescott was, but said, "God, poor Jim. Why did she jump, did anyone know?"

"There was a whole murder investigation, from what I heard. She didn't leave a suicide note, so I guess they had to wonder if she'd been pushed off that balcony. I say they should just tear down that whole monstrosity. Who puts balconies in student dorms to begin with? And Arnold Milner was a pervert, you know."

"Yes, I did know that."

"But they can't take his name off because he was never convicted. So I say just tear that whole dorm down and be done with it."

"I don't think anyone would complain."

"There'd be a celebration."

I took a sip of my cold tea. "Who was the woman who jumped, someone from around here?"

"No, she was an attendee. Josie Something. She was an art teacher from Woodstock."

"And did the police determine that it was a suicide, after all?"

"From what I heard it was eventually ruled a suicide. But I also heard that it was only ruled that because they couldn't find any solid evidence of foul play. Some people think she was thrown off. I know her husband made a big stink about it. He came down here, insisting she'd never have killed herself, and that some murderer had gotten away with it and was now out on the loose."

"Understandable," I said.

"Right, but what I heard, and this was not public information at all, was that that girl *had* been looking for company during the conference. Everyone knows that all these teacher-training conferences that Shepaug runs turn into Roman orgies late at night. I guess if you spend your time teaching sixth-graders to make collages you need to add some excitement to your life any way you can."

"So the rumors were that Josie Nixon was sleeping with someone at this conference?"

"Well, the rumors were that she was hoping to, that she was on the make, for lack of a better word. And, of course, she was naked when she jumped."

"And she was married."

"And she was married."

"So, it's possible," I said, "that she had sex with someone at the conference and then felt guilty about it and threw herself off the balcony."

"Right. Or *he* felt guilty about it and threw *her* off the balcony."

"Did her husband know about all this?"

Libby frowned, the tiny lines around her mouth contracting. "I don't really know. All I know is that he didn't believe she killed herself, so he probably also didn't believe she'd have an affair."

"Probably not," I said. "Maybe it was easier for him to believe that someone killed her than it would be to believe she took her own life. Or to believe she had an affair and then took her own life."

Libby got another one of her faraway looks and said, "Do you remember Eileen Morrell? No, you wouldn't, would you? She taught here before you were even born. Her husband shot himself and even left a note behind. Eileen must have felt guilty about it, because the rumor at the time was that she was sleeping with someone in the Science Department. She kept insisting that her husband had been killed, the suicide note faked. They gave her compassionate leave, or whatever they were calling it back then, but she never came back. I wonder what ever happened to her."

I was doubly wet and doubly cold when I made it back to Monk's House. I stripped down and took a long hot bath in the claw-footed tub on the second floor. I thought about Josie Nixon and her husband. And I thought about that summer conference for art teachers in July, the days filled with panels and classes, and the nights with social events. Josie Nixon, for whatever reason, had been excited about the prospect of a summer romance. She'd have met Alan Peralta, the man who set up his booth of funny T-shirts and quirky trinkets. Everyone attending the conference would have met him, of course. And was he there looking for a temporary fling as well?

The door to the bathroom swung inward and April padded in. She wasn't my cat, exactly, although I'd named her for the month, two years ago, when she'd first shown up at our house uninvited.

She came and went as she pleased, mostly visiting the barn, where I left her food, and it had been a while since she'd come inside the actual house. She sat on the bathroom tile and looked at me. "It's called a bath," I said.

When I got out from the cooling water, she sashayed back out the way she'd come in.

That night, while my mother watched PBS mysteries, I sat next to her on the couch with my laptop and found out everything I could about Josie Nixon and her husband, Travis. There were really very few newspaper articles about her death, but there was an obituary in the Albany newspaper, and there was a remembrance page on which people had left comments about Josie and the hole she'd left behind.

There were multiple images online, including several that came from Travis and Josie's wedding website. They'd met at art school five years earlier and gotten married two years after that. They both looked as though they were in their late twenties. Josie had a pale, round face and long hair that she'd dyed jet-black. She wore a lot of high-necked white shirts, but in the few pictures where she was showing some skin, it was clear that her arms were covered in tattoos. Her husband could have passed as her brother. Same sallow face but a little rounder, and he had a waxed mustache. On their wedding day she'd been in a traditional white dress and he'd been in a dark shimmery tux, but in every other picture of them he was wearing black jeans and graphic T-shirts, while she was usually wearing black velvety skirts, shirts with brooches, or vintage sweaters, her inky hair parted in the middle. Like Wednesday Addams, I thought, then remembered that Wednesday Addams had worn her hair in pigtails. Josie's husband was a graphic designer and aspiring comic book artist. They had lived in Woodstock, New York.

A little while ago I had created a false Instagram account under the name Rose Sheldon. This was back around the time I was helping Henry Kimball with the case that nearly got him killed. I logged on to my fake page, not entirely surprised to find that I'd acquired a few new followers, including a man who'd sent me a message that began, Hello, beautiful . . . despite there being only three posts on my page, two of April the cat, and one of the white rosebush in our front yard. I found Travis Nixon's page. It wasn't private, and I was able to scroll through hundreds of photographs. He'd been clearly enamored of his wife before she died, but since then *every* post was of her, along with a long text about how the police had stopped looking for her murderer. Every post ended with the hashtag: #JusticeForJosie.

I amended my fake Instagram bio so that instead of it saying "Gardener, amateur detective, adventuress," it read "Independent journalist. Looking for stories no one else wants to tell." Then I sent a message to Travis Nixon: Hi Travis. I'd be interested in doing a piece about the death of your wife. Would you consent to an interview? I have no agenda besides uncovering the truth. Regards, Rose Sheldon.

I sent it off, then immediately regretted it, thinking I should have given it a little more thought. All Travis would have to do was google "Rose Sheldon" to discover that she'd never published a single article. He'd identify me as an impostor, and probably conclude that I was some sort of con artist. I thought about other ways to approach him. I could be honest, of course, without giving him any real names. Just let him know that I had a friend who suspected her husband of targeting women at teacher conferences. But he'd insist on knowing more. From looking at his online presence, it was clear that he was deeply obsessed with the death of his wife.

I was thinking of closing my laptop and getting ready to go to bed when I received a response. Rose. Thank you, thank you for reaching out. I'd love to tell you my story. In person? On the phone? I live in Woodstock but would be willing to travel. Travis.

I wrote back that I'd be willing to meet him in Woodstock for lunch at noon the following day. He seemed ecstatic and named a place called the Dove and Hare.

After sending that text I decided to call Martha. She picked up right away, and there was a breathless quality to her voice, as though she were waiting for bad news.

I told her what I'd learned, and my plans for tomorrow.

"Okay, wow," she said. "But even if he's convinced she was murdered, it might not mean she was."

"I'll talk to him and see. But, yes, he's obviously going to try and plead his case. In the meantime, you and I should start making some phone calls, do some research."

"Like what?"

"We could call the police departments in the cities where you found those crimes. Tell them we're working for a private investigator, and ask for updates. They'll either talk to us or they won't, but you never know. We could also call crime reporters in those cities. That might work."

"I think I could do that," Martha said, but she sounded doubtful.

"It's worth a shot. We might get a chatty cop. Stranger things have happened."

"Okay, sure," she said. "I could definitely try. I can actually start tomorrow. Alan's here, but he'll be gone most of the day tomorrow. He told me he's doing an inventory count and that will take him most of the day. I've already told him I'm coming down with something, so I'll call in sick to work."

We talked some more about questions to ask, and I could tell that she was starting to get excited about the assignment I'd given her. She was a librarian, after all, and there's nothing a librarian likes more than an assignment.

CHAPTER 10

In the morning Martha emailed the library to let them know she was taking a sick day, then she let Alan bring her breakfast in bed. After he had left the tray she listened to him move around downstairs, preparing to leave for the day. Now that she'd decided to make some calls she was nervous, but wanting to get a start on her research.

At last she heard the front door open and shut and then the faint sound of his car starting up. She quickly got out of bed, dressed in yoga pants and a sweatshirt, and went downstairs to the computer. They still had a landline in the house, and there was a desk phone next to the computer.

The first few conversations did not go well. Martha tried her best to sound like a jaded investigator, someone who expected to receive information. The first police detective she reached was in the Atlanta Police Department, a Detective Gunter, who had worked the Kelli Baldwin case. She was the only victim on Martha's list who had been identified in the press as a prostitute. She'd died from blunt-force trauma to the head late at night while returning to her apartment in north Atlanta, three miles from downtown where the convention was being held. Martha asked the detective if he had any leads, and he'd told her that she was a junkie and a prostitute, and it could have been anyone she knew.

"Did she work the convention hotels?" she asked.

"The convention hotels? Nope. She was a strung-out street hooker who worked over by Piedmont Park."

"But it's possible that someone from a downtown hotel might have cruised that area looking for a pick-up?"

"Anything's possible, lady. For all I know, it was some tourist from China who'd read about the hot hookers on the Ponce de Leon. I can't help you."

Her next call was to Chicago, and she was shuffled around from department to department for thirty minutes before being connected with an Officer Wood, who was able to take a look at the file on Bianca Muranos, found dead in an alleyway behind the DoubleTree Conference Center in Chicago. She had been killed by blunt-force trauma, as well. And, as in Atlanta, no weapon had been found.

Martha asked Officer Wood if Bianca had been a prostitute, and listened while he whistled to himself, flipping through the case file. "Not according to this. She worked as a receptionist at one of the big downtown office buildings."

"And there were no leads?"

More whistling. "Well, nothing that came to anything. You know, though, there's pictures of the body here in the file and she was out to party that night."

"What do you mean?"

"I mean, it's possible that her skirt hiked up or something when she hit the ground, but even if it did, that skirt was shorter than my kids' attention span. She was either out clubbing or in the game."

The first informative conversation she managed to have was with Detective Melissa Cruz, who was in charge of the still-open murder of Nora Johnson in Fort Myers, Florida.

"We think the perpetrator was an attendee at a conference that was going on that weekend," the detective said, unprompted. Martha, who was taking notes, quickly scribbled that down.

"Why do you think that?"

"Because I've learned a lot about Nora Johnson in the last six months, and what I learned was that about eighty percent of her job was as a bartender, and the other twenty percent was running scams on married men attending conventions at the hotel she worked at.

She worked with a parking attendant named Dyson Holmgren, and he was the one who found the body. She was parked in the employee section of the belowground garage, and he told us that he spotted her car there long past the time her shift ended, so he went to check it out."

"She was dead in the car, right?"

"Yes. But we got witness statements from everyone who came and went from that parking garage from the time Nora Johnson's shift ended at eleven to the time that Holmgren called in the body. And one of our witnesses was another employee, a woman on the front desk who said that when she was leaving the lot at twelve she saw Holmgren peering into Nora Johnson's car."

"What time did Holmgren call in the body?"

"Not until about three o'clock."

"So, you think he saw the body was there at midnight?"

"At the time we thought it was a possibility, but he claimed he didn't. Regardless, it put Holmgren at the scene of the crime around the time it was probably committed. And then it turned out that Holmgren was friends with Nora Johnson, that she was the one who got him the job at the hotel in the first place."

"And you arrested him?"

"And we arrested him. His prints were on Johnson's car door, but that was because he'd opened it when he spotted her sitting on the front seat, not moving. There were no other indications that he'd been in the car when she was strangled."

"Was there any forensic evidence?"

"There was and there wasn't. There were a couple of fibers from whatever it was that had strangled her. Some kind of synthetic rayon. But other than that, we found far *too* much evidence. Hairs from at least fifteen different people. Multiple fibers. We even found semen stains, but they were all at least twenty-four hours old."

"Wouldn't that be common in someone's car?"

"You have sex with a lot of people in your car? I know I don't."

"I didn't mean the semen so much as the fibers and hairs."

"I guess so. Depends on how many people you drive around. Or, in Nora's case, depends on how many men she brought to her car."

"A lot of them?" Martha said.

"Yes, a lot of them. When we brought in Holmgren, he panicked pretty fast when we told him he was going to prison for first-degree murder. So he told us why he'd been snooping around her car. He and Nora had a little scam going at the Anhinga Hotel, pretty much the oldest scam in the oldest book. She would get to know one of the visiting conventioneers, preferably a married man, and after her shift she'd either go to his room, or, more usually, she'd ask him to walk her to her car. Then she'd get him inside the car for some extramarital activity, and that was when Holmgren would come in, crashing the party."

"Oh wow," Martha said, then gritted her teeth, telling herself to talk more like a fellow investigator.

"He's a big muscular dude. Sometimes he'd pretend to be her pimp. The guy almost always ended up emptying his wallet to get out of the situation. If he didn't have money on him, Holmgren would confiscate his driver's license and ask for a thousand dollars or something before he left Florida or else he'd make his life miserable. It was all pretty small-potatoes. According to Holmgren they only did it about once or twice a month. Sometimes they got a thousand and sometimes it was a couple of hundred bucks. Oh, hold on a moment."

She could hear Detective Cruz talking to someone, her hand held over the phone. When she got back on, Martha said, "You still got time?"

"Yeah, a little."

"So what do you think happened the night that Nora Johnson was strangled?"

"Well, that's why I said I think one of the attendees at the conference did it. She picked up the wrong guy."

"Then why wasn't Holmgren on the scene to stop it?"

"He tried to get there right away, but he didn't always manage it, depending on what was happening with work. That night he got sent the text from Nora saying that she was bringing a man with her to her car. This was right around eleven forty-five. He claims it took him fifteen minutes to get to the car and she was already dead."

"Why didn't he call the body in then?"

"He said he panicked, that he didn't want to get involved. Et cetera, et cetera. And then, at three, his better nature won out, I guess."

"And you don't think it's him?"

"I don't. If you talked to some of my colleagues you'd get a different story. Holmgren is a scumbag, but he's not a murderer. She got killed by someone who was staying at the hotel."

"You've been through the list of the attendees of the conference?"

"About a hundred times."

"No names jumped out at you?"

"Not really."

"Did you look at a guy called Alan Peralta?" Saying his name out loud made Martha feel like all her muscles had simultaneously clenched a little.

"That name's a little familiar. He was at the conference?"

"He wasn't an attendee. He was working at the conference. He sold novelty teacher items from a booth."

"Got it. Yeah, he was a guest at the hotel. We did look at him, only because he spent some money at the hotel bar."

"On the night of Nora Johnson's death."

"On every night he was there, if I remember. Should I be looking at this guy?"

"Maybe. You'll be the first to know if I find out anything." Martha stumbled over the words, but the detective didn't seem to notice.

"I'll take any leads. This one feels pretty cold."

She muffled the phone again and Martha could hear a muted conversation. "Sorry," Detective Cruz said when she was back on. "I need to get going. We good here?"

The final person Martha managed to speak with that morning, a Linda Callahan, turned out to be as uninterested in speaking to her as the first two detectives had been. Detective Callahan had worked the suspicious death of Mikaela Sager, the massage therapist who had turned up washed ashore by the Imperial Beach Pier in the South Bay of San Diego.

"It looked like a drowning at first, but the coroner found a head contusion, so now it looks like someone walked her to the end of the pier, bopped her on the head, and dumped her."

"And there are no suspects?"

"Nope."

"She was a massage therapist."

"Yep."

"Any chance that her calling herself a massage therapist was a euphemism for some kind of sex work?"

"It's possible, I guess. She worked out of her home."

"What about the night she died?"

"What about it?"

"What was she doing? Was she out with friends, out on a date, working? How'd she end up at the pier? Did she drive there?"

"She drove there. We don't know what she was doing that night except getting herself killed. And before that, we know that she ate fried calamari and drank tequila. That's what her stomach contents showed us. Oh, and she hadn't had sex, at least not recently."

Martha paused slightly after she'd finished this answer and the detective quickly added, "We all good here?"

"One last question," Martha said. "What was she wearing when she was pulled out of the water?"

"Okay. Let me see. She was wearing jeans and a green cotton top. And she was wearing a white sweater, a cardigan. Nothing fancy or distinctive. Her shoes weren't found."

Martha decided to give up and said, "Detective Callahan, you've been remarkably helpful. Thanks for talking to me."

The detective's voice brightened a little and she said, without a touch of irony, "Hey, no problem. Being helpful is my job."

"Well . . ." Martha said, and then couldn't think what to say to finish the sentence.

"Oh, and she wore a pin," Detective Callahan said, as though she'd just remembered that particular fact.

"Who?"

"The victim. You asked me what clothes she was wearing. I'm looking at the file right now. She wore a pin on her sweater. Like a . . . like a brooch."

"What of?" Martha said, trying to keep her voice neutral.

"Ah, let me see. It's a woman's face. She has white hair. No, it's some kind of hat she's wearing."

"A photograph?"

"No, it's a brooch."

"Can you do me a big favor, Detective? Can I give you my cell phone number and can you text me a picture of that pin?"

"It'll be a picture of a picture."

"That's fine. I just really would like to see it."

After they hung up, Martha stared at her phone until the text arrived. It was a picture of a brooch, not a very good picture, but good enough so that Martha knew exactly what she was looking at. It was a Jane Austen brooch, her hair in a white bonnet, the kind of brooch you might sell to an English teacher.

She sent a text to Lily, five words: I think I found something.

CHAPTER 11

I was crossing over the Hudson River on the Kingston-Rhinecliff Bridge when my phone made a sound. I was so unused to receiving messages that I didn't know at first where the singsong alert had come from, but when I looked down at my phone that was lying across the unused cupholder, I saw that I'd received a text from Martha. She'd written, I think I found something.

I almost picked up the phone to call her right then and find out what she'd discovered, but I'd gotten a late start that morning and was rushing to get to my lunch with Travis Nixon in Woodstock. Over breakfast I had told my parents that I was meeting a friend, and that I'd be gone for some of the day. It probably would have been fine, but my mother, unbeknownst to me, had also made lunch plans, meeting one of her old college friends two towns over in the town of Bethlehem. My father, for most of his adult life, has had a deep phobia about being left alone, especially overnight (pretty much unthinkable at this point), but also around any mealtime. He claimed it was because he didn't believe drinking to be a solitary act, and any meal naturally involved drinking. He generally had his first cocktail of the day, a single malt with water, around eleven thirty, after spending the morning reading and dozing in his office. Neither my mother nor I had a drink at that time but usually one of us was there to keep him company.

This morning, when he'd figured out that we were both going to be away, I saw a startled look in his eyes, a combination of fear and sadness. The closest I can come to describing it is that it looked like grief. And I think in a way it was. I spend too much time with my father to waste time analyzing him, but I do think that when he is alone, he is consumed with visions of death, both his own and those of the people he loves, and it's too much for him to bear.

"Mom," I said, "why don't you bring Dad to lunch?"

She looked horrified, so I said, "Or maybe we could see if Stanley wants to come over?"

"I'll be okay," my father said, not very convincingly. "I'll make myself a ham sandwich."

Nevertheless, I managed to get Stanley, David's friend and the owner of the Stone's Throw Bookstore, on the phone and he agreed to come over around eleven thirty and have a drink with David. He's a slow talker, Stanley, and we were on the phone for about ten minutes while I convinced him he didn't need to bring anything in particular, or to wear a collared shirt. And because of all that, I was late heading into Woodstock, and then it took me about ten minutes to find the Dove and Hare, an ivy-covered one-story brick restaurant just off Main Street.

"I thought you weren't going to show," Travis Nixon said. He'd been waiting for me at the front entrance. Because I'd looked at so many pictures of him on Instagram, mostly posing with Josie, I was startled by how thin he was now, a ghost of himself.

"Sorry," I said. "Late start, but I'm here now."

I followed him to a table in a nook just past an ornate bar decorated with twisting branches and Christmas lights.

"This was our favorite place," he said, taking a seat across from me.

"Yours and Josie's?"

"Yes." Even though he'd lost weight, apparently, he hadn't gotten new clothes, and his T-shirt, with an image of a crow under the words SAY NEVERMORE, swam on him.

"First off," I said, "I'm really sorry for your loss." He nodded at me. "And I also want to come clean. I'm primarily a fiction writer, poetry mostly, but I went to school at Shepaug University, and when I heard about Josie . . . I don't know, I just kept thinking about her. So the thing is, I asked around a little, just people I used to know from there, and I started to think that maybe it wasn't what it seemed. I mean, that it was more likely a murder than a suicide, and that meant that someone had got away with it. Then I looked you up, and it's clear that you feel the same way."

"I do," he said. A waitress was hovering near us, but she must have seen the intense look on Travis's face and she backed away.

"I didn't know Josie, and I don't know you, but I thought that maybe I could write a piece about what happened, and try to get it published. And that way I could help you out a little."

"That would be great," he said, leaning across the table between us. "It's actually good that you don't know us, that you didn't know Josie. I keep telling the world that she was killed, but I'm biased because I was her husband. No one believes me. But if you said something . . ."

"I agree," I said.

The waitress finally approached, and I quickly looked at the menu, ordering some kind of mocktail that was made from a blackberry shrub, and the chickpea burger. Travis ordered a dark ale and the soup of the day. While we were ordering I started to feel a little guilty about lying to this man, but I also told myself that I was trying to find Josie's killer and if I managed to do that, it would be worth a whole lot more to him than an article.

"So why don't you believe Josie kill herself?" I said after the waitress left with our order.

I expected him to talk about how much she loved life, or how she wasn't the type, but the first thing he said was, "She was scared of heights. Deathly scared. There's just no way in hell she would have gone out on a balcony, let alone jumped from it. I mean, that was the first thing I thought when I heard what had happened. Also, if she had been so unhappy that she wanted to kill herself, then I would have known about it. I know you won't believe that, no one does, but she would have told me. I know it.

"We even talked about suicide once. She said she used to think about it all the time back in high school. She said that if she ever did it, it would be with drugs, something that would put her to sleep. There's just no way she would jump from a balcony."

"What would you have thought, then, if she went to this teachers' conference and took an overdose and died there?"

He pursed his lips so hard that his upper lip pressed up under his nose. "That's a good question that no one has asked me. And I'll say this: I still think that she wouldn't have done it. Our lives were good, and she was really excited about that trip."

Our drinks arrived, and after tasting the blackberry mocktail I was a little regretful I wasn't drinking a beer. Travis's had come in a glass shaped like a shoe. "Cool, huh?" he said, catching me looking at it. "This place is so awesome. Josie didn't like beer, but she ordered it here because of these glasses."

"Why was she excited about the trip?"

"Can I ask *you* something? You said you talked with some people at Shepaug. What did you hear? What's the gossip from there? Was it just that she was some freaky goth girl who jumped from her dorm?"

I had been expecting Travis to ask me this question, but I hadn't decided yet what to tell him. But knowing him for five minutes I thought that he could handle what Libby Frost had told me. "What I heard," I said, "was that maybe Josie had hooked up with someone at the conference, or that she was looking to hook up with someone at the conference. And if that was the case, then I think people feel like maybe she was consumed with guilt and jumped, or maybe someone pushed her. Had you heard this before?"

I asked because he was nodding solemnly while I spoke.

"Yes. And those rumors are correct. Not that she would have felt guilty, but that she was probably looking for someone to have sex with."

"You knew about that?"

"You've heard of polyamory?"

"Sure," I said.

"I don't know that we were calling our marriage polyamorous, exactly, at least not yet, but we had started to experiment with being with other people. I went to a comic convention in Las Vegas and hooked up with someone and told Josie about it and it made her really excited. I'm sure you're judging us—"

"I'm not judging you. I promise. My parents were polyamorous long before there was a word for it, but for them a lot of it was about hurting the other person. Revenge. One-upping one another. This new version seems preferable."

"Josie and I just knew that we were going to spend our whole lives together no matter what, and that we were going to share everything with each other, so why not openly expand our sex lives? It seemed a natural thing to do."

"Josie was interested in finding someone during the conference at Shepaug?"

"Yeah, she was psyched about it. I was, too."

Travis was halfway through his beer but hadn't touched his soup. He seemed grateful to be talking about Josie, but his eyes, with deep shadows around them, were frightened and sad. I thought of my father's eyes that morning.

"Did you tell the police this?"

"Of course I did. And the way they looked at me, I knew what they were all thinking. That I changed my mind about the whole thing and drove down to Shepaug and killed her myself."

"You think that's what they were thinking?"

"Sure. But they checked my alibi and I was here in Woodstock, at a friend's game night. Lots of witnesses."

"It didn't bother you thinking about what Josie might be doing at her conference?"

He shook his head. "It didn't."

"But there's still a possibility, right, that Josie was excited about having a sexual adventure, and then after she did, it made her feel terrible? It wouldn't be the first time something like that happened."

"I think it's much more likely that she picked the wrong guy, or maybe even the wrong girl. And then something went wrong. But I know in my heart that it wasn't something that went wrong with her, it was with the other person."

I was nodding, and he continued, "Maybe I'm wrong. Maybe I pushed her into this thing and it freaked her out. It's not like I haven't had a few sleepless nights wondering about that. But let's say she did meet someone and something got triggered inside of her, something so terrible that she decided to take her own life. She was never going to go over a balcony."

I believed him, maybe not that he knew everything about his wife, but that he knew that she wouldn't jump from a building.

"Let me ask you," he said, "what do you think happened?"

I finished chewing a bite of my chickpea burger and said, "She met the wrong person. And now that I'm talking to you, I feel like I know more about this person."

"Like what?" Travis said.

"Well, I know that whatever happened to her wasn't a spur-of-the-moment, impulsive thing. It wasn't some guy who suddenly went into a rage. Because if that had been the case, then there would have been a fight, and there would have been evidence of that fight. No, I think that whoever killed her was someone very smooth who knew what they were doing. Maybe they lured her out on the balcony, said that the railing was really high and she'd be fine, and it was a beautiful night. Something like that. She was unaware of what was about to happen. She was taken by surprise."

I was worried that I'd said too much, but Travis was rapt, nodding his head. "That's what I think. Someone clever killed her. And he got away with it."

"You said earlier that she might have hooked up with either a boy or a girl . . ."

"I just said that because it's a possibility. Josie pretended she liked girls, just to be open to them, but I don't think she really did."

"It was a guy, then," I said. "Statistically, that makes the most sense."

"I'd agree with that," he said.

"Travis, did you have much contact with her while she was on this trip?"

"Yes and no. The first day, yes. We texted back and forth some. She sent me pictures of the campus, stuff like that. But the day it happened there wasn't much contact at all. I thought she'd probably met someone, and I didn't want to bother her." Travis cupped his mouth and nose with one of his tattooed hands, and squeezed his eyes shut. I thought he was about to cry, but then he took his hand down and said, "It's actually good talking to you about this. I know that my friends want me to move on, but I can't."

"It's hard to move on when there are unanswered questions."

"It is."

"If I find any answers, you'll be the first to know."

"Okay," he said. I ate some more of my burger and he moved his spoon around his soup bowl. "You'd have liked her if you met her," he said. "You'd have liked Josie. She was fire."

CHAPTER 12

After sending the text to Lily and before hearing back from her, Martha, suddenly physically exhausted, went to the living room sofa and lay down. Until she had seen that photograph of the Jane Austen brooch, a part of her believed that she'd concocted the whole thing out of her overactive imagination, that her husband was exactly who he seemed to be, and that the crimes (the *murders*) that had taken place in cities where he'd traveled only represented an odd coincidence. But now she lay on the couch, her mind both numb and somehow spinning, and looked up at her ceiling with its tiny cracks and realized that her world had altered forever.

Gilbert jumped onto the couch by her feet, startling her. He gave her a cursory glance, then folded his paws under his chest and settled into a meat loaf position on the very edge of the sofa cushion. Martha concentrated on her breathing, telling herself to not overreact until she spoke with Lily. Maybe she wouldn't be as convinced by the significance of the brooch as Martha was currently feeling.

After lying on the couch long enough that Gilbert had fallen asleep, curling onto his side to catch the sliver of sunlight that was coming in through the south-facing window above the alcove, Martha forced herself to stand up. She went into the kitchen, opening the refrigerator even though she wasn't hungry. Then she wandered the house, half in a daze, mostly berating herself for having the audacity to actually get married. She'd long known that her life was meant to be lived alone. Did she think that particular curse had a time limit on it? But then she told herself that maybe things really did happen for a reason, the type of thing her religious sister was always saying. Maybe the reason for her marriage to Alan Peralta was so that she could be the one to stop him from continuing to kill women. From now on, that was what Martha decided to tell herself.

When her phone finally rang, she was back in the living room, on the computer, looking for anything she might have missed in the articles that had been written about the drowning death of Mikaela Sager.

"What did you find?" Lily said.

"I found out a lot," Martha said, annoyed to hear that her voice was shaky, "but the reason I sent you that text was because of something I found out about Mikaela Sager, the massage therapist."

"Uh-huh, what was that?"

"So, the night she was drowned . . . the police officer was describing the clothes she was wearing, and apparently she was wearing a brooch. I asked the detective what kind, and he sent me a picture."

"What was it?" Lily said.

"It was a brooch, or like an enamel pin, of Jane Austen's face."

"Is that something Alan sells?"

"I mean, it's exactly the kind of thing he *would* sell. I don't actually recall ever seeing one before, but I rarely see the stuff he sells. Still, the conference he attended in San Diego was for high school English teachers. He could have had that pin in his booth."

"Okay, slow down. Remind me: Mikaela Sager was a massage therapist, right? She didn't attend the conference."

"She didn't, but that doesn't mean anything. Maybe Alan took her out, or he booked an appointment with her, and that's when he gave her the pin. Or, who knows, maybe he killed her on the pier and then put the pin on her before throwing her body in the ocean."

"Why would he do that?"

Martha, gesturing with her free hand even though she was on the phone, said, "Honestly, I don't know, but I keep coming up with scenarios. Maybe he wants to get caught? Maybe he's just a cocky bastard, or he's totally insane. Maybe nothing means anything. All I really know is that it's a huge coincidence, if it even is a coincidence."

"I'm not saying it's a coincidence. I do think it's a pretty strong connection between Alan and this woman who died, but it doesn't prove anything. I mean, if you want to go to the police now, I will support you one hundred percent—I'll even make the call, if you want—but just putting Alan on their radar won't necessarily produce anything."

"Yeah, I know," Martha said, rubbing the back of her neck. "So what do I do now? I mean, I'm more convinced than ever that my husband has killed women. I can't go on living with him. What do I tell him if I just up and leave?"

"Let me think for a moment, okay?" Lily said in a slow, measured tone. Martha knew that Lily was trying to calm her down, but she didn't mind, exactly. "Why don't you tell me what else you found out today?"

"Okay," Martha said. "First of all, I got the feeling that there's a reason none of these cases have been solved. There's not a lot of evidence, or leads, or patterns, and since some of the dead women were prostitutes, then I think the police departments don't care as much."

"The women were all prostitutes?"

"Not exactly. Mikaela Sager wasn't, but she was an in-house massage therapist, so it's a possibility. Kelli Baldwin, the Atlanta victim, was a streetwalker. Nora Johnson, who was a bartender at the hotel Alan was staying at in Fort Myers, was running a kind of side hustle with a parking attendant who also worked for the hotel. She'd pick up some traveling conventioneer and bring him to her car for sex or a blow job, and then this attendant would crash in and get money from them. I didn't learn a whole lot about Bianca Muranos, who was killed in Chicago. I got passed off to someone in the department who seemed to be looking at the file for the first time. But what I got was that she was killed in the alleyway behind the hotel that Alan was staying at, and that she was wearing clothes that suggest she was either a prostitute or else just out at the clubs. I mean, short skirt and stuff. Not much, I know."

"You've done some good work," Lily said.

"Have I? I don't know. Tell me what you found out."

"I met Josie Nixon's husband today. I'm in the car right now driving back from Woodstock."

"How'd that go?"

"She didn't kill herself. At least, I'm ninety-nine percent sure she didn't. But the biggest takeaway was that she was in an open sexual relationship, and she'd been looking forward to meeting someone during the conference."

"To have sex with?"

"Yes, that was the idea."

"The husband told you all this?"

"Uh-huh. He said she was excited about it."

"Which means she fits in with all the others. It means my husband hunts women to have sex with, and then he kills them. It doesn't matter to him if they're prostitutes or just up for sex, or even if they're just massage therapists he thinks might have sex with him."

"You're making some leaps."

"I know, I know. I think my mind just needs to conjure up the worst, somehow. But if Alan is responsible for these deaths, then the pattern is that he looks for someone sexually available, a young woman. I mean, he's not out there killing sixty-year-old department heads."

"Right. I see what you mean," Lily said, then added, "Josie Nixon was also deathly afraid of heights."

"Meaning she wouldn't have willfully jumped from the dormitory balcony?"

"Meaning she wouldn't have willfully gone out on the balcony in the first place."

"Okay."

"At least that was what Travis Nixon said. He was convincing. I thought he was going to be someone who just couldn't accept the fact that his wife might have been suicidal, but that's not how he came off at all."

"But if she was deathly afraid of heights it's like what you said: She might not have gone out on the balcony at all. How did someone get here out there?"

"Oh, there's my exit. Sorry, I'm driving."

"Should we talk later?"

"No, this is fine. Yes, I've thought about that, the balcony thing. It gives us insight into what kind of killer your husband is, if he even is a killer. I'd wondered if he was someone who compulsively cheated on you and was then consumed by guilt and lashed out at the women. That killing them was a way of punishing the act, and that would make sense with the bludgeoning deaths. But if he got Josie Nixon onto a balcony when she was afraid of heights, and he did it without any force, then that meant he talked her into it. I can kind of imagine it, him saying something like, 'You have to come out here and see the stars. Just don't look down,' et cetera. And then he throws her off. It would mean he wasn't in some kind of fit of homicidal mania—he was calm, and it was premeditated. How are you doing with all this?"

"I'm okay, just listening."

"Maybe I'm making too many leaps, as well?"

"No, you're okay. You're speculating. And if he's doing this, he's incredibly good at it. He doesn't leave any evidence behind at all, and the crimes he commits don't fit a recognizable pattern. The deaths are different enough that no one would connect them. So what do we do now?"

"Can I call you back? I might be lost."

Martha paced some more, thinking. She went and stood at the rear door at the back of the kitchen, looking through its glass panes into her backyard. An unchanging view, except that it *had* changed. Her life had changed. There was before she knew who her husband really was, and now there was only after. And the rest of her life would be spent in the after. She told herself that for right now, her only job was to find out the truth. She didn't have to do it alone. She had Lily. And when she did find out the truth, then she would make sure that Alan was put away for good. And then what? Then she'd have been the wife of a serial killer, the stupid librarian who didn't know who her husband really was. A panic rose in her, and she shut it down. It didn't matter what other people thought. Her mission now was finding out who Alan really was. Soon she'd talk some more with Lily. They'd form a plan. And then she'd greet her husband on his return, and make sure he didn't suspect a thing.

As she walked back into the living room, with a yogurt from the fridge, her phone rang.

"I'm home," Lily said. "How are you since we talked?"

"I'm good," Martha said. "We just need to do what we need to do."

"Right. Tell me again when Alan leaves for his next trip."

"He's going to Saratoga Springs on Monday morning. I can look it up, but I think it's a math and science conference."

"I'm going to go to that conference," Lily said.

"What do you mean?"

"I'm going to go to Saratoga Springs. I need to at least look at him, Martha, maybe get a sense if he's on the make or not. And I need to keep an eye on him, make sure he doesn't hurt someone. I won't take risks."

Martha couldn't think what to say.

Lily said, "I'll follow him. If I see anything suspicious at all, I'll call the police right away."

"You promise?" Martha said.

"Yes. The moment I think he's up to something bad, I'm calling him in. I'll lie if I have to. It won't necessarily get him arrested, but I'll stop him from hurting anyone else. That's the most important thing, right?"

"I agree, I'm just . . . I don't know what I am."

"Look, I'll be careful. But we need to know for sure, don't you think?"

"But what if he just attends the conference, sells his T-shirts, then goes to bed early each night?"

"Then we'll know a little bit more about him."

"Okay," Martha said. Then, "Oh shit."

"What?"

Martha watched through her bay windows as Alan pulled into their driveway, back from whatever he'd done with his day. "Alan's back."

"You can handle it," Lily said.

"I know I can."

"Just make it through the next few days, and one way or another we'll know more about what's going on by this time next week."

CHAPTER 13

It was raining when I reached the outskirts of Saratoga Springs. I didn't know a whole lot about the area except that it was a resort town that had originally been built as a destination for its natural springs, and then had transformed into a town known for its horse racing. I imagined that right now the city was desperately looking for another dying industry to base their economy on, and maybe they'd found it in convention-hosting. I drove past the giant conference center with its massive electronic sign alternating between WELCOME K–12 MATH TEACHERS, and WELCOME NEW YORK STATE POULTRY BREEDERS. About two miles from the center, I hit a stretch of road devoted to the smaller hotels and national chain restaurants. Outback Steakhouse. Buffalo Wild Wings. Another mile, and I was in the land of single-story motels, sex shops, and bars without windows. I pulled into the front of a motel offering rooms for $59.95 a night.

Inside, a bored-looking teenage girl checked me in for two nights. She was wearing earbuds, and when we'd begun to interact, she pulled one of them out and let it dangle over her shoulder, while keeping the other earbud in. When I told her I wanted to pay in advance with cash, I caught a flicker of eye movement as she looked over my shoulder to see if there was some kind of clandestine lover waiting in my car. After giving me my change, she said that she needed a credit card for incidentals.

"Like what?" I said.

"I guess like if you trash the room or steal a lamp or something." She smiled at me, and I saw that she was missing several teeth.

"Right," I said, and handed her my card. She took an impression of it with one of those old-fashioned credit card machines, putting a slip of paper over the card, then sliding a metal bar across to get an imprint.

"We'll just toss this if the room's fine after your stay," she said.

"Thank you," I said, and took the key from the counter. I moved the car so that it was now parked in front of my room's door. It was surprisingly clean inside, but very plain. There was only one piece of art, a racehorse print that had been screwed into the wall.

I did briefly wonder if I was being overly cautious, finding a no-tell motel and avoiding toll roads on my drive up from Shepaug. All I planned on doing in Saratoga Springs was to put eyes on Alan Peralta, get a sense of how he acted when he was on the road, away from his wife. Maybe I'd meet him. Maybe not. And then Martha and I could use that information to make a decision on whether to turn her husband in. I had no intention of taking care of Peralta myself, the way I'd taken care of a few predators in the past, even if I did discover he was a murderer. This time, I would find another way. Still, you never know what might happen, and I'd learned that being anonymous was far better than being noticed.

I unpacked in the motel room, then sent a text to my mother telling her that I'd safely arrived. My parents thought I was going to a friend's house in the Berkshires. I'd used Martha's name as the friend, reminding them that we'd gotten back in touch after having known each other in graduate school. They'd both looked suspicious, I thought, although my mother's suspicion was probably that I was having some torrid affair that she wasn't privy to, while my father's suspicion was most likely that I'd gotten tired of being a caretaker and was abandoning him.

The conference didn't officially begin until noon, but Martha had told me that the vendors set up early on the morning of the first day. Alan had apparently flirted with the idea of driving out the night before the conference but had decided to save money and leave very early the day of. My plan was to get a look at him this morning, maybe let him look at me, and then return to the conference center at five o'clock, when the vendors would knock off for the day. Really, I just wanted to keep an eye on him.

After changing into my convention-goer's outfit—black skirt, silky green blouse, three-quarter heels—I left the motel and drove downtown and parked at a meter that took quarters. I went through the revolving doors and stepped inside the cavernous convention center and hotel. Wide stairs led to a main floor that must have been the size of two football fields. To the right was check-in and reception, plus a large seating area dotted with plush chairs and sofas and delineated by lines of potted plants. To the left, across an expanse of brightly patterned carpeting, was a two-level bar and restaurant that, according to some cursive script etched into a large glass barrier, was called *Faces*. Teachers and administrators were lined up in front of the registration tables, or else were milling about in small groups, chatting and looking at their programs. The air was filled with the din of a thousand voices, mingled together into a meaningless hum. The sound of droning insects in summertime.

I followed a sign that pointed me toward Concourse A and Concourse B and the exhibition hall. As I got to the end of a long, carpeted hallway I saw a steady stream of conventioneers, most with tote bags strung over a shoulder, coming and going through the wide rolled-out doors of the exhibition hall. I walked in, trying to look like I belonged there. The hall was high-ceilinged and larger even than the expanse of the lobby/bar area I had just come from. There were row after row of exhibitor booths, mostly textbook publishing houses or software companies. The largest booths had podiums for presentations and seating areas, along with patches of carpeting brought in and taped down to cover up their sections of poured-concrete floor. Some of the booths were still being set up but most looked ready to go, hopeful vendors doing last-minute adjustments of their wares or standing out front of their booths ready to deliver their pitches. The conventioneers meandered aimlessly up and down the rows.

I left the area where the highest-profile exhibitors seemed to be and wandered to the back of the hall. It took me about five minutes, but I eventually found Peralta's booth, at the far rear of the allotted exhibitor space. It was a simple setup, just a white folding table with one chair behind it, and behind the chair a black backdrop, hung with T-shirts and ties and even some framed posters meant for classrooms. One read WEAPONS OF MATH INSTRUCTION and had pictures of rulers and graphs and compasses. Another said LET'S HAVE A MOMENT OF SCIENCE. Alan Peralta was there as well, arranging items for sale on the table that fronted the booth.

I was hoping that maybe no one would be there and I'd be able to talk to him alone, but there was a small loud coven, three middle-aged teachers laughing uproariously as they read out loud the T-shirts and badges on displays. Peralta seemed intent on finishing his unpacking, and ignored them. He was in dark suit pants and a white collared shirt and was wearing a tie decorated with math equations. Ever since Martha had shown me a picture of him, I'd been trying to figure out who he reminded me of, and watching him now it suddenly came to me. He looked like the young J. D. Salinger I'd seen in pictures. Same hairline, same long forehead and heavy brow, same slender, almost emaciated frame.

I wandered away, buying a burrito for lunch from one of the vendors set up just outside the convention center. It wasn't raining, but I had to wipe down a bench in order to sit and eat my food. After eating, I closed my eyes for a moment and tilted my face toward the sun that had just burned through the clouds to make an appearance. Then I steeled myself to reenter the exhibition hall. I'd been to large conferences before, but not for a long time, and I was reminded how the fluorescent lighting and the cacophony of voices combined to sap me of all my energy. Inside, I waited in the endless line at Starbucks and ordered the same thing that the woman in front of me had ordered, something cold with double shots of espresso and lots of flavored sugar syrup. Not my type of thing, but I needed fuel.

The crowd in the hall had thinned out now that the first sessions had begun, and when I reached Peralta's booth, I was happy to see that there was only one customer there, a man wearing a sweater vest who was half-turned to look at the merchandise, a smirk on his face. I walked up to the booth and looked down at the display items. There were numerous ties, all with either science or math themes, and then there were scarves meant for women. Sweater Vest reached out and touched a tie, then moved past me and away.

"Are you math or science?"

I looked up at Peralta. He was tall enough that I saw he'd missed a spot just along his jawline when he'd shaved that morning.

"Math," I said, then took a step backward and surveyed some of the posters that were featured on the booth's black backdrop.

"There's a rack here, with *all* the posters," he said, showing me one of those racks that you could flip through like a giant book.

"Hmm," I said.

"Where do you teach?"

I looked at him for a few seconds, as though I were deciding whether it was worth my time to answer his question, then said, "Actually, I'm between jobs right now. It's a long story, but in the last month I left a state, a job, and a relationship, and now I've moved near here and I'm wondering what to do next."

"I don't know much, but I do know that they're almost always looking to hire teachers in Albany."

"Oh yeah?" I said.

"That's the extent of my knowledge on the subject, I'm afraid."

"Well, it's helpful. Are there Albany teachers here at this conference?"

"Oh yeah. Huge contingent."

"Thanks," I said, moving down to look through a box of pins.

I thought Peralta might try to sell me something, but he was keeping quiet. "Truth is," I said, "I just don't even know if I want to keep teaching math or keep teaching at all. I like math. I'm good at it, but I don't think it's a passion for me anymore."

"So, what's your passion?" he said.

I looked up at him, his eyes showing nothing but some mild interest. "I know this is crazy, but I'm a math geek who's fallen in love with literature. Sometimes I think I got my life totally wrong."

He smiled. "I do conferences for English teachers, too."

"Oh yeah?"

"Same booth. Different wares."

"I'd imagine."

I was jostled from behind as a woman carrying two enormous and overfilled tote bags crowded in to look at the scarves on display. She began to laugh. I looked Peralta directly in the eyes, long enough to register their color, then raised my eyebrows slightly and said, "I'm Addie."

"Alan," he said, and I watched his eyes move, suddenly scanning my body, not obvious about it, exactly, but not unnoticeable, either. He blinked rapidly, maybe knowing that he'd been caught. I told him I hoped to see him later and moved on.

I walked along the outskirts of the exhibition hall to the exit, thinking about Alan's reaction to me at his booth, how he'd seemed both harmless and on the make at the same time. I think a part of him wanted me to see him check out my body. What I couldn't figure out was if he'd also wanted me to see him suddenly get flustered by it. The animal he'd reminded me of was a rabbit, partly because of his long thin nose and oversized ears, but mostly because he'd gone from calm to skittery before my eyes. Rabbits are prey, I told myself, as I merged in with a large slow-moving pack of teachers working their way from the hall back to the lobby of the center. But lots of prey animals are also predators. Cats, for instance. And it seemed clear to me that Peralta might be one of those humans that were both. We can't all be apex predators in this world.

CHAPTER 14

I stood at the edge of the bar area, wondering where to sit. I wanted to somehow be both visible and isolated at the same time. A small group got up from one of the high-top tables just beyond the empty hostess stand, and I went and sat by myself. I was there for about twenty minutes before it was cleared and cleaned, and I ordered a ginger ale in a lowball glass on the rocks with a lime. I'd brought a book with me, a paperback copy of *Death of a Naturalist* by Seamus Heaney.

When my drink arrived, I opened the book randomly, landing on the title poem. I thought maybe I'd read it before, since back at Mather College I'd taken a contemporary Irish poetry class. It didn't ring a bell, though, and I read it twice. It was a poem about that point when a child's interest in the natural world suddenly turns to disgust. I thought that maybe that had happened to me a little bit, way back when, but it was more that I'd discovered what humans were really like and found that disgusting. Animals and plants have no say in what they do. I tried to remember what my father thought of Seamus Heaney, and could somehow hear his voice saying something like, "That man knows all the nature words." I didn't know if it was something he had actually said, or just something I could imagine him saying.

I looked up from my book, the bar filling up, the voices combining into that unmelodious din. It was only about six P.M. but it was clear that all the sessions for the day were over and that the vast majority of conference attendees had converged on the bar. I scanned the room for someone who looked like Peralta but didn't see him.

"This seat taken?" It was a man about my age, still wearing his name badge, and carrying a light-colored beer.

"No," I said. "Please sit."

He settled onto the chair, his white shirt straining at the buttons as he sat. "Reading poetry at a math and science conference, I see?"

"How do you know I'm not here for the poultry breeders' convention?"

"Right, I forgot about that. You don't look like a poultry breeder, but I'm not sure you look like a teacher, either."

I gave him my spiel, all the while keeping an eye on the masses of people coming and going. He listened intently, peering over his wire-rim glasses. He had a well-trimmed beard, the skin of his neck pocked with razor burns. He told me he was a high school math teacher from Vermont, and I could instantly picture him in front of his classroom, disheveled and sweaty. He wore no wedding ring, but I thought I could see a faint line where he usually wore it. I wondered if he was recently divorced, or if he was married and looking to cheat. I asked him if he thought his students had changed over the years just so he'd talk for a while and I could scan the crowds.

"Oh my God, they have, don't you think?" he said, finishing his beer and glancing around for a server.

As he spoke, I watched the room. Peralta was tall, so I kept my sight lines high, scanning the tops of heads. A waitress idled by and the math teacher ordered another beer, offering to buy something for me. There were still two sips left in my glass of ginger ale, so I told him I was fine.

He was in the middle of a story about taking a student's phone away, when I saw Peralta at the bar. He'd just arrived there, trying to get the attention of a bartender. When he finally did, he pointed at one of the beer pulls. He paid in cash, then turned and leaned his back against the bar and sipped at his beer, surveying the crowd. I thought it was a possibility he might be looking for me and wondered if I should say something unforgivable to the math teacher so that he might go away. But as I watched, Peralta quickly finished his beer and put the empty glass back on the bar. He was wearing a collared white shirt like he'd been wearing earlier at his booth, but it was tucked into dark jeans instead of suit bottoms. It looked as though he was carrying a leather jacket, held under his left arm. He began to move with purpose across the expanse of the lobby, heading to either the elevators or the front entrance.

The math teacher had just asked me a question, and I said to him, "Sorry, I'm about to be very rude. I just saw someone I know leave and I'm going to track him down. Will you be here later?"

"First to the bar and last to leave," he said, puffing his chest, and laughing at his own joke.

By the time I was up and moving I spotted Peralta exiting the hotel, walking at a brisk pace. I sped up, pulling on my coat, and as I descended the wide carpeted stairs that led to the exit I was passed by a man walking even faster than I was, his shoulder brushing mine as he went past. He arrived at the revolving doors just before me and pushed his way through. I let a group of women through ahead of me, then passed through the revolving doors myself and out into the cool night. I turned right and about a block down the street I could see Peralta in his black leather jacket, now strolling, his hands in his pockets. I began to follow him, buttoning my own coat.

We were on a wide thoroughfare, lined with shops and restaurants, but the sidewalk was mostly clear, and I could keep an eye on him. Between us was the man who had nearly knocked me over on the stairs. He was tall as well, but wore a tan raincoat over a suit and carried an umbrella. Up ahead Peralta suddenly slowed down, bending over slightly to peer at something in the window next to an awninged entrance. He was probably reading menus. I slowed my pace, then stopped, pretending that I'd been distracted by the empty window of a defunct department store. When I looked up, Peralta was on the move again, and that was when I noticed that the man between us, the man from our same hotel in the tan raincoat, had stopped as well, bending down to tie his shoe.

We all kept walking, the three of us. After five minutes Peralta took a right onto a side street, and so did the man between us. I was now a hundred percent sure I wasn't the only one following Peralta. A flutter of nervous excitement went through me. Why was someone else interested in Peralta? Was it a plainclothes police detective? Maybe he was a lover, another married man, the two of them headed to a bar to meet.

The street we'd turned onto was tree-lined and clustered with smaller, more interesting-looking bars and restaurants and shops. Peralta slowed his pace, and so did the man following him. I crossed over to the opposite sidewalk, figuring I could watch them both from a better vantage point. I sped up a little to try to get a good look at the stranger from the hotel, but all I could really see was that he had short dark blond hair and wide shoulders. He had to keep slowing down, since it was now clear that Peralta was looking for a restaurant, stopping often to read menus. Eventually Peralta selected a winner, a barbecue restaurant called Red's, its crowded interior visible behind a large plate-glass window. He pushed through its front door, and then the stranger walked past the restaurant, glancing through the window, pausing a little. I thought he might follow his quarry inside, but instead he ambled toward a crosswalk and made his way to my side of the street.

I was in front of a closed clothing boutique and there was a bench on the sidewalk, probably situated so that husbands could wait while their vacationing wives shopped. I took a seat and pulled out my phone and studied it, the stranger doubling back toward me, walking slowly, and it was the first time I saw his walk from the front. Only his long legs moved, his hips barely swiveling, his arms swinging in small arcs. He moved with immense confidence, something catlike about him. As he got closer, passing below a streetlamp that had just turned on, I got a good look. His hair was different, a little darker, and he was wearing glasses, but the face was the same. Wide jaw and high cheekbones. A little more wrinkled than I remembered, but still startlingly handsome.

Ethan Saltz.

He passed by me, not looking in my direction, and ducked into a bar called Lost and Found. I was frozen to my bench, my mind spinning out possibilities. Why was Martha's ex-boyfriend from graduate school following Alan Peralta? It couldn't possibly be a coincidence, could it? I slid my phone back into my jacket pocket and tried to think. Yes, he had been following Peralta. I was sure of it. And now he'd ducked into a place across the street, probably to eat a quick dinner while Peralta dined nearby.

In the middle of these thoughts, the door to the bar that Ethan Saltz had entered swung open again and he emerged back onto the sidewalk. I had turned at the sound and we looked directly at each other.

"I thought you looked familiar," he said, walking toward me.

"You're familiar to me, too," I said.

"Did you go to Birkbeck College, about a hundred years ago?" He smiled as he said it, like he was delivering a pre-rehearsed line.

"I did." He nodded slowly, and I said, "Do you live here?"

There was the slightest flicker in his eyes, his mind calculating what to tell me. "I don't, actually, but I like to visit. What about you?"

For a moment I thought of telling the truth, simply saying, "Oh, I'm here to follow Martha's husband, Alan Peralta. We think he might be a killer, but you know something about that, don't you? You were following him as well."

Instead, I said, "I'm a teacher now and I'm sort of attending a conference here. I'm looking for a job."

"That's interesting," he said, his wide wolfish grin making it clear he didn't believe me. We both stared at each other quietly on the sidewalk in the dusk for a moment. I knew he was lying, and guessed he must have known I was lying as well. And maybe because our situation wasn't quite absurd enough, the door to Red's barbecue swung open and Alan Peralta stepped onto the sidewalk across from us, apparently only having had a drink at the bar and nothing more. We both looked across at Alan and then we looked at one another, and Ethan laughed.

"Something funny?" I said.

"Are you telling me you don't know who that is over there?"

"The guy across the street who looks like J. D. Salinger?" I said.

He laughed again, clearly enjoying himself. "That fucker does look like J. D. Salinger. You know, I obviously picked the wrong student to pursue when I was at Birkbeck. You're coming back to me now. I remember that you meddled in my relationship with Martha Ratliff."

"There was a reason I did that," I said. "I'm sure you don't need me to remind you of that."

"I think you're meddling now, too."

The wind changed direction and a dusting of rain moved across the two of us. Neither of us flinched, though, and Ethan's umbrella stayed down by his side.

"Honestly, I have no idea what you mean."

"What's your name again?" he said.

"Why would I tell you that?"

"Because I can find out anyway. I think I know why you're really here, and all I'm going to say to you is that you should mind your own business." He made a sudden move, raising his umbrella, and for a moment I thought he was going to strike me, but a yellow taxicab pulled up to the curb next to us. "Can I offer you a ride somewhere?" he said, as he opened the door.

"No, I'm good right here," I said.

"Nice seeing you again, Lily. You haven't changed at all." He said this just before his taxi knifed away from the curb.

CHAPTER 15

The text read: Give me a call when you get a chance. I have an update.

Lily had sent it at six thirty, almost three hours earlier. But Martha had been out to eat by herself, her phone untouched in her purse that hung on a hook beneath the lip of the bar. She was only looking at it now because she'd just settled the bill.

"Husband wondering where you are?" the bartender said.

"Oh no. Something else." One of the reasons Martha hadn't checked her phone all night was that she'd been talking with the bartender. She was at a restaurant walking distance from her house, a place she'd never been to before. Earlier in the evening, Martha had found herself wandering her house in a daze, unable to decide what to do next. After deciding to eat, she found herself staring into her cupboard, frozen. Her breathing was shallow.

Then she was grabbing her coat and her purse and the house keys and within minutes she was outside in the dusk, walking from her house to the waterfront. After she'd gone about half a mile she felt as though she could fully breathe. She turned a corner and slowed her pace. There was nothing she could do tonight, nothing to do but wait to hear from Lily, who had yet to check in with any kind of update. Not that she was supposed to. Lily had told Martha that she shouldn't wait for reports, that she'd only send a text or call if it was important. But despite the fact that she'd said that, Martha had still expected to hear something, anything. The silence was unbearable.

Despite her anxiety, or because of it, Martha had realized she was hungry. She walked past a local tavern called Muriel's, a place she frequented with Alan, then stopped outside a steak house she'd never gone into called the Flagship. Without hesitating, she stepped inside, and a hostess in a crisp white shirt and a black vest looked up at her from behind her station.

"Just one," Martha said. "For dinner."

"I can seat you at a table or at the bar, if you prefer."

Martha said she'd prefer a table, not wanting to speak with anyone, and she was led into a dim room outfitted to look like a library and was given an oversized menu. It was a Monday night and the place was quiet, just one couple a few tables over, silently dismantling their steaks. When a waitress shimmied over, Martha said she'd changed her mind and maybe she'd like to eat at the bar. The waitress, peeved, pointed her in the right direction, and Martha was instantly happier after she slid onto a large high-backed stool and ordered a glass of red wine from the bartender. After the wine was poured, she ordered a rare sirloin steak with béarnaise sauce and a side of creamed spinach. She felt calmer, confident that Lily was going to find out the truth, no matter what that truth was. The wine was helping as well, that first sip sinking her into the womb-like atmosphere of the dark bar. Lily could handle herself, whatever the situation turned out to be. And there was another feeling, one she was having a hard time admitting to herself. Regardless of what the truth was about Alan, she was starting to wonder if she needed him in her life at all. It wasn't as though she were madly in love with him. No, she just liked his company. Why had she thought they needed to get married? She hadn't, actually. But he'd wanted to, and she'd agreed.

When her steak came, she thought of her father, how much he'd like this restaurant, although he'd be drinking a dry Gibson with his meal. She sliced into the very pink steak, sopped up a little of the sauce, and took a bite. How strange life was, that on the night when she might find out if her husband was a serial killer, she could enjoy something as heavenly as steak with béarnaise sauce.

"All good?" the bartender said. He was about forty she thought, one of those heavyish men who made the extra weight sexy. It didn't hurt that he had great hair and a beautiful gray beard.

"Perfect," she said, "and another glass of wine when you get a chance."

After her meal was finished, she didn't want to leave, so she ordered a glass of port, still thinking of her father, a fan of the post-dinner drink.

He'd been talkative, her father, toward the end of his life, as though making up for years of silence. Even though he'd had two daughters, Martha's sister was all the way in Alaska, and since he'd never remarried after her parents' divorce, Martha was really all he had as he had succumbed, pretty rapidly, to pancreatic cancer. Not only was he suddenly open with her, but she found herself telling him things about her life that, before his diagnosis, she would never have considered speaking out loud to anyone. She told him about Ethan, her horrible boyfriend when she'd been at graduate school, and she even told him about how she was convinced Eve Dexter put a love curse on her back in high school.

"I actually remember Eve Dexter," he'd said. "Only because I knew her mother. Kit Dexter. I did her will."

"Did she leave everything for Eve?"

"I don't remember."

"She really did curse me, you know."

"You actually believe that?"

"That she put a curse on me, or that it worked?"

"Either. Both."

"Yes, I believe she put a curse on me. I kissed her boyfriend and the first thing she did was get every kid in school to shun me, but I guess it wasn't enough. It was confirmed, you know. A psychic spotted it on me."

Her father frowned, but his eyes were amused.

"You think I'm silly?"

"No, I believe you. And I believe that little harlot Eve Dexter cursed you."

"But you don't believe that it affected my love life."

"If it did, it's because you believed it would. No, I don't really believe that love curses work. What I do believe, though, is that we're all cursed, anyway. At least in love."

"Ooh, dark, Dad."

"Sorry," he said, but he'd been laughing as he said it.

Martha paid the bill at the steak house, having just read Lily's message. She left Jonah the bartender a whopping tip and promised to be back soon. As she moved from the dim lighting of the bar through the yellow glow of the restaurant, then out into the misty night, she still felt as though she were in the unreal bubble created by that first glass of wine. Once outside, she called Lily, who picked up right away.

"Oh, you had me worried."

"Sorry," Martha said. "I went out to eat and wasn't checking my phone. What's going on?"

"Well, there are developments," Lily said slowly.

"Okay."

"I waited in the hotel bar for your husband tonight. He went to the bar and got a drink and then he left. I followed him. He was going down the street, looking for a restaurant to eat at, from the looks of it, and I started to notice that I wasn't the only one following him."

"What do you mean?"

"Someone else, another man, was following him as well."

"That's strange."

"Anyway, I'm going to cut to the chase. The person following your husband was Ethan Saltz."

Martha stopped walking. She was baffled for a moment, wondering if Lily had misspoken. "Ethan? From Birkbeck?"

"Yes."

"I'm confused. He was following Alan?" Martha could hear her own voice rise in pitch. Just hearing Ethan's name was like feeling the earth shift under her feet.

"I was confused, too."

"Are you sure it was him? Did you get a good look?"

"I talked to him, Martha. It was him. And he knew that I was there to watch Alan."

"But why?"

"That's what I've been asking myself. But now that I've had time to think, I believe that Ethan has something to do with what's been happening."

"What?" Martha was still standing, a man with a dog on a leash trying to navigate past her.

"Are you outside walking?" Lily said.

"I am," Martha said, the question prompting her to start moving again.

"Do you want to call me when you get home?"

"No, no. I want to hear what you think."

"Okay, it's crazy, but I'll tell you. What if Ethan kills women that your husband comes into contact with? What if he's trying to frame Alan?"

"Why would he do that?"

"He's not targeting Alan, he's targeting you. He likes to play creepy games, right? He's a manipulator. For whatever reason, he wants you to think that your husband is a serial killer. It's a game to him."

"I'm sorry, Lily. I'm trying to catch up here. But, I mean . . . how does he even know who my husband is? I'm just . . . Oh, sorry, I didn't see you there."

"You okay?"

"I'm walking into people on the sidewalk," Martha said.

"Let's hang up, and you call me when you get back, okay?"

"Okay."

Somehow she made it back to the house, navigating turns with no memory of doing so. She unlocked her door and stepped inside, turning on the lamp nearest to the door. Gilbert meowed loudly at her, but when she picked him up and carried him to his bowl to show him he already had food, he sniffed at it and turned away.

She wandered through the downstairs, pulling curtains and turning on lamps. Twice, she nearly tripped over Gilbert, who was right underfoot. She kept thinking about Ethan Saltz following Alan in Saratoga Springs. Maybe Lily had been wrong. Not about seeing Ethan, but about thinking Ethan had anything to do with her husband. She used to think about Ethan a lot, about how quickly he'd consumed her. He'd come along and simply taken control of her life and her emotions. If it hadn't been for Lily she often wondered what would have happened between the two of them. For a long time she vacillated between a feeling that she'd escaped something truly evil, and another feeling, that maybe life under Ethan's spell would have been okay. He would have controlled her, and there was something tempting about that, about giving over your agency to another human being.

She sat on the edge of Alan's recliner and looked at her phone. She was about to call Lily back when she realized she was still wearing her jacket. She got up and took it off, along with her boots, then decided to quickly go upstairs and change into some elastic-band pants and a sweatshirt. If she was going to have her world entirely turned upside down, she might as well be comfortable.

She entered her bedroom, flicking the switch next to the door. The man in the hooded sweatshirt stood between her and the bed she shared with her husband. There was a relaxed toothy grin on his face and he held a knife casually by his side. In Martha's mind she had already turned and begun to run away, hightailing it down the stairs and through the door and out into the night, where she could scream for help. But she hadn't run. She was standing still, her legs immobile.

Oh, it's over, she thought, almost casually. The man moved, inhumanly quick, the knife piercing her throat so fast that she didn't even have time to say his name.

PART 2

LISTEN TO ITS THROAT

CHAPTER 16

The first person he killed was his grandfather. Ethan was eleven years old.

He didn't particularly dislike Grampy, who, when he had been healthy and living in his own house, had always let Ethan play with his collection of military weapons and even given him a boxful of toy metal soldiers—British and German and French ones—that for about a year had been Ethan's favorite possessions in the world.

But Grampy had a stroke—a bad one, his father said—and now he had to come and live with them. And because Ethan had the only bedroom in the house that was on the first floor, he'd had to move out and relocate to his older brother's room on a trundle bed with a saggy mattress. He wasn't mad at his grandfather for taking his room, although it did occur to him that the sooner Grampy died, the sooner he'd get his room back. No, what really bothered Ethan about having Grampy living in his house was that his mother made him go into the smelly room every afternoon when he got home from school and sit with his grandfather for a while.

"He doesn't do anything," Ethan said to his mother.

"No, but he's your grandfather, and even if he doesn't show it, I'd bet it makes him feel happy as a clam just to have you in there next to him. Tell him what you studied at school. Just because he can't talk doesn't mean he can't hear what you say and understand."

So Ethan would sit with his grandfather, who just lay there, one part of his face slacker than the other, and with drool on his lower lip. Sometimes Ethan would use the time to get a start on his homework, but often he would actually talk to the old man, tell him about some class, or how much he hated his classmate Karen Armitage, who thought she was better than everyone else. And sometimes he would read out loud to him. Ethan, in his twelfth year, had discovered that he actually liked to read. Part of that was discovering the Goosebumps series, hand-me-downs from his brother who was now thirteen and reading Stephen King. But the books that Ethan had fallen in love with most were his sister's old books. She had a bookshelf full of them in her single bedroom. Judy Blumes and Lois Duncans and all of the *Flowers in the Attic* books. She even had some pretty dirty books, like *Lace* by Shirley Conran (Ethan had flipped through it, just reading the sex stuff) and *The Clan of the Cave Bear* and *Endless Love.*

What the books taught him was that there was a whole world out there, an adult world, of sex and death and betrayal and lies. It was like a playground where you got to do whatever you wanted, and it made him want to skip right through the rest of his childhood and be an adult. But, instead, he was an eleven-year-old who had to go and sit next to his dying, smelly grandfather because his mother thought it would make him happy as a clam, one of his mom's weird expressions. So Ethan read stuff aloud to him, and it was pretty clear to him that Grampy didn't understand a word. He was practically dead already. Ethan thought, If I was like this, I would want someone to come into this room and put me out of my misery. Once he had that thought it became a permanent part of his mind. It was like reading that scene in *Lace* where the man puts the goldfish into the woman's private area and she loves it. That was part of his mind now, too.

Over time, Ethan began to enjoy going into Grampy's room after school. It was funny that Scott, his brother, never had to do it, mostly because he was now in high school and had a lot of homework. His sister Vicky didn't seem required to make visits, either, and Ethan wondered if that had something to do with the fact that in the last year something had gone decidedly wrong with his sister. She was out late all the time, and when she was home, she and his mom just yelled at each other. She smelled of cigarettes and booze and hair spray. Ethan had decided that Vicky was stupid, maybe even stupider than Scott, and that was saying something. If she wanted to sneak out of the house and smoke cigarettes and get drunk and meet boys, why wasn't she better at it? Why did she get caught? Ethan's father, who worked in the city, was always exhausted when he came home. All he cared about was drinking whiskey, watching sports highlights, then going to bed. Ethan's mother was around more, that was true, but she was always humming to herself and swaying around the house and, honestly, it didn't take a genius to slide right past her without her even noticing. Ethan did it all the time.

Ethan thought about these things while sitting next to his grand-father. He thought, If I were Vicky and had just gotten my driver's license, then I'd be able to get away with anything. He hadn't really had thoughts like this before, not about what it would be like to be someone else, and he wondered if it had something to do with all the reading he'd been doing. Because, honestly, it had never even occurred to him until recently that other people had thoughts at all. He stared at his grandfather and tried to imagine it, tried to imagine words and ideas moving through his brain. All he came up with was that he must want to die, lying in bed being unable to move.

In October his mom had a screaming fight with Vicky that was so bad that his father came home early and Vicky ran out the door. Ethan asked his mom, her face all wet with tears, if he could eat in his room, and she said, Of course, honey, and hugged him in a way that Ethan knew had more to do with his sister than with him. Once he was in his room with his microwaved meat loaf, Ethan climbed out the window and onto the porch roof. It was steep, but not so steep that you couldn't slide along it. He went to his sister's window, which was never locked, opened it, and snuck into her room. He wanted to look at her books, but he was also a little curi-ous about what all the screaming had been about lately. He turned on her desk lamp, not worrying about getting caught because his sister had put a padlock on the outside of her door to keep her parents out of there.

He went through her underwear drawer, mostly filled with stained white underwear, but toward the back she had a couple of lacy things from Victoria's Secret. Something about that was funny, and then Ethan realized that her name was Victoria and so was her underwear. At her bookshelf he found this small dark paperback called *Go Ask Alice*, a book he'd heard about that was all about drugs. He put it in his back pocket, then went to his sister's unmade bed. She still slept with the stuffed dog—Doggy—she'd had since she'd been little. It had floppy ears and weird plastic eyes and was so old that it was coming apart and had been sewn back together so many times it looked like an accident victim. Ethan slid his finger into one of the sewn-up seams and ripped it a little more, then put it back where he'd found it. But then he had another idea and hid Doggy under the bed. There was a ton of crap down there, old T-shirts his sister had slept in, a few textbooks, and a hundred dust bunnies. He covered the stuffed animal under one of the disgusting T-shirts.

In Vicky's bedside drawer he found her old diary, and cracked it open, wondering if she'd written anything new in it. But she hadn't, at least not for a couple of years, and Ethan had read most of what was in there, anyway. There were some tampons in her drawer as well, and Ethan looked at the directions on the back of the box, glad that he wasn't a girl. There wasn't much else in the drawer that he hadn't seen before, just a bottle of something called Midol.

Before leaving, he looked through his sister's trash bin, filled with damp Kleenex and gum wrappers and at the very bottom a piece of plastic, half-blue and half-white. Ethan almost picked it up but decided it was somehow related to tampons, so he covered it up again.

Back in his own room, he ate some meat loaf, then started to read *Go Ask Alice*.

The next week was crazy because one night Vicky didn't come home, and Ethan's parents called the police. Then there were more fights and screaming and even one moment when Ethan snuck down late at night and saw his mother holding Vicky on the couch almost as if Vicky was still a baby. They were both crying and rocking each other, and Ethan watched from the doorway, more confused than he'd been by the fighting. All he knew was that what he was looking at made him feel queasy.

It was around this time that he first came up with the idea of killing his grandfather. That would show them, he thought. Everyone's freaking out because Vicky can't control herself, and meanwhile Grampy dies all alone in his room. The thought of it made Ethan feel like he was smiling inside of himself. Also, if Grampy died, then he'd get his own room back. There had been at least two times in the past month when he'd woken up in the middle of the night and heard noises coming from Scott's bed, bedsprings squeaking and little groans. He knew what his brother was doing because he'd read one of his sister's books all about puberty. It was disgusting to him, and he'd already vowed that it was something he would never do himself. But what it mostly made him feel was that he wanted to get back into his own bedroom on the first floor.

It was either on Halloween or maybe it was the day before that Ethan sat in his old bedroom listening to his grandfather breathe. In and out. In and out. Like some kind of machine that keeps running long after it's stopped being useful. While Ethan listened, he thought about other stuff, like how they'd learned in history class that a million people had starved in Ireland because the potatoes went bad. Ethan was pretty good at math, so he kept trying to picture what a million people looked like. He laid them side by side over rolling hills, and that helped. And sometimes he let one candy corn represent a person and then tried to picture what a million candy corns would look like. That actually wasn't helpful at all.

His grandfather made some sort of snorting noise and Ethan looked at him. But his expression hadn't changed. Without thinking too much about it, Ethan stood up, walked over to his grandfather, and pinched his nose shut. It didn't really do anything, because Grampy's mouth was always open. With his other hand Ethan pushed his grandfather's mouth closed and held it that way. Nothing happened at first, and then his grandfather's head moved back and forth a little and a strange rattling sound came out of his throat. Ethan thought about letting go, but he wanted to see what would happen next. About a minute later it was pretty clear that his grandfather was dead. He left the room and walked to the bathroom, where he washed his hands. He only went back into Grampy's room to get the book he'd brought in there with him, his English textbook, all about grammar rules. Then he went to the kitchen and told his mother that he was going up to his room to study.

"You visited Grampy, right?"

"I did. Told him all about my day."

"Thanks, honey."

Up in his brother's room Ethan shut the door and lay down on his cot. He wondered how long it was going to be before his mother discovered that her father was dead. He was glad he was dead because it would mean the house would go back to the way it was before, but he wasn't excited about all the things that would happen first. Crying and a funeral and other relatives. Still, it would go back to normal in time. He'd get his room back on the first floor. Scott would get his own room all to himself and be able to do disgusting things to himself all day long. His sister wouldn't be the most important person in the family for at least a few days, although she'd probably try. What about Grampy? Ethan tried to examine his feelings about what he'd done to his grandfather. He held the feeling like it was a Rubik's Cube and looked at it from every side. At first he told himself that he'd done his grandfather a favor, the same way his parents told him they were doing Sparky a favor when they took him to his final visit to the vet. But in the end, after looking at every side of the cube, Ethan decided that it hadn't been a favor, but it also hadn't been much of anything. All he'd done was kill someone, someone who was going to die anyway.

He'd finished his English assignment and was starting on his history assignment when he heard his mother wail from the first floor.

After the funeral, and when things had gone back to normal just as he'd predicted, Ethan took out his feelings again to look at them. He still didn't feel bad about what he'd done. His mom had been pretty sad at first, but at the reception after the funeral she'd seemed pretty happy, laughing and drinking wine with his two aunts. He'd brought them together by what he'd done, and he tried to understand if that made him feel good. It didn't, exactly. But he did feel something, and he wasn't sure what it was.

Before he fell asleep that night, he carefully tore a blank page from the back of his English notebook. At the top of the page he put his own name, *Ethan Conor Saltz*. He underlined it. Then two lines down he wrote the number *1*, and following that he wrote his grandfather's name, *Martin Conor Byrne*.

He folded the paper so that it was a fourth of its original size, then slid it between the pages of one of his old picture books, *There's an Alligator Under My Bed*.

CHAPTER 17

The first person he'd killed was his grandfather. The last person he'd killed was Martha Ratliff. In between them he'd killed twenty-four others.

The names of all those people, and the place and date where each died, were on a list that Ethan hid in a hollowed-out hardcover copy of John Cheever's stories. That list was his life's work, the thing of which he was the proudest. Sometimes he fantasized about turning himself in when he was seventy-five years old. The list would be much longer then. He'd bring it with him when he stepped inside the police station, or FBI headquarters, or whatever place he chose. He'd deliver the list, his curriculum vitae, his autobiography. Then the interviews would begin. Endless conversations with detectives and investigators from different jurisdictions. Not to mention the psychiatrists who'd be lining up to hear what he had to say. He'd explain to them just how easy it had been to kill so many people. He'd tell them his rules. For example, never do it the same way twice and always disguise it as something other than what it was. That was the important one. And because he'd followed that rule, at this point in his life—twenty-six murders in—Ethan was not on any investigative body's radar. He was a nobody. He'd never been arrested. He had no internet presence. No, that wasn't entirely true. *Ethan Saltz* had *some* internet presence. He was listed in a few obituaries, and he was the author of a number of well-received articles, including one that had been published sixteen years earlier in *New York* magazine. Ethan Saltz, as a name, as a citizen, *still* existed. He paid taxes on the relatively small annuity he received from his inheritance, and he held a post office box in Boston. But Ethan Saltz the flesh-and-blood man currently lived his life as Robert Charnock, an art dealer with a residence in Philadelphia. The real Robert Charnock had been a germophobic recluse who was currently at the bottom of a kettle pond in Wellfleet, Massachusetts. Robert, the person who Ethan now was, had much shorter, darker hair than Ethan, and a flat California accent. And he had actually become relatively successful in the art world, having sold several genuine pieces of art along with several very good forgeries. It went against Ethan's philosophy to engage in other criminal pursuits besides the art of murder, but forgery was surprisingly easy, especially, or only, when it was done on a small scale. He'd made a fair amount of money simply inventing mid-century artists and selling their forged art directly out of the gallery. Why anyone attempted to produce forgeries of well-known artists was beyond him.

The most surprising thing—surprising to Ethan, at least—about his life as Robert Charnock, was that he was married. His wife was older than him, with two children from a previous marriage, both of whom boarded at private high schools. He'd married Rebecca Grubb because she was rich, and because she owned a brownstone in Rittenhouse Square, and because she accepted him as a rather eccentric art dealer who never talked about his past. (He'd insinuated childhood trauma and she bought it hook, line, and sinker.) And she also accepted that his passion in life was meandering around the country, seeking hidden gems from flea markets and junk stores. She had never complained about his trips away. He suspected she liked the time alone. Rebecca's only expectations for her husband was that he attend the annual Christmas gala for the charity she ran, and that he spend two weeks with her every February at whatever tropical resort hotel she'd decided she absolutely had to visit.

The best part of having a wife was that men without wives were always a little suspicious. Wives were gatekeepers, really, telling the world that the man they had married had been thoroughly vetted and passed some sort of test. This only worked if the wife in question was a person of character. And Rebecca had character. In her case, that meant she had money and clout. And since she'd chosen Robert to share her life with, she'd conferred on him an extra layer of authenticity. She was his disguise.

Ethan's gallery was managed and staffed by his longtime assistant, Chris Salah, another person in his life, like Rebecca, who seemed perfectly content with being left alone for long stretches of time. God knows, and who cares, what Chris got up to when Ethan was away.

Ethan had now been Robert Charnock for six years, although he had credit cards still in the name of Ethan Saltz, and a bank card and a very convincing Illinois driver's license in the name of Bradley Anderson, another one of Ethan's previous victims. In Philadelphia, as Robert Charnock, he drove a two-door Jaguar XJ, but Brad owned a white Kia Forte that he parked at a run-down house north of the city with a single-car garage, a house in Brad Anderson's name. Ethan used the place as a place to swap identities and to swap cars.

In the first five years that Ethan had lived in Philadelphia as a married art dealer, he'd killed nineteen people in various locations, mostly along the East Coast. The easiest people to murder were those on the outskirts of society, drug addicts, teenage prostitutes, all those clichés from the serial killer handbook. And occasionally Ethan did indulge in some of those down-market victims. How hard was it, after all, to find some passed-out vagrant in a department store doorway and pummel him with a brick? The problem, Ethan had found, was that these victims often had no identifiable names. He'd lucked out once, after pushing a teenage drug addict off a bridge in Minneapolis, to discover her name in that week's newspaper, but there had been occasions when the murders he'd committed had never even been reported to the local press.

For that reason, Ethan looked for victims a little higher up the food chain. People with Social Security numbers and friends and family. People the police would care about. He had his rules. There could be no connection between him and the victim, no possibility that his name or even his description could ever come up in an investigation. He took this rule very seriously.

What was equally important to him was that his homicides appear to be something that they weren't. They didn't need to all look like accidents or suicides, although he'd engineered plenty of killings that did just that, but they needed to point in some direction other than random killing. For that reason, Ethan often chose his victims from newspaper stories. Somewhat prominent people going through ugly divorces. Wealthy businessmen being investigated for fraud. They were easy to spot if you knew what you were looking for. Down in Ocean City he'd picked up a newspaper left on a bar and read about a man, Dominic Salamone, recently released on bail after violating a restraining order issued because of domestic abuse. Ethan located Salamone's address in a White Pages phonebook, and cased the shabby little stucco house that, if Ethan didn't know better, he'd have deemed unlivable, and at one in the morning a cab dropped off Dominic Salamone, who entered through the front door. An hour later Ethan entered the house through a back door, let his eyes adjust to the darkness inside the house, then went upstairs to Dominic's bedroom, and strangled him with one of Dominic's own cheap ties.

He was back in Philadelphia the next day. Two days later he bought a copy of a Maryland newspaper at one of the few remaining news merchants in the city, and read a story about the death of Dominic Salamone, thought to be a revenge killing. The story hinted at Salamone's ex-wife being potentially connected to a local criminal enterprise.

It was all so easy.

And, truthfully, it had started to get a little boring. A year ago,

Ethan had been in one of his periodic downswings, the world colorless and dull. He'd gone onto Facebook, logging in as Barbara Smith, an entirely made-up person who had somehow still managed to acquire about four hundred idiotic friends. He liked to go on Facebook and browse around. It was stunning to him how much information people gleefully offered up. About where they lived, where they traveled, what their kids were up to, whom they loved. Mostly he used Facebook as a place to fantasize, and sometimes he used it to read remembrance boards on people he had killed—all those clichéd sentiments unspooling because of what he'd done. That was his favorite thing to do on Facebook, honestly, although he did occasionally take a look at people from his past, kids he'd gone to high school with, and sometimes even his brother and sister, both of them entirely out of his life.

On that particular day in springtime—Ethan's least favorite season—a name had come to him: Martha Ratliff. Ethan found her on Facebook. There was a picture of her, still a little brown mouse, still a librarian. She rarely posted. In fact, it had been a year between her last post and her most recent one, but the latest post was a marriage announcement, accompanied by a picture, her and some gaunt, vapid businessman. They'd honeymooned at Niagara Falls, the picture of them swallowed by mist, and Ethan supposed that the choice of Niagara Falls was partly because it was such a funny place to honeymoon, because, ha ha, people in the old days used to do it.

Ethan had eliminated most of the rage in his life, but it reared up in him now. Martha, back when he was Ethan Saltz the writer, back when the only person he'd killed was his grandfather, plus that one Vermont townie his junior year of college, back then Martha had been his special project. This was when his favorite pastime had been seducing mild-mannered girls, then slowly and completely taking them apart, corrupting them, making them do things they'd regret for the rest of their lives. Like everything else in his life, it had been far too easy, really. He'd always been handsome. There were always eyes on him wherever he went. Covetous eyes. He could have his pick of available girls, and for a time, toward the end of high school and the beginning of college, he'd picked the most popular girls, the prettiest, the ones who wanted him because he was a prize as well. But those girls, he found, were uninteresting to him. They were self-absorbed, and scorekeepers, and already prone to cruelty and extremes. Then he discovered the subset of girls who'd been ignored their whole lives, the wallflowers, and he found that they were far more interesting to him. He could talk them into the only kind of sex he enjoyed, sex that hurt, and he found that sometimes he could even talk them into hurting other people with him.

He'd found Martha during that one semester when he'd been an adjunct professor at Birkbeck College, back when he was going by his real name. He'd been a writer then. It was something he was good at, had always been good at, and it allowed him to openly and publicly investigate some of the seedier sides of the world we all lived in. His most famous piece, the one that was published in *New York* magazine, had been an exposé of a nascent cult that had sprung up among high school students in rural Texas. It had been started by the local minister's kid, who'd convinced more than ten fellow students to commit animal sacrifice, and join in orgies, at an abandoned farmhouse on Friday nights, while the rest of the town watched high school football. That story had gotten him a lot of attention, plus a now-expired film option. Writing it had been easy. Writing was just manipulation, in a way. The key was to seem objective while all the time leading your readers to the conclusion, and the emotions, that you wanted them to have. But Ethan, at that point in his life, knew he was bound for greater things, and being a writer was not quite as anonymous as he'd hoped it would be. He took the teaching gig to get out of New York City and to rethink what he really wanted to do with his life.

Martha Ratliff had been so promising to him, her self-esteem so low that she believed she'd actually been the victim of some kind of love curse. She was an ugly duckling who had given up all hope of a relationship. He'd spotted her at a table in some bar, surrounded by a bunch of prettier students, and he'd seduced her without so much as talking to her. And things had gone well for a while. He'd talked her into rough sex and into some pretty interesting threesomes with drunk locals. He hadn't seen it in her eyes yet, that moment when she gave in to the transgressions and began to enjoy them. But that was why she was a project. He had time. And then, suddenly, out of the blue, she'd told him that she didn't want to see him anymore. It was a laughable performance. She'd been coached by some do-good friend of hers who'd clearly become concerned. That friend had shown up on the night of the breakup, conveniently arriving just in time to usher Martha home and out of his grasp. He didn't remember the friend's name, but he remembered what she looked like, red hair, strange green eyes, skim-milk skin. She'd scared him just a little. What was her name? Some kind of flower, he thought.

What was funny was that he remembered Martha Ratliff's name but not really what she looked like. Of course, when he saw her on Facebook it all came back to him. There she was, the little mouse, survivor of some silly love curse, and survivor of a pretty exciting relationship with Ethan Saltz. Maybe he shouldn't have let her go so easily. He clicked over to her new husband's profile. It was actually a business page. He sold novelty items for teachers at conferences. There was a picture of him standing in front of some booth, and Ethan had an idea, a really interesting idea. It would be dangerous, more dangerous than his current hobbies, but then again, it might be far more satisfying. There was a calendar of upcoming conferences on Alan Peralta's Facebook page—the man traveled constantly—and Ethan began to formulate a plan.

CHAPTER 18

The first convention that Ethan went to—the first convention when the purpose was to tail Alan Peralta—was some sort of math conference in downtown Atlanta. On his first day there, he checked into a nearby hotel as Brad Anderson, and, wearing a purple turtleneck tucked into some very loose jeans, Ethan visited Peralta's booth. He'd only do it once, he told himself, get close enough to Peralta and maybe even speak to him. The booth was crowded, Peralta making money hand over fist, apparently, and Ethan lingered awhile, long enough to notice that Peralta, whether intentionally or not, focused on his female customers much more than his male ones. Nothing unusual in that, of course, but Ethan thought there was something a little pervy about the way Peralta's eyes raked over the poorly dressed female teachers. Peralta appeared to be on the prowl.

It turned out he was right about Peralta's appetites, although Ethan hadn't been sure about that until midway through the conference. Ethan shadowed Peralta from afar throughout the three days in Atlanta. It was easy to do, the convention center teeming with people who didn't know one another. The trade hall closed each night at six, and Ethan would take up position on one of the faux-leather couches in the lobby near the entrance. He pretended to read the conference program and kept an eye out for Peralta. The first night he didn't spot him, but on the next Peralta got a table by himself in the lobby bar and Ethan watched as Peralta approached a lone woman carrying a conference tote bag and drinking a margarita by herself. They spoke for about twenty minutes, then the women was swallowed up by a group of her colleagues sweeping through. Peralta faded back.

On the last night of the conference, Peralta, having changed from his cheap suit into jeans and a winter jacket, slipped through the lobby and exited into the mild February evening. Ethan followed him to a strip club that was about a twenty-five-minute walk away, hesitated for a while outside, but then decided to go in and see what was happening. It was quiet inside, and even though Ethan was using his fake ID and was in one of his semi-disguises as a fashionably challenged middle school math teacher, he still hated the scrutiny one received in strip clubs. Not from the strippers, of course, who just looked out from their poles and saw blurry men in either expensive suits or cheap ones, but from the bouncers who were paid to get a good look at the lone men who entered the establishment.

Ethan went straight to the empty bar, sat at one of the swivel stools, and ordered a fifteen-dollar Heineken, then turned and watched the action. The stage was an elevated platform that jutted out into the center of the bar; there were seats around it, and he expected to see Peralta in one of them, but he wasn't there. There were just two other lone men and then a couple, the female half the most vocal audience member, yelling encouragement and waving dollar bills at the stripper, currently a top-heavy woman with very little natural rhythm. It took a minute before Ethan spotted Peralta at a table against the back wall, talking with one of the roving strippers, probably negotiating a closed-door lap dance. But the stripper took off, and Peralta leaned back into the shadows, sipping what looked like a Coke.

"Hey, handsome." It was the same stripper who had just been propositioning Peralta. She was young and thin, with dyed-red hair and caked-on makeup that made it hard to imagine what she really looked like.

"You probably call all the guys handsome," Ethan said.

"I do, but you actually are. Handsome."

"Aw, thanks. What's your name?"

"Debbi."

"Debbi, I'm just here to drink a beer and watch the dancers, for now. When are you up?"

"I just danced, two girls ago, so I won't be back up there for at least an hour. But I could give you a private dance."

Ethan considered asking her what she knew about the guy she was just talking to, but it wasn't worth the risk. Besides, what would she possibly know except that he'd passed on a lap dance, just as he was about to. "No, thanks, Debbi," he said.

"Well, if you change your mind . . ." She strutted off, looking around the half-empty bar before making her way backstage.

Ethan began to consider options. It did occur to him that this might be the end of the sexual adventures for Alan Peralta. He'd struck out at convincing a lonely math teacher to come hang with him, so for his last night of freedom from Martha Ratliff he was enjoying the meager delights of the Rockstar Strip Club. If that was the case, then Ethan could wait for Peralta to get his eyeful and maybe a private dance or two, and leave, and then later on he could swan back at closing time and hope one of the strippers decided to walk home alone. Still, he hated that plan, mostly because he was a visible customer at the Rockstar right now, and on a slow night, to boot. He finished the Heineken and left.

Directly across the street from the strip club were two bars side by side. One of them was windowless and promised cheap pitchers and pool tables. The other bar was more of a dining establishment. It was called Mac's Chicken and boasted a large window with seats that faced the street. Ethan went inside, was told he could sit any-where, and grabbed one of the window seats. He could see the entrance to the Rockstar. A waitress showed up, far prettier than any of the strippers he'd seen across the street, and he ordered a local IPA plus a grilled chicken salad. Just as he was finishing up his meal, he spotted Peralta leaving the strip club, standing for a moment on the sidewalk as if deciding which way to go. It gave Ethan time to flag his waitress and quickly pay his bill in cash. When he emerged out onto the street, he still had an eye on Peralta, although he'd headed farther uptown and was turning at a corner. Ethan followed him.

After about a twenty-minute walk, it was clear to Ethan that Peralta was looking for something he hadn't been able to find at the Rockstar. The neighborhoods were getting seedier—more abandoned storefronts, more pawnshops and cash-checking estab-lishments, more busted streetlamps—and Peralta was slowing his pace, either out of fear or because he was searching for someplace specific. They were on the outskirts of a park when a small woman approached from the other direction and began to talk with Per-alta. Ethan was near a bus stop and leaned against the opening of the shelter there, keeping an eye on both of them. After about thirty seconds of conversation they went together into the dark park through a stone arch. Ethan considered following them, but he knew exactly what they were doing, so he decided to stay put. He'd actually gotten a decent look at the street prostitute. She wore a tiny skirt and high heels, no surprise there, but was wearing a winter puffer jacket on top, probably just because she was cold from being on the street all night. And she was small, almost child-sized, but with a lot of dark hair that was either some kind of wig or had been sprayed into a helmet. He'd even gotten a look at her face, enough to see that she had glittery makeup on her cheeks.

He waited.

After ten minutes, maybe less, Peralta emerged from the park the way he had entered it. He was walking much faster than he had before, heading back south toward downtown, and keeping his head down. Ethan moved farther back into the bus-stop shelter as Peralta passed by, although it didn't matter. Peralta didn't glance his way.

Ethan stayed where he was, and after about five minutes the prostitute emerged from the park and back out onto the street. A car pulled up and she went and talked to the driver, but then the car pulled away again, and she was alone. This was too easy, Ethan thought, and made his way to her.

"You're in a good mood," Rebecca said.

"Am I? I thought I was always in a good mood." Ethan was a little annoyed by the comment. He'd always hated when people pointed out his moods to him.

Rebecca, wearing a dark gray tunic over jeans, and, with her hair up, was sawing through her chicken piccata, taking little bites. Chicken piccata was the only dish she cooked, and she made it a lot.

"You are *always* in a good mood, but tonight you're in a better mood. You had a good trip?"

Ethan had returned from Atlanta in the late afternoon, having driven through half the night and most of the day. He called Rebecca when he was about an hour away, just before switching cars at his secret house an hour away in Tohickon, and told her he was coming home. He didn't think Rebecca had affairs while he was gone, but if she did, then the last thing he wanted was to actually catch her at it. Their marriage was good as it was, and he had no reason to add any messiness to their trouble-free lives.

"My trip was fine. The problem is that every owner of every junk store can now just go online and look up what everything in their store is worth. It's a lot harder to find gems."

"Still fun to look, though, right?"

"Always. And I did buy some paintings—they look like Chagall rip-offs done back in the 1970s—and if I change the frames and call it folk art, some Philadelphian will definitely overpay for them."

"See what I mean?" Rebecca said, leaning above her plate to take a minuscule bite. "Good mood."

Ethan squeezed his left hand into a fist under the table but nodded at his wife.

After dinner that night, Ethan went up to his office on the top floor of the brownstone. He got the lighting just right and put on his ambient mix. First he unwrapped the three small paintings that he'd actually bought at an antique store just outside of Greensboro on his drive back to Philadelphia. They were crude approximations of Chagall's style, probably done by an amateur painter half a century ago, but as he'd said to Rebecca, sometimes changing the frame was all it took to persuade a nouveau riche local to overpay for them. He stared at the three small canvases for a while—they were growing on him. Floating horses and lurid suns.

After rewrapping the paintings, he poured himself a scotch and sat at his computer, immediately finding the article he'd been looking for, the one that let an uninterested public know that a prostitute named Kelli Baldwin had been found dead in Piedmont Park, bludgeoned to death. The article listed her age as twenty-nine. He got up and went to his built-in bookcase, pulled out his hardcover of *The Stories of John Cheever*, modified into a hiding place, and opened it up. Inside was the handwritten list of the people he'd killed, the list he'd begun so many years ago. He added Kelli Baldwin's name to it, including the date and place of her murder, then cast his eye over the names, noticing how his handwriting had changed over the years. Sliding the book back into its place on the shelf, he wondered if he was being too careless. There was a good safe in his office, protected by a combination that only he knew, but safes could be cracked. Besides, the list was his secret, but it wasn't going to be his secret forever. One day the whole world would know just how many people he'd killed in his lifetime. Either he'd eventually get caught—not the worst thing in the world if he was very old when it happened—or he would die and the list would be found.

Sometimes he worried that his hidey-hole, his first-edition Cheever collection, was actually too good a hiding place. What if he died and no one ever bothered to look at his books? He'd thought of this before and told himself that he'd eventually make a copy of his list and add it to his safe as well. It was very important that one day he be given credit for the sheer audacity of what he'd done. Legacies were all people left behind.

He poured a little more scotch into his glass. Yes, he *was* in a good mood that night. Not only had things gone well in Atlanta, but now he had a project for the discernible future. Why had he never thought of doing this before—shadow someone who travels for a living and kill people they come into contact with? It met his criteria perfectly—no contact with the victims, except for killing them, and making it look like someone else was responsible. In this case, making it look like the work of a serial killer. Of course, it helped that Peralta was halfway to being a serial killer anyway. It was very clear that he hunted women on his trips, just to fuck, of course, but he was still hunting. Ethan wondered if he ever succeeded at scoring with one of the other conventioneers on his trips, or if he always resorted to prostitutes. It would be easier if he always went to prostitutes—easier for Ethan, anyway—but it would be far less interesting. He hoped that occasionally Peralta would strike up a classic extramarital romance and that Ethan would get to kill someone who mattered a little more to the world.

Against his better judgment, Ethan allowed himself to project a little, to revel in the future instead of the past. He could already imagine it. How many women would he get to kill before Peralta got busted for the crimes he hadn't committed? For all Ethan knew, the game might be over. Maybe Peralta's DNA was on file for some reason (unlikely but possible) and he'd be picked up for the prostitute's death in Atlanta. Ethan doubted it, though. He thought he'd be able to get away with this game for a while until some police detective figured out that Peralta had just happened to be at the scene of a string of nationwide crimes. There'd probably be a *Dateline* episode about it.

He told himself to calm down, and not fantasize about the future. That was what normal people did. Small people. Still, if it actually worked out, nothing made him happier than thinking about mousy Martha Ratliff, the horror she would feel when it was revealed that her husband was actually a prolific serial killer. That was who he was doing this for, really. For Martha, the love-cursed. For Martha, the one who got away.

CHAPTER 19

The Peralta killings, as Ethan had come to think of them, had been some of the best experiences of Ethan's life. The conventions were easy places to remain anonymous. Peralta was so fixated on his own sexual pursuits that Ethan was never concerned about being spotted. He'd watch Peralta from afar (and sometimes fairly close up) and over time realized that the man had a pattern. First and foremost, he would flirt with conventioneers, hanging out at the hotel bar, looking for someone who would sleep with him. If that didn't work out—it rarely did—he would leave the vicinity of the convention, go to dive bars late at night to look for easy prey, or check out strip clubs and massage parlors. From there he would keep lowering his sights.

In Chicago, three months after he'd killed Kelli Baldwin in Atlanta, Ethan watched Peralta spend a late night at a bar buying drinks and making out with a local. Ethan, disguised in a hockey jersey and a baseball cap, sat at a table near the back by the pool tables. He followed them out of the bar, watched them stagger back to Peralta's hotel, arms around each other, hips bumping. Ethan found a place to camp out across the street from the hotel, and kept an eye on the revolving doors, hoping that the woman didn't decide to stay the night, assuming, somehow, that she wouldn't. Ethan turned out to be right—at three A.M. the woman emerged from the hotel, stepping into the light cast on the vacant valet stand. Ethan, worried that she'd ordered a car to pick her up, moved fast, then lucked out when the woman started walking. He dragged her down the alleyway by the hotel, put her in a choke hold that knocked her out, finishing her with a brick. Her name was Bianca Muranos, and there were a fair number of stories about her in the press. Ethan kept wondering if Peralta would be identified. Plenty of other patrons at the bar had seen them together. They'd entered the hotel together. She'd have been lousy with Peralta's DNA. But nothing came of it.

Ethan found himself torn between enjoying his new game and wondering when someone would identify Peralta as a suspect. He'd always thought that most police officers, despite what television shows and detective novels would like you to think, were neither smart enough nor particularly driven to solve crimes. In Fort Myers, Ethan went so far as to kill Nora Johnson while Peralta was right next to her in the car. He'd watched the whole scam unfold in the bar, Peralta smitten with the gorgeous bartender, her flirting back. After last call he'd followed Peralta to the parking garage where he'd met the bartender. She led him to a parked car, the two of them getting in the front seat. Ethan had been surprised they hadn't gotten into the back and he'd waited for a moment before approaching the car, but after a few minutes it was clear they weren't going anywhere. Knowing how dangerous it was, but thrilled with the idea, he'd removed his own tie, then simply slid into the backseat and managed to get it around the woman's neck while her hands were down Peralta's pants. Peralta never looked his way, just scrambled out of the car when Ethan told him to run. And, not surprisingly, Peralta had never reported the incident.

It was a genuine shock when Ethan heard that a parking lot attendant had been arrested for the crime. Less of a shock that he was eventually released. As far as he knew, the case had stalled.

Getting a little bored, Ethan had decided to see if could point the finger in Peralta's direction a little more forcefully. In San Diego Peralta had visited a woman's house on his second-to-last night there, a woman who turned out to be a massage therapist who worked out of her home. Judging by Peralta's body language as he left her house, he'd been expecting more than he'd received. From that point on, Ethan decided to shadow the massage therapist, who he later learned to be Mikaela Sager—she had a small business sign next to her front door. Ethan trailed her the following night to an oceanside bar, where she ordered a glass of wine and pulled out *Bring Up the Bodies* in paperback from her hobo bag. He'd grabbed the seat next to her and started a conversation.

"You're not . . . ?" she said, an anxious expression on her face.

"I'm not . . . who?" Ethan said.

"Oh, sorry. This is embarrassing but I'm meeting someone here, not for another hour, but I thought you might be him."

"You're on an online date?" Ethan said.

"Not yet I'm not," she said, and then he told her he was a school administrator from Northern California and that he was here for the English teachers' conference. A flicker of recognition crossed her eyes at the mention of the conference—Peralta must have told her he was attending—and Ethan watched her think about telling him about her bad experience with a massage client but deciding not to. They had a couple of drinks and split an appetizer, then Ethan told her he'd better get out of the way before her real date showed up, and how he'd really come down here in hopes of walking out along a pier at night to see the stars. She'd taken a guilty look around the bar and asked him if she could come with him. The rest was easy.

Before he tipped her into the water, he'd pinned a Jane Austen brooch that he'd stolen from Peralta's booth onto her blouse. It was time to finally get someone to pay attention.

After returning from San Diego to Philadelphia he waited to hear news, but none came. In the meantime, Ethan had become distracted by an interesting development in his life as Robert Charnock. One of his longtime clients, Jane Hillerman, a very bored middle-aged wife of a financial adviser, had fallen in love with the paintings of an obscure mid-century Canadian artist named Donald Carlyle, who'd painted misty seascapes (and practically nothing else) of the Nova Scotia shoreline. Ethan traveled up to Halifax on Jane's dime to see if he could purchase some paintings for her. While he didn't find any unclaimed artwork, he did find Carlyle's nephew, a watercolorist himself with a knack for painting seascapes very similar to the style of his deceased uncle. He was selling them in two or three touristy galleries under his own name, but Ethan, after bedding the nephew and buying the underfed youth some very good meals, convinced him to produce a few works just for him. Works that would pass as original Donald Carlyles and with Carlyle's distinctive scrawled signature in the lower right-hand corner. And he had returned to Philadelphia to a very giddy client, happy to overpay for the forgeries.

In April Ethan went to Denver the night before the last day of one of Peralta's conventions, and as he joined the throng at the Southwest English Teachers Symposium, trudging their way through the exhibition hall, he was overcome with weariness at the whole prospect of following Peralta on his philanderer's tour around the city. He wanted Peralta caught. He wanted news stories, and he wanted to know that Martha Ratliff had become more convinced than ever that she was truly cursed. That was why Ethan went to Denver on the last night of the convention only. He'd come to realize that, unless Peralta got lucky with a convention-goer (chances of that: close to zero), most of the hunting took place on the last night. And that was the case in Denver, when Ethan followed Peralta to the Five Points neighborhood, where he disappeared into a single-story corner tavern with stucco siding and a red neon sign that simply said BAR.

For two hours Ethan waited across the street in the window seat of a coffee shop. Peralta emerged near closing time accompanied by two women, one on either of his arms. They all walked together, Peralta noticeably unsteady on his feet, to a liquor store two blocks away. Ethan watched a conversation ensue in front of the store, and then the three walked another block and wound up at an ATM machine,

Peralta no doubt pulling out the maximum withdrawal his bank allowed. The girls took the money, then shoved Peralta to the ground and walked casually away. Ethan had never seen Peralta that impaired and he assumed that the two hustling girls had roofied him.

He followed the girls, who ducked into an empty parking lot. Ethan crouched behind a car and watched them split up the cash. One girl took off, while the other one stayed in the lot for a moment, pulling out a cigarette from her bag and lighting it. Earlier that day Ethan had passed a pile of free junk on a residential street and pocketed a meat tenderizer that had been in a box filled with other kitchen implements. It was in his pocket now, as he came out of the shadows and approached the girl. She jumped a little when she saw him, and he halted, held up his hands, and said, "Sorry. Didn't mean to scare you. I hate to ask, but can I bum one of your cigarettes? I'll even pay you for it."

She smirked in his direction, swaying a little on her heels, wondering if he was someone else she could con. "They're menthol," she said.

"Menthol, Jesus. One of those isn't worth a whole lot more than a buck." Ethan pulled out his wallet, fishing through it.

She laughed. "You really going to pay me for a cigarette?"

"Sure. Why not? I'm rich."

"Are you?"

"Not really. Maybe just drunk."

She laughed again and held out the hardpack of cigarettes. Ethan took one with his left hand while removing the meat tenderizer from his jacket pocket with his right. He hit her square across the jaw, and she dropped down to the ground in a heap. He crouched next to her. He'd hit her with the serrated side of the tenderizer and a flap of skin hung from her cheek. Without thinking too much about it, Ethan wiped the tenderizer clean of fingerprints, using the girl's cheap skirt, and hurled it down to the other end of the alley. Then he lightly pressed his hand up against the welling blood on her cheek, getting his fingers wet. He stood up and left the parking lot, holding his hand down by his side.

When he got back to the ATM, he didn't immediately see Peralta, but he knew he couldn't have gotten far. Ethan wandered back in the direction of the liquor store and spotted Peralta leaning up against its brick siding. Ethan walked up to him, placed his right hand on the small of his back, and said, "Hey, man, you okay?"

Peralta looked at him through glassy eyes, void of recognition—whatever the girls had slipped him was pretty potent—and said, "I just got robbed, I think."

"Looks like you did," Ethan said. There were sirens in the distance, and he added, "Don't worry, the police are coming." He wiped blood from his hand onto Peralta's shirt.

Walking briskly away, he wondered if he'd gone too far, but, honestly, he really was getting tired of this game. He wanted Peralta on the national news. And it wasn't until he was back at his hotel room that he remembered he'd left a witness alive in the parking lot. It was such a stupid thing to do that it actually made him laugh out loud.

The next morning, flying back from Denver to Philadelphia, he was nervous at the airport for the first time in a long time, somehow waiting for his name to trigger an alert to the TSA officer. He really had been careless in not finishing off the girl in the parking lot. He'd also let her look at him. He wasn't as worried about Peralta, who most probably had zero recall of the events that had transpired the night before. But Ethan made it home unmolested by the police, and in his office that night he decided that he needed to end the Peralta killings sooner rather than later. It had gotten too risky. The next convention that Peralta was going to be at, according to his website, was in Saratoga Springs, New York. Well, at least he wouldn't have to fly there. And it was an area he knew well. He decided to go, and he resolved that it would be the last time he committed a Peralta killing. Somehow he'd make it so fucking obvious that even an upstate New York police detective might be able to figure it out. Maybe he'd shove one of Peralta's business cards in the victim's pocket.

But when he got to Saratoga Springs something very interesting happened. Alarming as well, but mostly interesting. On his first night there, he discovered that he wasn't the only one keeping an eye on the roaming salesman. He'd been following Peralta at dinner hour, idly, not giving it too much thought. But Peralta often found someplace to eat dinner before making his way to the part of town where he might find a strip club or a prostitute. So, it was important to keep an eye on him from the get-go. But that night, hanging about a block back, Ethan had the unsettling feeling that *he* was being watched, that someone was following *him*. At one point, bending down to tie his shoes, he saw a woman a block back from him, staring into an empty window. After Peralta finally picked a restaurant, Ethan doubled back across the street and got a brief look at the woman who'd been behind him. She was now sitting on a park bench, pretending to look at her phone. Red hair, small frame, a composed stillness about her. He ducked into the next bar and was about to order a drink when a name came to him.

Lily.

She'd been Martha's friend back when he had that teaching gig in Maryland.

He told the bartender he was still thinking and stayed at the bar for a moment. It couldn't be a coincidence, Lily being here. He actually did believe in coincidences—they happened all the time in his life—but not this particular one. His mind raced, creating a possible narrative. Martha must have become suspicious of her husband. Maybe she found the bloodstain on his shirt. Maybe she read about one of the unsolved murders and realized that her husband had been there at the time. Maybe some cop had actually zeroed in on Peralta and asked her to provide an alibi. It didn't matter. Martha suspected her husband. So, she did what she'd done fifteen years earlier when she'd gotten involved with a scary man. She ran to her best friend, who got her out of the situation. Was Lily there to keep an eye on Peralta?

Complicated emotions flooded through Ethan. He felt some satisfaction that his plan was finally coming to fruition. Martha had discovered her husband was a potential serial killer. Her love curse had returned, and now it was only a matter of time before Peralta was actually nabbed for one of his crimes. But there was another feeling that Ethan had, one that was familiar but rare. He was angry. Seeing Lily had brought back the feeling he'd had all those years ago when she'd taken Martha away from him. He remembered it so well. Her smug look from across the table at the bar where Martha had just broken up with him. She'd provided the words and Martha had said them. But it wasn't just that she'd interrupted his fun and games; he remembered being a little scared of her at the time. He'd tried to stare her down and it didn't work, her green eyes looking right back at his with no fear in them. He'd called her a monster, he remembered that, and without hesitating she'd said back to him that she was a monster, and that he needed to remember that.

He went back out to the sidewalk, not surprised to see Lily still on the bench. She turned to look at him and he said, "I thought you looked familiar."

She hadn't admitted anything, of course, pretending that she was randomly in Saratoga Springs for the same conference that Peralta happened to be working. In the middle of their conversation, though, he was suddenly filled with certainty that it was now time to put an end to this whole fucking Peralta caper. He saw a taxi with its light on cruising down the street. He hailed it and jumped in.

During the ride back to his own hotel, and to his Kia, Ethan thought about Martha. At the time he'd walked away from her, he told himself that she'd been too easy to manipulate anyway, but the truth was that he'd been one-upped by Lily, a fucking librarian who looked like she'd get blown over in a sharp breeze.

He'd been mad then, and he was mad now.

He thought about killing Lily. He could double back and follow her to wherever she was staying, probably at the conference hotel. But that would be almost too easy. No, he got another idea, one that would take the legs right out from under her and teach her to not play Nancy Drew with her friends. He needed to show Lily that she'd made a big mistake.

And, suddenly, he wasn't angry anymore. He was happy as a clam.

CHAPTER 20

Martha didn't call me back after I told her that I'd spotted Ethan Saltz. I tried several times to reach her and even sent her a text. But somehow I knew in my heart she was dead.

I didn't even try to sleep that night. I was waiting for my phone to make a noise that would tell me Martha was okay, even though I doubted that she was. Just after dawn, I opened up a browser on my phone and did a search for Alan Peralta and Martha Ratliff, adding Portsmouth, figuring that their purchase of a house would be public record. It came up almost immediately: 55 Birchvale Road. They'd paid $650,000 for it the previous year.

I checked out of my motel, and got into my car, the address loaded onto my phone. I drove as fast as I dared and made it to Portsmouth by ten that morning, driving through the center of town on cobblestone streets, brick buildings on either side. It was sunny, but the kind of misty sunshine that indicated that it had probably been rainy in the recent past. After passing through the center, I took several turns along residential streets, eventually finding Birchvale, a lightly wooded street of modest homes that all looked like they'd been built in the 1950s. The address on Birchvale was one of the spiffier houses on the street, freshly painted an olive green, daffodils poking up in its neat front yard. There was a Subaru Outback in the driveway. I drove past the house about half a block and pulled up beneath a large maple tree on the edge of a small cemetery.

If I was about to find what I thought I was going to find inside of the house, then it made sense to not draw attention to myself. I reached back and unzipped my bag that was resting on the backseat of my car. Inside was a blue baseball cap without a logo. I could at least tuck my red hair up under the hat. It wasn't exactly a disguise, but if I were identified later, it might muddy the waters a little bit.

I left the car and walked down the street as casually as possible, skirting puddles on the sidewalk. When I reached Martha and Alan's house I turned down their driveway, then crossed the small yard that led to the front door. The bland façade of the small pretty house filled me with even more dread than I'd been feeling. I somehow knew what I was going to find behind its walls. I rapped on the door, then turned the doorknob. It wasn't locked, so I pushed the door open and yelled "Yoo-hoo," into the house as I stepped inside. I closed the door behind me.

I was in a dim living area, the curtains still pulled, a stairway to my right. A cat padded heavily down the stairs, stopping at the bottom and meowing.

"Hey, there," I said, crouching and holding out my hand. "Where's your mom?"

I yelled another hello into the house, then listened. The cat had sniffed at my fingers and was now rubbing up against one of my ankles. I stood up, deciding to look upstairs first.

At the top landing there was a wide carpeted hallway, three doors leading off from it on one side, and one on the other. Only one of the doors was opened, the one to the right, and judging by its position in the house it made sense that it was the master bedroom. I took a step toward it, suddenly wishing I'd brought my Mace, or even my stun gun. I didn't think there was anyone behind the door, at least no one alive, but I couldn't be sure. I pulled down the sleeve of my sweater, covering my hand so as not to leave any prints on the knob, and pushed the door open.

I could smell the blood before my eyes adjusted enough to see the room. The curtains were open, light from outside illuminating Martha, lying on the floor, blood soaking an area rug that framed her with almost precise geometry.

I looked around, moving carefully. There was a spray of blood across the hardwood floor and even along some of the beige wall beside the door. Martha had bled out from a major artery. Nothing else in the room seemed disturbed. Not that I'd known what the room looked liked before, but it was neat, the bed made, no clothes on the floor.

There was no sign of a struggle.

A wave of faintness passed over me, and I shut my eyes for a moment. When I opened them, nothing in the room had changed. Martha was still dead. As I turned to leave, I noticed a framed print on the wall next to the door, a pen-and-ink drawing advertising the Berkshire Literary Festival. It was familiar to me, and then I remembered that it was a piece of art that Martha had hung in her dorm room back when we'd been students together. I wondered if Martha's killer had seen the print as well, and if he remembered it as I had.

Back downstairs I looked around for the cat, but didn't see him, then I peered through the strip of beveled glass beside the front door, just to make sure that there weren't immediate witnesses in the area. I pulled my sweater down over my hand again and exited the house, walking briskly back down the road to my car.

I drove for a while, not in any particular direction, then I pulled into the empty parking lot of a clam shack that hadn't yet opened for the season. I shut off my engine and thought about Martha, taking a moment to digest the fact that she was longer alive. My hands shook, and I rubbed them on my legs even though they weren't sweaty.

I sat in the car for ten minutes, just staring through my windshield. I had several decisions to make. One of the decisions was whether I was going to call in to the police and report a dead body at 55 Birchvale Road. It would spare Alan from coming home and discovering his wife's corpse, but on the flip side, it might hurt the investigation, especially if I called in anonymously, which was what I would do. The other possibility was to simply go to the police with everything I knew, but I was not inclined to do that, partly because what I was thinking still sounded so ludicrous to me that it was hard to imagine the police believing my story. I decided not to make the call, as myself or anonymously. It wouldn't help Martha, and it wouldn't help me in finding the person who had killed her.

My next decision took a little longer for me to make. Over a year ago Henry Kimball had come to me for help when he'd been entangled with Joan Whalen Grieve and Richard Seddon. I'd helped him, but not until after he'd nearly died. I didn't particularly want to get Henry involved in something dangerous—I believe he'd suffered enough because of me—but (a) I knew that he would help me no matter what I asked him to do, and (b) I knew that he would keep whatever we found out together a secret. It was hard to explain our relationship, even to myself, but it was an alliance. Maybe for Henry it had to do with love. Maybe for me as well. But most importantly we trusted one another. And he knew things about me that no one else in the world knew.

Before I left the parking lot, I'd made my decision. I drove to Arlington, a suburban town next to Cambridge, and parked outside the office building where Henry now worked. I thought about just knocking on his door but decided to call instead. He picked up right away.

"Hey," he said.

"Are you in your office?"

"I am."

"I'm outside. Do you mind if I come up?"

"No, not at all. When you get to the door press the button next to my name and I'll buzz you up."

When I stepped into his office, we did a slightly awkward dance that involved a kiss on the cheek and a half hug. "Everything okay?" he said, stepping back. We looked at one another. He was basically unchanged since I'd last seen him, his brown hair a little shorter, eyes a little wearier, but wearing his usual uniform of a tweed blazer over old jeans. He'd referred to his style once as "dissolute poet."

"I'm fine," I said. "But I think I might have a job for you, if you're interested."

We moved to separate sides of his desk. The office coloring was beige and there were built-in fluorescent lights in the dropped ceiling. I was looking around, and Henry said, "New office. My last one blew up with me in it."

"I remember. This new one is . . ."

"Maybe it needs some new paint."

"Yes."

"It's nice to see you in person," I said, not willing to get down to business just yet. Maybe I didn't want to say the words about my friend Martha out loud. I knew it made no difference, but I still wasn't quite ready.

"Thank you for all the letters. They make me feel like I'm living in a different, better time."

"We might be the last letter writers on planet earth."

"We might be."

"How are David and Sharon?"

"My mom fell and broke a hip about six months ago—I probably wrote and told you that already—and now she's much better but likely a pill addict. David's just about the same. I've been reading him Anne Sexton poems. He talks about you."

I saw a slight flush of red cross his cheeks. He admired my father a lot, despite having met him on several occasions. "What does he think of Anne Sexton?" he said.

"He says she keeps his attention, which is his highest praise. And, oh, he met her once, but that's not that surprising, because he's met everyone."

"Did you read him my limerick?"

I laughed and told him I hadn't, at least not yet. Henry had once been an aspiring poet, but these days he only wrote limericks. Most of his letters included at least one.

"I'm glad you're all doing well," he said. "I had this horrible feel-

ing when you buzzed up that you were going to tell me that someone died."

"Someone has died," I said. "No one you know, but that's why
I'm here."

"Okay," he said.

"Her name was Martha Ratliff. Do you have a moment to hear
the entire story?"

I saw him hesitate briefly, then say, "Yeah, tell me all about it.
I'm free."

I told him all about it. How Martha had come to me with a suspicion that her husband might be responsible for up to five murders
across the country. How we'd researched those deaths, together,
finding some evidence that suggested Alan had most likely been
responsible, but not enough evidence to know for sure. And then
how I'd gone to a conference in Saratoga Springs to at least look at
Alan, to follow him, see if I could find out anything.

"Did you think you'd look at him and know the truth?"

"A little bit," I said. "Foolish, I know."

"So what did you think?"

"Let me tell you another story first. Back when I first met Martha, she began dating one of the adjunct professors at our school. He
was this very good-looking guy, and it was obvious to me, but not immediately to Martha, that he was bad news. He got her into all sorts
of sexual things she was uncomfortable with. She became a project
for him, someone he could manipulate and change. It was all a game
to him. He was a sociopath, or maybe just a sadist. I helped her get
out of the relationship."

"And you're telling me about this guy now . . ."

"Because he was there at the conference in Saratoga. Because
he was following Alan as well. And now I have a theory."

"Okay."

"It sounds ridiculous, I know, but I think he's killing the women."

"Okay," he said again, this time with some skepticism in his voice.

"Hear me out. He's not picking them. Peralta goes on trips and cheats on Martha. With a woman he picks up at a bar, or a prostitute, or a stripper from a club. Peralta is picking the victims. This other man is killing them."

"Because of Martha?"

"Because of Martha."

"And now he's killed her. Why didn't he just start with that?"

"I have a sick feeling he did it because of me."

"Because of you how?"

"I didn't just spot him trailing Peralta, he spotted me as well. We spoke."

"Jesus."

"Right."

"How was that?"

"It was awkward. Neither of us admitted why we were really there, but we both knew. He seemed amused, pleased almost. After our conversation he must have driven straight to Portsmouth and killed Martha. He did it as a challenge to me, I think."

"Why wouldn't he think you'd just turn him in?"

"I don't know. Cockiness, I suppose. I have no proof. Plus, I think it's possible that he's no longer going by his old name, that maybe he's disappeared."

"Why do you think that?"

"Because I was up all night trying to find him online. There's stuff from fifteen years ago, but nothing new. That's why I'm here talking with you."

"You want me to find him?"

"Yes. I want you to find him, then I'll do everything else."

"What's his name?"

CHAPTER 21

Two days later I was standing outside the Fix and Finesse hair salon in Cresskill, New Jersey, trying to figure out the best way to approach Ethan Saltz's sister.

After leaving Henry's office, I'd driven back to Shepaug and spent a couple of hours listening to contradictory narratives of what had happened while I'd been away. My father claimed that he'd been fed nothing but salmon and kale salad for my entire absence, while my mother said that she'd gone to the diner twice to get my father double cheeseburgers. Neither account sounded remotely feasible to me. After my mother had retired for the night and after my father had fallen asleep in front of the television, I spoke with Henry on the phone to hear what he'd learned about Ethan Saltz. The man was a ghost. No current address. No arrest record. No car registration. There were a number of articles still available from when Ethan Saltz had been a journalist, mostly longer pieces with clickbait hooks. He'd profiled a woman who had married the drunken driver who had killed her first husband. There was an article about a group of pagan teenagers in Texas that had been anthologized in that year's *Best American Essays*. He'd interviewed a Harvard student who claimed to have made over a million dollars running a sports betting operation from his dormitory room. But then, sometime around 2005, there were no more pieces. He'd stopped writing, or at the very least stopped publishing. And it seemed he'd changed his name.

Henry had found the same two photographs of Ethan Saltz that I had found online. One was a headshot that he used for his articles—Ethan looking very much the way I remembered him—

and one was a group shot from his alumnae magazine, Vermont's Camden College, Ethan in the back row of one of those wedding photographs that gathered all the alumnae of one college for a shot.

The most promising information that Henry had come up with were the names and locations of Ethan's brother and sister. Scott Saltz taught literature arts at a community college on Cape Cod, and Victoria Andrucci, née Saltz, was a hairdresser in Cresskill, New Jersey. The Saltz parents were both dead, within a month of each other in 2012. Ethan had been mentioned as a survivor in both of their obituaries.

If anyone knew what Ethan was doing now, it would be his family. Henry had work numbers for each sibling, but we agreed that we'd have a much better chance of getting information if we saw them face-to-face. He was on the Cape now approaching the brother and I was in Cresskill outside Victoria Andrucci's salon.

I'd already called and asked if she was working today and found out that she was. But simply entering the salon and asking her if she had time to talk—or time to give me a haircut—wasn't going to work. Even if she did agree to talk, she might not open up inside the salon with other people around. I wanted to get her on her own. So I decided to wait.

It was just past three and the salon was open until six o'clock. But that didn't mean Vicky would stay until closing time. If she didn't have appointments, she'd probably leave early. Two store-fronts down from Fix and Finesse was a bakery shop that looked as though it was also a café. Out front were two cast-iron tables, each with two chairs, all of them currently occupied. It was a beautiful day, the still-high sun bathing that side of the street in late afternoon light. I crossed over and went inside the bakery, buying a Earl Grey latte and a fresh cannoli. I sat just inside the plate-glass window that fronted the shop and kept an eye on the tables outside. I watched a pair of women talk away, empty plates and cups in front of them. One was wearing lots of makeup and a Burberry coat that probably cost more than two thousand dollars. The other was dressed in running clothes and doing most of the talking, while the Burberry lady tried to suppress yawns and kept surreptitiously checking her watch. Eventually the talker paused long enough for her friend to tell her that she had to get going. They stood up and finally left. I went outside and sat at their uncleared table.

It was a perfect spot. I could see the women that were coming and going from the salon. There had been a picture of Victoria on the website and, unless she'd changed her hairstyle, she had long blond streaky hair. Her face, wrinkled and overly tan, was unmistakably similar to Ethan's. High cheekbones, light eyes, squared-off jaw. I thought I'd be able to recognize her.

I sipped my drink and picked at my cannoli. I wished I'd brought a book. But I did what everyone else in the world now did when they had time to kill and looked at my phone, googling random names from my past, and checking, as I sometimes did, if anything new was being written about my father. His name did show up in reviews of other books, and sometimes even academic studies, but these days it was more common to see his name prefaced by something along the lines of "literature's oldest enfant terrible David Kintner." Today I found a new piece, a top ten list on the *Guardian* website that called my father's novel *Left Over Right* one of the top ten books about style. I made a mental note to mention it to him later, knowing that even though he'd pretend not to care, he would be pleased.

By five o'clock the sun had sunk below the old Sears building across the street and it was suddenly cold. I buttoned up my cardigan and stayed where I was, carefully watching the front entrance of the salon. It occurred to me that there might be a back entrance as well, but there was nothing I could do about that if there was. It was just past six when a woman with long blond hair exited onto the sidewalk, pausing to light a cigarette. I got up briskly from my chair and walked over to her. She was having trouble with her lighter but had finally lit her cigarette by the time I was within speaking distance.

"Are you Vicky?" I said.

She looked up, her eyes suspicious, and said, "Maybe."

"Hi, sorry to jump out at you like this. My name's Addie Logan. I'm sure you've never heard of me, but I used to date your brother, Ethan."

"Oh," she said, and I couldn't quite read her expression. "Bully for you," she added.

"This was a long time ago, about twenty years," I said, putting a little desperation in my voice. "And I would really like to talk with him. Will you help me out?"

The door behind us swung open and we both moved out of the way of a woman trailing a waft of perfume, who said, "See you tomorrow, Vic," as she passed by.

"Let's move down the street some," Vicky said.

I followed her as she walked, then stopped under the awning of an abandoned storefront. She had finished half her cigarette. "I haven't heard from Ethan in over ten years," she said, in a flat dismissive tone. "I don't have a phone number for him or an address or anything. He didn't come to my dad's funeral or my mom's. Not surprising, and frankly no one wanted him there. For all we know, he's dead, and forgive me for saying it, but it might be for the best."

"What did he do?" I said.

"You knew him, right? What did you think of him?"

"We dated for a little while. He was decent to me."

Vicky took a long, cheek-imploding drag of her cigarette, and said, "Then you were the only one. Sorry I can't help, but I don't know where he is, and I don't want to know. He's just a bad seed. He made all of us miserable, and I suspect he'd make you miserable if you managed to find him. I gotta go, hon. Sorry."

"I have a kid, and I'm pretty sure it's his," I said, the words just coming out of me. I knew that if I didn't say something dramatic, I was going to lose her. Still, she didn't immediately react, except for jutting out her lower lip as though she were thinking about what I'd just said.

"Your kid okay?"

"It's a girl, her name is Lily and she's great."

"Then don't ever introduce her to the evil fucker that is her father," Vicky said. "And now I really got to go. Good luck to you."

She took off down the street, flicking her cigarette away, and taking a left so that she was out of sight. I crossed quickly to my own car, sliding into the driver's seat and starting it up. I couldn't decide whether to stay put or to follow Vicky down the side street, but while I was figuring out what to do, I spotted a white pickup truck moving through the intersection, Vicky's blond hair visible through the side window. I followed her, wanting to see where she lived.

We'd only gone about a mile when she pulled into the driveway of a modest single-family house on a street of similar houses. I drove past, catching the number on the mailbox. It was thirty-five, and the street was called Tenafly Avenue. I found a small park with an empty lot and sat in my car for a while. I put the address into my phone and found a listing on a real estate site that said the house had been sold to a Victoria Andrucci by a Caroline Saltz for one dollar back in 2012, which meant that this was most likely the childhood home of Ethan Saltz.

It was dark now and I got out of the car, donned the hooded fleece jacket I'd brought, and walked back along Tenafly Avenue to Vicky's house. There was now a second car in the driveway, a beat-up-looking Dodge with a New York Yankees bumper sticker. The house itself was well lit by a streetlamp; the first story was orange brick, and the second was painted white, or more likely it was vinyl siding. The driveway culminated in a single-car garage, and there was about two feet of clearance between the garage and a thick hedge that separated the property from its neighbor. I skirted along the garage in the dark, a thorny branch from the hedge scraping along my cheek, and emerged into a small rectangular garden, fenced on three sides. It was much darker in the garden than it had been at the front of the house, but I still hid myself behind a damp stack of wood with a view through two large windows at the back of the house. I could see into a small living room dominated by a large sectional sofa, and I had a partial view into an overly lit kitchen through a sliding glass door. It was in the kitchen where I could see the back of Vicky's head. She was talking and gesturing wildly with another blond woman, who looked mid-twenties, at least. The other woman, maybe Vicky's daughter despite how close in age they looked, had a sour expression on her face. She was drinking from a large lime-green water bottle. They talked some more and then they both disappeared from the kitchen toward the front of the house. Five minutes later the younger woman reappeared, wearing a denim jacket now, and retrieving her water bottle. She flicked the lights off in the kitchen. I moved back down along the side of the garage, scratching my other cheek on the same hedge, and peered out in time to see Vicky and her probable daughter driving away in the white truck.

I returned to the backyard and immediately went to the back door. It was locked. I found a basement bulkhead at the edge of the house and pulled it open. It creaked as though it hadn't been used in years. I walked down the poured concrete steps through a network of old spiderwebs. The door at the bottom was unlocked as well and I stepped into a dark basement. Using my phone's flashlight, I found the stairs that led up to the first floor of the house.

I shouted a quick hello into the house to make sure no one was there. After not getting an answer, I moved into the living room. If this had been Ethan Saltz's childhood home, then maybe there was something here that would be helpful. And maybe there would even be some indication that Vicky was actually in contact with her brother, although that was a stretch.

I moved fast through the house, focusing on desk drawers and closets that might be used for storage. I didn't find anything interesting on the first floor and made my way up the stairwell. A hanging light had been left on and I looked at an array of family photographs that decorated the wall next to the stairs. Most of the pictures were of Vicky with her now-confirmed daughter. One of them showed Vicky holding a baby in which she looked to be about sixteen years old, at most. There was one wedding photograph on the wall that looked as though it were from the late sixties. The general color palette of the wedding guests assembled in the shot was brown and yellow. The couple, who I assumed were Ethan Saltz's parents, were surrounded by older relatives. No one looked particularly happy. I wondered if anyone in that photograph was alive, and I remembered looking at my parents' own wedding photograph, from around the same decade, and my father commenting that all wedding photographs were just pictures of dead people. ("You could say that about every photograph," I'd said to him.) I kept moving up the stairs, looking at all the pictures. Unless I'd missed one, there were no pictures of Ethan, either as a boy or as an adult.

There were no lights on in any of the rooms upstairs, so I used my phone again. I bypassed the two bedrooms that appeared to belong to mother and daughter and found myself in a room that was partly a storage area and probably also a guest room. The walls were papered in a swirly geometric pattern of light brown and dark orange. There was a trundle bed against the far wall, and the floor was covered with old boxes that had helpfully been labeled with a black marker. *Xmas Stuff. Victoria—Elementary School. Taxes 1999–2009.* Et cetera. None of the boxes said anything about Ethan. Still, I kept looking through the piles, listening for the sound of a car pulling back into the driveway. If they were out to dinner, I was fine. If they were picking up takeout, I was in big trouble.

Just when I had convinced myself that Victoria had scrubbed

any and all reminders of Ethan from her home, I moved two framed travel posters that had been leaning against a bookcase and spotted three Cresskill High School yearbooks crammed in between old Stephen King paperbacks and romance novels. I grabbed the 2000 yearbook, the most recent of the three, and quickly flicked through the senior photographs, and found Ethan Saltz, looking very clean-cut and handsome. I rifled through the pages and spotted a few signatures here and there, including two that contained that timeless phrase, *I wish we'd known each other better.* But one of the seniors, a girl named Alice Gilchrist, had written a long paragraph to Ethan, beginning with, *To the Talented Mr. Saltz* . . . I wanted to read it all but was starting to get very nervous about being caught in the house. I put the posters back over the bookshelf and left the way I had come, taking the yearbook with me.

CHAPTER 22

After dinner I went to my bedroom and cracked the window, the air still warm for this time of year. I could hear a chorus of chirps, the spring peepers down by the marshy pond at the edge of our property, a sure sign that winter was over. I called Henry, who picked up after one ring.

"Any luck?" I said.

"Finding Ethan: not yet. But I got some information from his brother. You?"

"I didn't find him, either. He has no contact with his sister and she called him an evil fucker."

"Well, that's pretty much what I found out, too."

"Tell me more."

"I went to the brother's office at the college and asked him directly about Ethan. I told him I'd been hired by someone to locate him, but that I couldn't disclose the name of the client. He didn't seem surprised, exactly, definitely not surprised that I couldn't find him, but he did seem rattled. Emotionally rattled. His office hours were starting, so we made plans to meet at his bar at four o'clock."

"What do you mean, his bar?"

"The bar that Scott Saltz hangs out at. It's a dive called the Bullpen. He's an alcoholic, or else working real hard on becoming one. We actually had a lot in common. I'm not calling myself an alcoholic, but there were other things."

"Like what?" I said.

"He'd wanted to be a writer, and at one point he was teaching high school English, but it was too hard and he felt as though he never had time to do his own work. So he got a job at a community college hoping he'd have more time to write there, but . . ."

"He's filling his extra time with drinking."

"He didn't say that exactly, but that's what's happened. He was a sad guy."

"When was the last time he'd seen Ethan?"

"He said it was about twelve years ago, that he just showed up randomly at Christmastime. This was in Cresskill when his parents were still alive. He said that the only person who was happy to see him was his mother."

"What was he doing then, did he say?"

"For work? Scott didn't know. He knew about Ethan's journalism career, obviously, and said how jealous that had made him. Scott is Ethan's older brother and he'd always talked about how he wanted to grow up to be a writer."

"So it felt like a personal slight to Scott when his brother became a writer as well?"

"I guess that was what he was driving at. Or maybe just everything about his brother agitates him. He basically told me that he considers Ethan to be pure evil."

"He used that word?"

"He did. Same as Vicky, right?"

"Yeah. Did he tell you why he thought he was evil?"

"He had a hard time describing it, but did say that even when Ethan was a toddler, sometimes he'd just stare at the rest of his family like they were exhibits in a zoo. Scott thinks he was born bad. I kept pushing him for specific examples of things he'd done, but he said that he would just quietly and subtly undermine everyone around him. He had one story, though. Scott's senior year of high school he had a steady girlfriend. I wrote the name down. Here it is—Samantha Perry. Scott said he was in love with her, and it was pretty clear he's actually still in love with her. During his senior year Scott went to California over spring break to visit cousins.

Ethan had wanted to go as well, but his parents had told him that it was a special trip just for Scott. And while Scott was away on this trip apparently Samantha got really drunk at some house party and ended up having sex with two guys. It was huge gossip when he got back and he was crushed and he dumped Samantha, even though she claimed she didn't really remember the party and she thought she'd been raped. He feels bad about it now, but at the time he was a teenager and his knee-jerk reaction was to blame his girlfriend.

"So the reason Scott told me this story was because months later he heard that Ethan had been at the same party where it had happened, which was strange because Ethan was younger and he wasn't friends with seniors. And then he also heard that Ethan had been hanging out with Samantha while he had been in California. He said that when he'd heard that, he knew, without a shred of doubt, that Ethan had somehow arranged the whole thing. He didn't know how he'd done it, but he knew. Maybe he'd been the one who drugged her and put her in that room. Maybe he'd told guys at the party that there was a passed-out girl they could go take advantage of. And Scott said something else. He said that when he got back from California he thought Ethan would still be pissed that he hadn't been allowed to go, but Scott remembers that Ethan was in a great mood when he got back. At the time he didn't think too much of it, but then he realized that his brother was happy that he'd found a way to wreck Scott's life."

"It sounds like he kind of did wreck his life."

"Before I left I asked him if he wanted to try to find Samantha Perry, this old girlfriend. He told me she ODed years ago."

"Sad," I said as I walked across my room and shut the window against the cold.

"The only other useful thing I might have found out was that Ethan had been a writing major in college, or something like that, but that he'd minored in art history. Scott said that Ethan had always been fascinated with beauty, with looking at things. And not just looking but appraising. He remembers his brother talking about how the art world was this incredible grift, with art only being worth what people would be willing to pay for it. He said it wouldn't surprise him if that was what his brother was doing now, something with art."

"Huh," I said. "That kind of chimes in with something I found out."

I told him about my day, about my brief chat with Vicky, about breaking into their house. And then I pulled out the yearbook I'd stolen and opened it up to the page with the interesting inscription I'd found that had been written by an Alice Gilchrist. I read it aloud to him.

"*To the Talented Mr. Saltz, I look forward to following your exploits on* America's Most Wanted *and to seeing your face circled in that group shot of the art club on the glossy pages of a trashy true crime book. I'll be the smudged face next to you that no one remembers. But no, really, I wish you a life of successful thievery and forgery. I wish we'd gotten to know each other just a little less. Love, the unnamed narrator. XO.*"

"Wow," Henry said. "Lots to unpack there."

"I'll take a picture of it and send it to you, but we obviously need to talk with her."

"You think it's a reference to *The Talented Mr. Ripley?*"

"I'm assuming it is. Even if they hadn't read the book, there was a movie out around that time."

"I remember it. And how did she sign it, *the unnamed narrator?* That's interesting. By the way, how do you know who wrote the inscription if they didn't sign it?"

"She drew one of those comic book bubbles coming from her picture. I'll photograph it and send it to you. And then we need to find Alice Gilchrist. Let's hope she's still alive."

After ending my call with Henry, I googled Alice Gilchrist and found her right away. She was a tattoo artist living in Queens, and

also selling artwork on Etsy. She had her own website that confirmed she'd graduated from Cresskill High School the same year
that Ethan Saltz had. I sent her an email asking if I could see her
the following day, not specifying exactly why I wanted to meet.
Then I went back downstairs and joined my father in the living
room. I got us two tall, weak whiskey-and-waters, and settled in
across from him on the less comfortable sofa. Something moved in
the shadow cast by a tall bookshelf and startled me. It was April the
cat darting out of the room.

"I didn't know she came in here," I said.

"Who?"

"The cat."

"Was that a cat? I was betting on raccoon, and worried that
Monk's House had finally gone the way of *Grey Gardens*."

"No, it's a semi-feral cat I've called April. She comes and goes as
she pleases, but mostly avoids Sharon."

"Clever girl."

"Dad," I said

"Daughter," he said back.

"If someone sent you a letter that began, *To the Talented
Mr. Kintner*, what would you think?"

"I'd think they thought I was talented. And then I would read
on with heightened interest."

"But you wouldn't think of any particular reference if someone
addressed you as the talented Mr. Kintner?" I said.

My father raised his drink to his lips, then lowered it without
taking a sip. "Oh, you mean Pat Highsmith."

"That's who I was thinking of."

"It didn't immediately jump into my mind, but now that you
mention it . . . You always liked her books, didn't you?"

"Some of them," I said.

"Do we have any here?"

"Sure, probably."

I got up and went to one of the built-in bookshelves that lined the south-facing wall of the room. We had two Highsmith firsts, *The Cry of the Owl* and *The Talented Mr. Ripley*, both British editions. I pulled out *Ripley* and looked at the frontispiece. Cresset Press, 1957. The dust jacket was a very nice drawing of the Italian seaside town where most of the story took place. I brought the book over to my father.

"Is this mine?" he said.

"I doubt it belonged to Mom," I said.

My father started to flip through the book while I continued to think about the yearbook inscription from Ethan Saltz's friend. As I'd said to Henry, it might have been a reference to either the book or the movie. Certainly the rest of Alice Gilchrist's yearbook inscription to Ethan Saltz seemed to chime with the reference, mentioning that she looked forward to seeing him on *America's Most Wanted*, and that she wished him a *life of successful thievery and forgery*. It was clear that she had a very good idea about what kind of person Saltz was.

Since my father now seemed to be immersed in his book, I flipped through the Anne Sexton collection that was still hanging around on the coffee table. I found a poem called "It Is a Spring Afternoon," and read its first few lines: "Everything here is yellow and green. Listen to its throat . . ." I put my finger on that line and thought some more. Even though people can talk, can actually tell you what they are thinking, I still have a hard time understanding them. When I look at an animal, even something as inscrutable as a cat, I feel as though I comprehend the basic way they see the world, a place that flickers between danger and comfort, a place of hunger. Humans, the humans of the world today, seem alien to me. But I did think I knew Ethan Saltz a little, that I'd comprehended him back when I first met him. He was driven by cruelty, but also desire. And even though I thought he worked very hard at hiding it, there was some rage there as well. I'd seen it in him the night that I pulled Martha Ratliff out of his reach. But if Ethan was really shadowing Peralta, and killing women he'd come in contact with, then he was patient, too, willing to play a long game to get his revenge. And that meant that he had control over his emotions, at least he did until we met up in Saratoga Springs. Because, as soon as that happened, he drove straight to Portsmouth and killed Martha. Was it rage that caused him to do that? I didn't think so. I thought he'd lost interest in Martha, so when he saw me he discarded her, doing it in a way that would get my attention. He wanted to play. With me.

I considered what else I knew about Ethan. It wasn't just killing he desired. It was killing someone and then getting away with it. His primary end goal was to fool people, to feel superior to them. And it made sense that his alter ago, the fake person he had become, was also someone who felt superior to those around him. Whatever name he was going by, whatever life he was pretending to live, it wouldn't be a small life. He wasn't some warehouse worker with a basement apartment in a small town. No, he'd probably be working in some kind of profession in the arts. Maybe someone who worked in the movie industry, or television. Maybe an artist, like Alice Gilchrist. Maybe he was still writing, but under a pseudonym. But whatever he was doing it would be important that he be successful at it.

Before getting into bed that night I spent some more time on my laptop, not really knowing what I was looking for, but trying out searches anyway. First I used an anagram generator on the name Ethan Saltz to see if it generated a possible fake name he might be using, but it turned out that Ethan Saltz is a poor name for anagrams. Then I did multiple searches such as "Hollywood screenwriter pseudonym" and "artist criminal" and "scandal art world," and came up with a glut of stories, real and unreal, unspooling in front of me. I switched the stories over to images and looked for Ethan's face, but there was nothing. He was in this strange machine somewhere, I knew that much, but didn't know where to find him.

Just when I was going to give up, Henry called.

"A *Globe* article just appeared on Martha Ratliff," he said.

"About her murder?"

"Yes, just a few hours ago. Apparently the manner of death is similar to an unsolved homicide in the Portsmouth area from over a year ago. A woman alone, her throat cut during a home invasion."

"That tracks," I said. "I've been doing nothing but thinking of Ethan Saltz. He likes to fool people. My guess is that as soon as he figured out that he wanted to kill Martha Ratliff he checked up to see if there were unsolved cases close to her. And he found one, and he copied it. He did all this in about four hours, of course. But I think that fooling people—manipulation in general—is more important to him than the killings."

"I can see that," Henry said. "Or maybe he was the person who killed that other woman."

"It's all possible, I suppose."

While we were talking, I checked my emails and saw that Alice Gilchrist had gotten back to me, saying she'd be happy to meet the next day at eleven in the morning.

CHAPTER 23

I got to Queens at ten thirty and found a parking space half a block from the storefront where Alice Gilchrist worked. The studio was called Fledgling Ink, and I'd studied their website a little before leaving Shepaug that morning. I had no real interest in tattoos, but I'd scrolled through the designs and decided that I liked them.

Alice and I were meeting at a coffee shop just next door to the shop. We'd emailed a little bit back and forth and I'd told her that I wasn't a client, that I was interested in learning about Ethan Saltz. She'd immediately emailed back, Jesus, that's a name from the past. What did he do?

I told her I was just looking for information that might help me find him. She said she had no idea but that she'd be happy to meet up.

As I entered the small, packed coffee shop, I spotted Alice right away. She had white-dyed hair cut to shoulder-length, a nose ring, and was wearing baggy overalls. I was looking at the top of her head because she was bent over a sketchbook, but she must have sensed me looking, because she glanced up, her face a flat plane, wide, with smooth, shiny skin and pale brown eyes. I asked her if she needed another coffee and she said, "No, I'm good," so I grabbed myself a tea and joined her.

"Thank you for meeting me," I said.

"My shop is right next door, so it wasn't too much trouble. I know I asked you on email, but what did he do?"

"Ethan?"

"Yes." She smiled, revealing perfectly straight teeth. There was something disconcerting about her appearance, but I couldn't quite put a finger on it.

"I don't know what he did. All I know is that he's very hard to find." I'd identified myself to Alice as Addie Logan, journalist, having sent my email through my alternative Gmail account. I'd also told her that a friend of mine had asked me to find Ethan as a favor.

"I just assumed he was in some kind of trouble. Legally," Alice said.

"He might be, for all I know. When was the last time you saw him?"

"About five years after high school, and it was by accident. We were at the same gallery in New York. I don't even remember where it was, but he was there, and he looked exactly like he did in school. A preppy serial killer."

"You were friends in high school?"

"We were. Kind of. I thought he was funny."

"How did you two meet?"

She thought for a moment, taking a sip of her cappuccino. "We were in Art Club together, but that's not where we met. It's where we became friends, though. It turned out that the teacher who started Art Club would basically leave us alone in the room and let us do whatever we wanted. There were no activities or anything, except for the one time we all went into New York to go to MoMA. I think that's why most of us signed up in the first place, because of that trip, and because Art Club was something to put on our college applications. We kind of bonded on the trip to New York, I guess. I mean, we didn't bond, but we talked. We were looking at all these modern pieces of art and he was going on about how brilliant they were, how the art world was the greatest scam in the whole world, and that his dream was to make a fortune selling fake art. And I was like, good luck with that. I mean, he was full of shit, but he was very entertaining. He told me once that he was a sociopath."

"He did?"

"Yeah, but not on that trip, I think. It was when we knew each other better. There were two weeks in there when we were kind of best friends, inseparable, and then it just kind of ended. Or faded away. Or whatever you want to call it."

"Which one of you ended the friendship?"

"I think it was him, to be honest. One day he just seemed to lose interest in me. I was hurt, I guess, but it was fucking high school. We weren't married or anything."

"Do you remember what you wrote in his yearbook?"

"Oh," she said, looking surprised.

"That's how I knew you were friends with him, your inscription in his yearbook."

Her eyebrows rose a fraction as she tried to remember, and then I saw the memory pass across her features. "I kind of remember," she said. "Only because it was a joke that I was signing it in the first place. I mean, Ethan wasn't the type to go around getting his friends to sign his yearbook. He didn't really have friends. And even when I signed it, we weren't super-close. I think I ran into him after we'd all gotten our yearbooks and he was carrying his and I insisted that I get to sign it. I think I wrote something about how I'd one day see him on television when he was the subject of a manhunt. Something like that."

I hadn't brought the yearbook with me, but I'd photocopied the inscription, and I handed her a copy now. She laughed while she read it.

"I was a pretentious little shit."

"Why did you call him *the Talented Mr. Saltz*?"

"Oh, from that Matt Damon movie about the guy who kills his friend and takes over his life. We'd both seen it—not together, I think—but Ethan told me how much he loved it, and how it was probably something he'd do himself one day. He was always saying things like that. In a jokey way. Like, 'If I haven't buried someone alive by the age of thirty, then I'll be incredibly disappointed.' That kind of thing." She was still looking at the photocopy. "That's why I made that joke here about the Art Club picture. After it was taken, he said that in fifty years the picture would be in the middle of some book about his life of horrible crime, his face circled, and I would just be some anonymous student next to him. I thought it was funny, clearly, because I remembered him saying that. But you're here now, probably because he is some genuine psychopath and he wasn't actually making jokes at the time."

"I don't know about that," I said. "He does seem to have disappeared, which makes me think that maybe he is living under an assumed name. Did you ever talk about that?"

"You mean other than him saying that thing about killing a friend and taking over his life?"

"Yeah. Like, did he ever mention what name he would use as a pseudonym? Did he ever make a joke about that?"

She spun the pen in her hand while she thought. I looked down at her still-open sketchbook and saw that she had been drawing quick sketches of owls. "Not really. Nothing jumps to mind."

"Why did you sign the yearbook as *the unnamed narrator?*"

"Yeah, I was wondering that myself. Just being pretentious, I guess. I was a fan of *Rebecca* when I was in high school, the book *Rebecca,* and the narrator didn't have a name. So maybe it was that. I'm sorry I'm not being more helpful. I've always been curious about what happened with Ethan. It was a brief and platonic relationship, but it left a mark."

"Was it platonic for a reason?" I said. "I mean, did you ever wonder if the relationship would turn romantic?"

She looked at the dregs of her coffee and said, "I remember thinking it was strange he wasn't trying to get into my pants, only because he was a teenage boy, but he told me once that if he slept with me then he'd have to kill me. Like I mentioned already, it was the type of thing he was always saying. Also, I wasn't calling myself a lesbian back then, exactly, but the writing was on the wall. I never really thought of him that way."

I finished my tea, thinking about what other questions I had.

Even though Alice didn't know where Ethan was, she still might help in coming up with what name he might have picked for an alias. "You said you both liked that movie *The Talented Mr. Ripley*. Did he have any other favorite films or books that you remember?"

"Strangely, I kind of remember he had lowbrow tastes. His favorite film was *Ferris Bueller's Day Off*. Like, by far."

"What about books?"

Alice thought. "Sorry, I can't remember ever talking about books."

"Celebrities he loved? Historical figures? If he's changed his name, then maybe he changed it to something that has meaning for him."

Alice was shaking her head. "Sorry. All I remember was that he liked *Ferris Bueller* and he liked talking about himself."

I stood, thanking her and putting my coat back on, then I realized what it was that was strange about her appearance.

"Hey," I said. "You don't have any tattoos."

She smiled up at me. "That you can see."

"Right," I said. "That I can see."

"Actually, you're right. I have zero tattoos."

"That's strange, probably, for a tattoo artist. Don't you think?"

"Probably," she said. "I'm not against tattoos, obviously. I think I just have commitment issues."

When I got back to Shepaug, I went onto my computer and looked up *Ferris Bueller's Day Off*, a film I had never seen despite knowing a fair amount about it. I could picture scenes, Ferris at a parade in a city, and some teacher droning out the names of his students. Even knowing just that much, it seemed to me to be an odd choice as Ethan Saltz's favorite film of all time. *The Talented Mr. Ripley* made more sense, but I stayed on the *Ferris Bueller* page. Because I had nothing much better to do, I opened my notebook and wrote down all the character names from *Ferris Bueller*, then systematically I searched for all the names, adding words like "artist" or "forger" or "scam." It was a long shot at best, but one thing I'd learned definitively about Ethan from Henry's conversation with the brother was that he'd been fascinated by art, and particularly the commerce of it. It wasn't an enormous stretch to think that those enthusiasms would have lasted into adulthood.

Nothing really jumped out at me online. There were no Sloane Peterson galleries involved in forgery scandals, no notorious art world figures named Cameron Frye. I went back to the IMDb page and read the trivia associated with the film. One of the tidbits was that the Charlie Sheen character—apparently a druggy in the police station who flirts with Ferris's sister, Jeanie—was given a name in the shooting script, although it isn't mentioned in the film. That name was Garth Volbeck.

I entered "Garth Volbeck" and "artist" into my search engine and the first item that came up was a listing from the Charnock Gallery in Philadelphia. Two abstract paintings for sale by an artist named Gareth Vollbeck. I felt something in my chest as I clicked on the link. It brought me to the Charnock Gallery website, a very minimal site, but in a way that made me think the gallery didn't need the website as opposed to its being a gallery that couldn't afford a good site. Besides a few pages that showed available art pieces, there was just the landing page, which provided the name of the gallery and its address. There were no hours, since viewings were only available by appointment. And there was no photograph of the gallery owner, Robert Charnock.

I searched under that name and didn't find any photographs cropping up on other parts of the web except for one group photograph from a fundraiser in Philadelphia. The man who was identified as Robert Charnock was looking away from the camera. He had short dark hair and wide shoulders. I wasn't sure, but it could possibly be Ethan Saltz.

I did searches for the artist named Gareth Vollbeck, and hardly anything came up, the only mentions being ones associated with the Charnock Gallery. The whole thing seemed off. Actually, it didn't seem off. It felt as though I'd possibly found Ethan Saltz. I called Henry, and he picked up right away. I told him what I'd found out, and he said he'd start to investigate right away. I could tell from his voice that he was as excited by the possibility as I was.

It was afternoon and the weather was still good, and I decided to go for a thinking walk. When I was a young kid I used to call them daydreaming walks, knowing that if I went into the woods and began to wander, pretty soon my mind would wander, too, and I'd enter strange daytime fantasies, usually a scenario in which I could speak to animals and they'd tell me all their secrets. I'd given up on that particular childhood dream, but I did know that I did my best thinking on walks, so I found my mother and told her I was walking into town and asked if she needed anything. She said we needed more of the granola that they sold at the Carrot Seed.

From Monk's House you could reach Shepaug Center either through the woods or along Woodbury Road. The trail through Brigham Woods was faster, but I decided to set out along the road, make myself more visible rather than less. There were daffodils and tulips blooming in the front gardens of the houses on Woodbury Road, along with the occasional patch of wild crocuses. A few trees were beginning to show leaves in that soft green color that only happens in springtime.

In town I went straight to the Carrot Seed, our local organic grocery store, for the granola, picking up a hot tea as well that I didn't really need. I sat on the bench outside of the store, and it was there that I realized I hadn't brought my phone with me. I rarely did when I was out walking, but this time it meant that if Henry wanted to reach me, he couldn't right away. Just having that thought made me feel strange, like I was now uncomfortably part of the modern world. I sipped at my tea, alone with my thoughts, but not for long. Since I had grown up in Shepaug, coming into the town center meant that I would meet someone I knew and have to talk to them, and I suffered through two of those interactions that afternoon. The first was with my old math teacher, Mrs. Corrigan, who told me, for the second time, how the Shepaug regional school system was possibly going to have to merge with the Washington School system. "No one's having kids anymore," she said, and I thought I saw her eyes cast down in sadness in the direction of my empty womb. I also talked briefly with one of my mother's friends, Ginny Adams, who had just picked up the new Louise Penny book at Stone's Throw. Over the past year Ginny had begun to stoop, her body curling inward like an overcooked shrimp. She stopped by my bench and we caught up, her head cocked toward me in a way that reminded me of a turtle, and as Ginny talked, her voice now cracked with age, I had a vivid childhood memory of seeing her emerge naked out of our pool at one of the numerous parties at Monk's House, my father there to greet her with a towel and a drink.

After finishing my tea I began the walk home, leaving town along River Street, and passing the commons. I was aware that my thinking walk had not produced any significant thinking, but it had produced something else. A prickly sense of unease. I didn't believe that people knew when they were being watched any more than I believed in love curses, but it was what I was feeling at that moment, a palpable disquiet, a surety that there were eyes on me. When I reached Woodbury Road, clouds had moved into the sky and it was suddenly cold. I walked faster, staying to the left as I'd been taught. Two cars passed me going in the opposite direction, then the road was quiet for a while. I heard a car approaching from behind and squeezed up along the narrow shoulder that separated the road from an old stone wall and the dense woods. I must have heard something in the car's engine, because I knew it was slowing down, and I turned just as a shiny white sedan pulled dangerously close to me, its driver's-side window rolled down.

Ethan Saltz, with surprising speed, swung open the door and

stepped out, holding a pistol down near his waist. Something went over me, a wash of disbelief that it was all about to end, but then Ethan said, "I can shoot you right now or you can get into the trunk. Five seconds to decide."

"Trunk," I said.

He grasped my shoulder with his left hand and moved me around to the back of the vehicle. The trunk was already cracked open and he used his foot to open it all the way. I felt stupid being caught this way, but it also felt inevitable. Maybe I'd wanted it to happen.

PART 3

EVEN THE TREES KNOW IT

CHAPTER 24

It had taken him a few days to find Lily Kintner. She was living back at home with her parents in Shepaug, Connecticut. The mother, Sharon Henderson, was a sculptor, but not a very good one, Ethan thought, and her father was David Kintner, the English novelist, who, surprisingly, was still alive.

The reason it had taken him so much time to find her was that Lily owned a house in Winslow, Massachusetts, home to Winslow College, the last place she seemed to have had employment. He'd traveled there first, wasting a day keeping an eye on the small shingled cottage by a pond, only to discover that it had apparently been rented out to an elderly couple with two whippets. Ethan was well aware that it was a dangerous thing to do, but he'd gone into the CVS located in the Winslow town center, bought a celebrity magazine, plus a padded envelope, and returned to the cottage pretending to be a deliveryman with a package for Lily Kintner. The old couple straightforwardly offered up the information that Lily Kintner had returned to Connecticut to look after her parents, while one of the whippets sniffed aggressively at Ethan's crotch.

He left Winslow and made his way to Shepaug, elated by this new pursuit. He knew it was dangerous—everything had been dangerous since the moment he stuck a knife into Martha Ratliff's throat—but he also knew that he needed to get to Lily before she got to him. She'd know by now that Martha was dead, and she would certainly know who'd done it. Would she run directly to the police with the name of Ethan Saltz? A normal person would have. But he somehow didn't think Lily was quite normal. He thought she might try to find him herself. And while he doubted she'd be able to do that—Ethan Saltz had well and truly disappeared off the face of the earth—he wasn't one hundred percent sure.

When he got to Litchfield County he stopped first in a town called Washington, parking downtown to get a cup of coffee and to call his wife.

She answered, as she always did, as though he'd just interrupted her while she was in the middle of a good book.

"Darling," Ethan said.

"Oh, that's a bad sign. Is this about the dinner party?"

"I'm just giving you a possible heads-up that I might not make it. I've found this old coot in Maine who claims he owns an original Wyeth sketch, but he keeps putting off showing me. If it's real, I'm thinking of killing him for it. How do you feel about that?"

Rebecca was silent for a moment, but he could sense she was smiling. He'd obviously married her for her money and for the house in Philadelphia, but it didn't hurt that she enjoyed his occasional morbid jokes. At last she said, "I was already dreading this party, and the only thing that was giving me hope was that you and I could laugh at its awfulness during our post-party debrief. How long will it take you to murder this man and steal his painting?"

"My plan right now is that I'll be back for the party, but I did want to give you a warning in advance that there is the smallest chance I'll have to cancel. I really will try, but it's an *Andrew* Wyeth."

"No, I understand."

"What are you doing right now?"

"Sorting shoes, actually, and waiting for a call from Stephanie about the house in Great Barrington. Where are you right now?"

"I'm staring at the Maine coast and thinking about how much you would hate it here."

After ending the call, Ethan took a stroll. He wandered through a small parking lot behind the town pharmacy, then picked out a car, not in the lot but parked behind a residential building that abutted the lot. It was some old model of Lincoln, backed into a tight spot. The car was white, but there was a fine film of grime and dust all over its exterior. It looked as though it hadn't been driven in years. He crouched between the back of the car and the brick apartment building, took a screwdriver from his leather briefcase, and removed the license plate. He didn't know how long he'd be in Shepaug and it wouldn't hurt to have Connecticut plates.

It didn't take him long to find the Kintner residence. It was set far back from the road, an old farmhouse with several outbuildings, and Ethan didn't even slow down while he went by. Instead he parked in Shepaug's tiny town center and considered his options. His plan right now was to kidnap Lily if he had a chance. If he could get a tranq dart into her, then throw her into the trunk of his car, he'd drive her to his house in Tohickon, where he had a room waiting. It wouldn't be impossible, but the chances for something going wrong would be high. Still, if he could pull it off it would mean he'd get to talk with her, wipe all the smug off her face and let her know that she'd lost. Just thinking about the possibility made him almost hard. It would be nice to talk to someone about his achievements, even to someone not long for the world. It was vanity, he knew that, but if anyone deserved to be a little bit vain it was him.

Two teenage girls walked past his car yakking at each other, not even seeing him sitting there, but he decided that if he was going to stay in the Shepaug center he shouldn't just sit in his car attracting attention. He pulled the stiff mesh baseball hat he was wearing farther down on his head, stepped outside, and looked around for a store to browse in. There was a bookstore called Stone's Throw, but people noticed browsers in bookstores. It was probably filled with lonely Shepaug women hoping to find some man flipping through the latest Margaret Atwood book so they could strike up a conversation. The best stores to browse in if you didn't want to be noticed were drugstores. Everyone shopping in drugstores was in their own little bubble of solipsistic anxiety, just hoping to get out of there as soon as possible. No one wants to run into a neighbor while holding a tube of hemorrhoid cream.

He'd walked two blocks when he spotted a woman with red hair entering what looked like a small grocery store. He'd only seen her for a brief second, but something coiled in his chest. The color of her hair was unmistakable.

Back in his car, he did a U-turn and parked across the street from the Carrot Seed. If she was shopping she probably wouldn't be longer than fifteen minutes, and she'd probably come out and get immediately back in her car. He'd follow her and, if he could, pass her on the road and force her to pull off to the side. His tranquilizer gun and a Taser lay on the seat next to him, covered by a folded sweatshirt. He went over good and bad outcomes in his mind. She might spot him right away when she came out of the grocery store. She wouldn't really be able to do anything about it, but it would put her on guard. If she didn't spot him and he was able to run her off the road, then another car might pass by. If that happened he'd put a gun in the face of the driver and see how long they hung around. But what if Lily was carrying her own weapon, a real handgun? Well, he had one of those as well, in his glove compartment, and if he couldn't kidnap Lily, then he'd kill her and leave her body by the side of the road. He'd get out of Connecticut and ditch the car. There would be very little reason to connect Ethan Saltz to Lily Kintner, but absolutely no reason to connect Robert Charnock to Lily or even to Martha or Birkbeck College.

While he was going over pros and cons, Lily—it actually was her—came out of the store. Instead of making her way to her car, she sat on a sidewalk bench. She didn't have a grocery bag with her, just a takeaway coffee, the lid of which she pried off. Ethan slumped in his seat, angling his head so he could keep watch on her. She wore green pants and a raincoat. She sat there for a while, and at least two people came and talked with her. It occurred to him that maybe the smartest thing to do would be to leave the

Shepaug center and go wait by the entrance to her driveway, block-ing it. But he wanted to keep an eye on her for a while longer. It had been huge luck that he'd spotted her away from her house, and maybe there'd be more luck coming his way.

Twenty minutes passed. Most of the passersby didn't give Ethan a second look, but one old woman stared at him a little as she shuf-fled down the street using a cane. He stared back until she looked away. His mind, as it always did and always had, conjured up a sudden image. In this one he ripped the cane out of the woman's gnarled hands and pushed its rubber tip down her throat, pinning her to the ground until she choked. The image spread through him like a shot of whiskey and he was calm again, thinking about Lily and how long she was going to sit on that fucking bench.

When she eventually stood up, he thought she might turn to her right—it was where most of the town's parking spots were located—but instead she began walking away from town, cutting down a side street. Ethan lost sight of her. He got out of the car and crossed Main Street, then turned down the side street Lily had taken. She was up ahead, walking with purpose. It was a short street and Ethan could see that it ended at the road he'd taken to get to the town center after passing by the Kintner household. She was walking home.

He walked briskly back to the Kia, marveling again at his luck. Part of him wondered if he should just run her down in the street, make her a victim of a hit-and-run. But, no, he did want to spend some time with her in Tohickon before killing her. He felt he de-served that, like buying a painting he couldn't quite afford as a spe-cial treat.

CHAPTER 25

I had a faint memory of being walked through a cool misty night, my legs like jelly, a strong arm around my waist. Then there was a house that smelled of mildew and rot and there was a staircase that led down and then I was on some sort of cot and everything went dark again.

When I woke and opened my eyes I was on my side, staring at a wall that had been painted maroon. My body hurt and my mouth felt as though it were coated in glue. I didn't know where I was, but I remembered who had taken me there. I was surprised to find myself alive.

Moving my head made my stomach lurch and bile rise up in the back of my throat. I stayed still a little longer, until the feeling passed. I blinked rapidly because my eyes were dry, then I tried slight movements with my limbs, assessing my situation. I was still in the clothes I'd been wearing when I'd been on my walk: my green corduroys and white Irish sweater, plus my windbreaker, zipped almost all the way up to my throat. I could feel the zipper teeth against my neck. I moved my toes and my feet and could tell that my shoes were still on. There was another sensation as well, something cold and sharp around my right ankle, which meant I was most likely chained to the bed, or to the wall. I took deep breaths, in through my nose and out through my mouth, and then swiveled my head around a little more. The nausea had mostly passed, and now I was aware of how much my head and neck ached. I stretched my body out, listening to the crackle and pop of my back, then turned over onto my back, the cuff around my ankle cutting into my skin.

"You're awake," came a voice from a few feet away, and I was startled, only because I had felt that I was alone in whatever room this was. I turned my head to look at Ethan, sitting on a wooden chair about five feet away. The room spun some more and I squeezed my eyes shut.

"There's a bucket right below you if you need to throw up," Ethan said. "Or just go ahead and throw up on yourself if you'd like. I don't care."

I opened my eyes and the room stayed still. Ethan was sitting cross-legged, wearing dark jeans and a black hoodie. He had a to-go cup of coffee in his right hand that rested on his knee. There was another cup of coffee down by his feet.

"How do you feel?" he said, as though we were old friends, like maybe I'd had too much to drink at his house the night before and crashed in his guest room.

"Nauseous," I said.

"Yeah, well, I hit you with a tranq dart. Do you remember that?"

"Yes."

"I'm surprised it didn't kill you, that dosage, but I'm glad you're still with us. It's nice to see you again, Lily."

I closed my eyes, wondering if I should just keep them that way. I didn't particularly feel prepared for a genial conversation with Ethan. But something told me it was an opportunity, so I said, "Is that coffee for me?" Then I opened my eyes again.

"This one?" He looked down at the coffee on the floor. "It is, if you're up for it."

"Got any Advil as well?"

"That I don't have, I'm afraid. Depending on how long I keep you here, though, maybe I can get some next time I'm out."

"That would be swell."

"Are you up for the coffee now?" He bent down and put his

hand around the cup. It was one of those generic Greek diner to-go cups adorned with the words WE ARE HAPPY TO SERVE YOU.

"Let me see," I said, and swung my legs off the side of the cot, sitting upright, the room swimming. I spied the bucket on the floor and picked it up. I retched a little, but nothing came up. Still, I held on to it, and looked at the room we were in. It was a finished basement that looked as though no one had lived there in about ten years. There were patches of black mildew along one wall and the drop ceiling was covered with a network of water stains. But the electricity was working, two fluorescent lights filling the room with a sickly white light. I held on to the bucket—a small metal trash bin, really—and wondered if throwing it at Ethan would be a good idea. But if I was going to get out of this, it wasn't going to be through fighting my way out.

"I think it was a man cave of some kind," Ethan said, his head swiveling, and I was confused for a moment, before I realized he was talking about the basement. I looked where he was looking and saw a bar area backed by an enormous mirror, engraved with the logo of the Philadelphia Eagles. "Can you imagine being a suburban husband who has to create a subterranean space to get away from his wife and kids?"

"Can you imagine being a serial killer?" I said.

Ethan lit up like I'd just told him how good he looked for his age. "Oh, I knew there was a reason I kept you alive," he said.

"Whose house is this?"

"It's mine. I own it, even though the name on the deed is Brad Anderson. There are no other houses around, not for at least a half a mile. I'm just telling you this so you don't get ideas about escaping or screaming your lungs out down here. You're at my mercy. The sooner you realize that, the better we'll get along."

I looked down at the chain that was shackled to my leg. It was hard to tell from the angle, but it looked as though it was about five feet along and it was secured to some kind of bracket screwed into the floor. Next to the bracket was a bedpan.

"Do you need to go?" Ethan said. "I can leave for a moment if you'd like me to."

"I'm fine," I said. "How long are you planning on keeping me here?"

"I don't know. I've never kidnapped someone before, and I don't know how long this will stay interesting."

I arched my back and turned my head, my neck popping and strands of pain radiating up through me. I needed time to think, but I had already decided that if Ethan Saltz was keeping me alive in order to talk with me, then I should do what he wanted and talk back. And I'd decided to tell the truth, about everything except Henry Kimball. There was no reason to bring him into this.

"So I was right," I said. "You followed Alan Peralta from conference to conference and you killed women he came into contact with?"

" 'Came into contact with,' " he said, making quote signs. "He's a bit of a hunter himself."

"But not a killer."

"Doubtful."

"And you did this why?" I said. "To get revenge on Martha Ratliff?"

He was smiling, awkwardly I thought, like a politician in the middle of a televised debate. "How'd you get involved? Martha came calling for help again?" he said.

"She said she thought that her husband might be some kind of serial killer, that she'd found blood on one of his shirts—"

"Oh, she found that?"

"You put it there?"

"I did. Honestly, I was starting to get bored with the Peralta game. I mean, how many high school teacher conferences can one man take? I thought the Jane Austen pin might speed things along."

"We found out about that," I said.

"You two researched, like good little library students. And you found a long line of dead women."

"Basically."

A look of smug superiority was passing across Ethan's features. I told myself to keep telling the truth, though. That was why he'd kept me alive, wanting to hear about his triumph. Wanting validation.

"Why didn't she call the police?"

"She wasn't a hundred percent sure it was him, and she knew that if she called the police and he found out about it—which he would have—then that would mean the end of their marriage. She didn't want to lose that."

"He was a serial cheater, you know? Hit on women at the conferences, went to prostitutes, the whole thing."

"I know."

"So Martha Ratliff called you to bail her out, the same way you bailed her out when she was dating me?"

"Is that how you see it?"

Ethan finished the last sip of his coffee and put the cup on the floor, then picked up my coffee and said, "You ready for this now?"

"Sure," I said.

He stood up and brought it over to me, getting close enough so that if I'd wanted to, I could grab him, punch him, try to lash out. I took the coffee, the cup lukewarm, and Ethan settled back onto his chair, crossed his legs again. I opened the tab on the plastic lid and took a sip, and it tasted good, even though I preferred tea.

"Is it okay?" Ethan said.

"Not bad. I usually drink tea, but I like coffee fine."

"Ah, noted." He looked at his watch, then uncrossed and re-crossed his legs. He rubbed at the side of his neck as though he had a kink there.

"What were we talking about?" he said.

"I asked if you thought I'd bailed Martha out of her relationship with you back at Birkbeck College."

"Oh right. Yes, of course you did. You told her what to say and then you showed up that night at the bar and took her home with you. You remember all that, don't you?"

"I do."

"What did you think I was doing to your friend?"

"I knew what you were doing. You were manipulating her, talking her into sex games she didn't want to play, hurting her. I don't know what you had planned for after that."

"She liked it, you know."

"Yeah, I'm sure that's what you told yourself."

Ethan laughed, not performatively but in a genuine way. His laugh had an almost imperceptible snort at the end. "No, you're right. She didn't like it, exactly, but she would have gone farther if I'd gotten the chance. And you took that away from me. You took her away from me."

"I'm confused, Ethan," I said. "She meant so much to you that you waited fifteen years and then concocted an elaborate plan to make it look like her husband was a serial killer, all to do what . . . to get revenge?"

Ethan appeared to be thinking, his lips pressed hard together, and I wondered if I'd made a mistake by using his name. Finally, he said, "Do you want to know how many people I've killed in my life?"

"Sure," I said.

"Twenty-six," he said.

"That's a lot."

"Yes and no. I mean, twenty-six people probably just died in the last hour by falling down the stairs. But, yes, I've committed twenty-six separate murders and I got away with every one of them. I do think that's impressive."

"So, it's kind of like a sport for you. A game."

He uncrossed his legs and leaned forward a little. "That's it. That's why I do it. Do you have any idea how boring regular life is for someone like me? Actually, I think you might know. But when they write books about me, and they will, I'm sure they'll try to find something in my childhood, something that went wrong, but nothing in my childhood made me this way. I was just bored, and I found out how easy it was to play with people, to wreck lives, and eventually I figured out how easy it was to murder people."

"Who was the first person you killed?"

He leaned back a little and I thought he looked uncomfortable for the first time, as though he didn't want to tell me. Then he said, "I killed my grandfather. He was sick already, nearly dead, and I suffocated him. I was eleven years old."

"Maybe you did him a favor," I said.

"I definitely did him a favor. And I did myself a favor, because I got my own room back. He was living with us and he was in my bedroom. So, my grandfather . . . he's the first on my list."

"Have you actually kept a list, besides in your head?"

"I have, every name and place and date. I've hidden it in a place that will be found after I'm dead, and that's when they'll realize."

"You'll be like the Emily Dickinson of serial killers."

He laughed, the genuine laugh, again. "I like you, Lily. I didn't like you at all back when we first met, but now is different."

"Because now you've got me chained in a basement."

"Yes, that's true."

We were both quiet for a moment and I could hear and feel my empty stomach. "I'm hungry, Ethan," I said.

"When I come back, I'll bring some food," he said. "That's what you want to hear, right? That I'm not going to kill you right away. That I'm going to leave you down here and you'll have a chance to get out."

"I suppose so," I said.

"I do need to go soon. For one, I need a change of clothes and to check in with my other life. You understand?"

"I wondered about that. I couldn't find you anywhere and figured that you were going under a different name now."

"I haven't been Ethan Saltz for about six years."

"Who are you now?"

He hesitated briefly, then said, "My name is Robert Charnock. I run a gallery in Philadelphia. I'm married. My wife doesn't mind that I'm gone half the time."

"Your wife?"

"Does that surprise you?"

"Not really. You always struck me as the kind of man who had to have a woman in his life. I'm just surprised you're married."

"She insisted, but I find that I like it. There's a sense of comfort in knowing that I always have someone to have dinner with."

"And she knows nothing about Ethan Saltz?"

"No, why should she? Besides, Ethan Saltz doesn't do much of anything these days. All my wife knows is that she married a successful gallery owner who doesn't like to talk about his past. My Charnock birth certificate is real, by the way, as is my marriage certificate. I'd be worried about being found out, but normal people just aren't that smart. When they get introduced to someone at a cocktail party, they just assume that the name they've been given is a real one."

"And she doesn't suspect anything?"

"No, nothing. I mean, maybe she wonders what I get up to when I go off on my art-scouting trips but, honestly, I'm not sure she cares too much about it. She's got her own life to lead."

"So do you attend teacher training conferences as Robert Charnock, gallery owner?"

"Oh, I have other names as well. One of those is Brad Anderson. He attends the conferences. As I mentioned, he also owns this shitty house that we're in right now. And he has a very convincing driver's license. No birth certificate, but you can't have everything."

I shrugged, trying to look unimpressed, and decided to stop asking questions about how clever he was. Ever since he'd told me he was going to bring me food I was hungrier than ever, but I did want to keep him talking. I said, "You never answered my earlier question. Killing all those women and pinning it on Alan Peralta . . . you did all that just to get back at Martha Ratliff?"

"No, not really. I was annoyed when you pulled Martha away from me, but it was the same level of annoyance I feel when the kitchen at a pricey restaurant cooks my steak wrong. No, the truth is that I spotted Martha on Facebook crowing about getting married and then I saw that her husband was some kind of traveling salesman, and the idea just came to me. You didn't ask me how I got away with so many murders. It's something I've gotten very good at."

"Tell me, Ethan," I said. "How *have* you gotten away with so many murders?"

A corner of his mouth went up, listening to my tone, but then he said, "I disguise them as something else. Make it look like an accident or kill someone who's in the middle of an ugly divorce and it looks like someone else did it. Using Peralta was all about padding my numbers. I figured I could shadow him and kill people he came into contact with, and eventually he'd be nabbed for the crimes. It would wreck Martha's life as well, so two birds . . .

"But then it turned out that Peralta was coming into contact with the type of people easiest to kill, really. Street prostitutes, drunk women at bars. It's been almost too simple, and I keep waiting to see Peralta's ugly mug on the cover of *USA Today*, but *nothing*.

"And then there I was in Saratoga Springs, utterly bored, and who do I see? Lily Kintner, disguised—maybe?—as some kind of slutty teacher, and I knew that you were there to keep an eye on Peralta. It was too good to be true."

"Why was it good?"

He tilted his head back to think. "Because Peralta is boring, and Martha is boring, and I don't really know you, but I don't think you're boring."

"So you went and killed Martha?"

"I wanted to make you pay for poking your nose into my business again. I always thought I should have killed Martha after you took her away from me, back at college. Although then it would have been risky—I would have been a suspect, for sure. But not now. Now I have nothing to do with her or with you or even with Ethan Saltz."

"Did she suffer?"

"God, no. Do I look like a sadist? I'm a collector, Lily. Martha Ratliff is now on my list. That's all that matters." There was a smug look on his face, like he'd just placed the winning bid at an auction.

My mind conjured up a quick image of Martha, her limp body on the floor of her own bedroom in her own home. I pushed the thought aside, knowing that the only thing I could do for Martha at this moment was find a way to kill Ethan.

"So why am I alive?" I said.

"Well, I'm not going to torture you or anything. Maybe I just want to talk with you, get to know you a little bit."

"Okay," I said, then lay back on the cot. "You'll bring me some Advil when you get back, plus some food." I figured that if he wanted to hear me talk, I'd at least get something out of it for myself. I turned and faced the wall and listened as Ethan left the room.

CHAPTER 26

Henry Kimball was in Philadelphia, parked across the street from a building owned by Rebecca Grubb, when his phone rang. The number said it was from Shepaug, Connecticut, and he instantly knew that it was bad news.

"Hello," he said.

"Is this Henry?"

He recognized Lily's mother's voice. "It is. Hi, Sharon. What's going on?"

"Oh, sorry to bother you, Henry, but David thought it would be worth giving you a call and I guess that I agreed with him. Lily's gone missing. She took a walk into town this afternoon and she never returned."

"Did she have her phone with her?"

"No, of course she didn't. I've dialed her number, but she'd left it by the couch in the living room."

"Did you call the police?"

"Well, we did. They were here earlier, and they were helpful, but I'm not sure there's too much they can do right now."

"What time did she take the walk into town?" he said.

"Same time she usually does. Probably around three o'clock. She's usually back by five at the absolute latest."

"And she walks through the woods, usually?"

"I think so. Maybe she's there now. Maybe we should go look for her." Sharon's voice was rising in pitch.

"No, don't go look for her," he said. "The police can do that tomorrow morning, and if the police won't do it, I'll come down, okay?"

"Okay," Sharon said. She sounded scared. Henry felt as though she knew what he did, which was that something bad had happened to Lily.

"You don't think she's taken the train up to see you, then?" she said, as though the idea had just occurred to her.

"Maybe," he said. "If she shows up here, you'll be the first to know, okay? Try to get some sleep, and call me first thing in the morning."

"Thank you, Henry," she said. "You've always been such a good friend."

Henry sat in the car for a moment on the dark street, the phone in his hand. He tried to slow his thoughts down, to think rationally about what might have happened to Lily. If Ethan Saltz had gotten to her in Shepaug—and it sounded as though he had—then he had either killed her and left her, in which case she was probably lying in the woods, or he'd killed her and taken the body with him, in which case she was anywhere. Maybe in some dumpster or in a shallow grave that would never be uncovered. Or maybe he had taken her alive. If it was one of the first two options, then there was nothing much he could do now except make it his goal in life to find Ethan Saltz and make him pay. But if Lily was still alive—and until he knew otherwise, he would make the assumption that she was—then it was crucial that he find Ethan as soon as possible.

The fact that he was already in Philadelphia was a good thing. Before leaving from Cambridge to drive down here Henry had done research into the name that Lily had given him. Robert Charnock, owner of Charnock Gallery. It seemed possible, maybe even probable, that Saltz was Charnock, if for no other reason than the fact that there was so little information about Charnock and so few pictures of him online. He owned a high-end gallery, which would make one think he had a very public presence, but it was clear he avoided exposure. There had been, however, a wedding announcement from six years earlier—Charnock married a woman named

Rebecca Grubb. She, unlike her husband, had a fairly robust online presence. She was a divorcée with two children. She was on the boards of several Philadelphia arts institutions, including the Mütter Museum, and she ran her own charitable organization called SEAP, or Society for the Encouragement of the Arts in Philadelphia. Henry found her address, a house in Rittenhouse Square, one of the tonier parts of Philadelphia.

And that was where he was sitting, on a street of brick town houses that reminded him of Beacon Hill in Boston. His plan had been to sit and watch the front entrance. It was just past eight at night, and he was hoping to catch sight of Charnock coming or going, hoping to get a good enough look at him to see if he really was Ethan Saltz. But now that he'd gotten the phone call from Sharon, everything had changed. He got out of the car and crossed the road, going up the stone steps to Rebecca Grubb's front door.

There was a very old knocker on the door in the shape of a lion's head and he rapped several times, then waited. Just as he was about to knock again, the door opened a crack and a woman peered out from behind the door chain. Her skin had the glossy look of someone who had just removed all her makeup. "Can I help you?" she said.

"Hi, you must be Rebecca Grubb. I'm very sorry for the late call, but I was hoping to speak to your husband."

"Robert's not here right now. What is this about?"

"I'm a private investigator." Henry pushed one of his fake cards—identical to his real card but with a different name—through the crack in the door and she took it but didn't look at it. "I'm employed by someone who has been conned out of a great deal of money, and in my investigation it has become clear that the prime suspect is someone who has also had business dealings with your husband. Sorry for being so vague, but the reason I'm here bothering you is because I thought your husband would like to know as soon as possible that he might be in some financial jeopardy. I tried to find a phone number for him, but . . ."

"Yes, he likes to remain anonymous," Rebecca said. "He's really not here tonight. He's scouting for antiques on the Maine coast."

"Is it possible for you to give me his cell phone number? I really do think he'd like to hear what I have to say."

He watched her think about it. She had a bland but pretty face, her hair pulled back and held with a floral-print headband, and Henry thought that he'd never seen such a smooth forehead on someone who wasn't a child. "I'm sorry," she said, "I don't give out my husband's cell number, but I'm happy to get a message to him from you."

"Do you think he'll be at the gallery tomorrow?"

"Doubtful," she said, "but his schedule changes all the time. Chris Salah will be there, though—he's the one who really runs the gallery. In fact, he's probably a much better person for you to speak with than my husband if it has anything to do with a client of the gallery."

"Great," Henry said. "Chris Salah. I'll check in with him in the morning." He took a step back from the door.

"His phone number is probably on the website," Rebecca said, her voice suddenly friendlier now that Henry was backing away.

"Thank you again, you've been very helpful to someone who knocked on your door in the middle of the night."

"It's not quite the middle of the night," she said.

"How long have you been married to Robert?" Henry said.

She moved her mouth to the side while she thought, then said, "Four years now."

"Was he running a gallery here when you met him?"

"God, no. He was a dealer, though, an art dealer, but it was all online. I'm the one who convinced him to have a gallery. You don't really think he's in financial danger, do you?"

"Please don't worry about it. The person I'm looking into did take quite a lot of money from my client, and then your husband's name showed up as another potential client for this same person. Does your husband like to gamble with his money?"

"With my money, you mean?" she laughed. "No. My husband is only interested in art. I mean, he loves to sell a painting, but unless he leads some kind of secret life, I don't think he's investing in get-rich-quick schemes."

Rebecca didn't seem worried, and Henry thought it was probably because her husband had no access to her own wealth. He could also tell that she'd decided that he was harmless, and for a moment he considered pulling out his phone, showing her the old headshot of Ethan Saltz, then asking if that was her husband. He wasn't sure she'd tell him, though, and he *was* sure that as soon as he did that, she'd become very suspicious, probably warn her husband that someone had come around snooping. He decided he could wait until morning to confirm the identity of Robert Charnock.

"Well, that's good to know," he said. "I'll call on Chris Salah in the morning. You've been very helpful."

Henry had been parked outside of the Charnock Gallery since dawn when a stylish man he assumed was Salah bounded up the steps at ten A.M. and let himself in the front door. During the night he'd managed two fitful hours of sleep in the backseat of his car, then gone to a twenty-four-hour diner for coffee and to use their restroom to clean up.

He knew he would have to act fast if and when Salah arrived. The most important piece of information was whether Robert Charnock was actually Ethan Saltz. If he wasn't, then he needed to go back to the drawing board, also called the internet, and keep looking. But if Charnock was Saltz, then he'd need to find out where he was. Either he had kidnapped Lily, or he had killed her and hidden the body. Henry pushed that latter thought, the most likely scenario, to the back of his brain.

Henry got out of the car and walked across the tree-lined street to the stone steps that led up to the Gothic façade of the gallery. There was a simple sign by the ornate front door that indicated that the Charnock Gallery resided here, and below the sign was a doorbell and a speaker box. He pressed the bell.

A muffled voice came through the speaker box, saying hello.

"I'm looking for either Robert Charnock or Chris Salah," Henry said.

"Did you have an appointment?"

"I'm here on an urgent criminal matter," he said. "I'm a licensed private investigator and Rebecca Grubb told me to come here."

"I'll be right there."

The man who opened the door was about what you'd expect a high-end gallery manager to look like. He was dressed in salmon trousers and a linen-ish jacket in a blue check. He was very slender and had an impeccable haircut. "I'm Chris Salah," he said, as Henry stepped through the opened door. "Is Robert okay?"

"I don't know," Henry said. "I haven't spoken to him. Is there a place we can sit?"

"Sure, sure," he said, and they went down a short hallway tiled in black-and-white and into a cluttered office with two desks, one that sat in a bay window and one that was pushed against the opposite wall. "Robert's not here," Salah said, "so we can sit at his desk."

Henry looked around the small office space. It could have been the offices for an insurance company except that on the largest wall hung an enormous abstract oil painting and on Charnock's desk there was a small ballerina sculpture that looked like it might have been a Degas. Salah must have seen Henry's eyes go to the sculpture and said, "It's a fake, but Robert always says it's the best fake he's ever seen."

"First things," Henry said, and pulled up a photograph on his phone, leaning across the desk to show to Salah. "Can I confirm that this is your boss, Robert Charnock?"

Salah looked at the photograph and frowned, and for a moment Henry thought that he'd just run out of luck. Then Salah said, "About ten years ago, sure."

"Thank you," Henry said, taking a seat across from Salah. "I don't mean to be dramatic, but there's been some confusion about Charnock's real identity, and I wanted to make sure that we are talking about the same man."

"Is he in trouble?" Salah asked, his voice more excited than concerned.

"He isn't," Henry said. "But I do need to locate him as soon as possible. Do you know where he is?"

Salah sighed. "I *think* he's in Maine right now. He travels a lot, going to antique stores and estate sales. It's his absolute passion. I can call him for you if you'd like."

Henry had expected that and said, "No, that's okay. At least not right now. To be honest with you, the fact that you've identified his picture is very helpful. The case I'm looking into is some low-level financial fraud and there was some confusion over whether Robert Charnock was actually the owner of Charnock Gallery. Does the name Ethan Saltz mean anything to you?"

Salah shook his head, but then said, "The name's familiar. He might be one of our buyers. I can check for you."

"That would be great," Henry said.

Salah slid behind his own desk and booted up his laptop that was placed on top of a stack of art books.

"Let me see, let me see," Salah was saying as he punched at his keyboard. "What's the spelling of the name?"

"First name is Ethan, and second name is Saltz. S-A-L-T-Z."

"Huh, nothing," Salah said. "I could have sworn . . ."

"That's okay," Henry said. "It was probably nothing."

"Wait, let me try something else." He clicked some more, then said, "There's an Evan Saltzman in here. That's why that name sounded so familiar."

"Do you know Evan Saltzman?" Henry said.

"I don't. I mean, I recognized the name, but I've never met him. We recently sent him a refund for a painting he returned, which is why the name was familiar. It was a lot of money." Salah laughed.

"Would it be possible for me to get his address?" Henry said.

Salah seemed to hesitate. "Uh," he said. "I'm not sure I should give out that information. I probably shouldn't have given you his name at all."

"Why not?" Henry said. "You sell art, right? I mean, it's not exactly top-secret information."

Henry watched as Salah clenched his teeth slightly, and knew that unless he changed course this conversation was over.

"Listen," Henry said. "You seem like a smart guy, so I'm going to do you a big favor." Salah nodded. "Your boss is potentially in big trouble," Henry continued. "In *real* big trouble. It's a financial scam that he seems to be involved with, and I think he's going to go down with this ship. The question is: Do you want to go down as well?"

Salah pressed a hand to his chest. "I don't know anything about what you're talking about. Seriously, believe me. As far as I know, we just sell art here."

"I believe you, Chris," Henry said, "but that doesn't mean that you won't be implicated. You obviously have access to financial records because you just told me about a cash transaction that went to Evan Saltzman. I just don't think you're going to have plausible deniability."

"Why would I need to have plausible deniability?" he said, his voice rising a little in pitch. "Should I be worried?"

"Well, your boss should be very worried," Henry said, "and you should be a *little* worried. I'm going to be honest with you. There's a third party who is about to give up your boss for financial impropriety. The reason I'm trying to find Robert Charnock—the reason I *need* to find him—is to give him the opportunity to tell his story before this third party does. It's that simple. It's very, very important that I find him, and soon."

"I can call him," Salah said, pulling his phone out from his pants pocket.

"It would be much better," Henry said, "if I could just go find him and speak with him. If you call him, I think he's going to shut down immediately, and that is not going to go well for him. Do you really think he is actually somewhere on the coast of Maine looking for art? Is it possible he's somewhere else?"

"It's possible," Salah said, "but I have no idea. I think you think I have more involvement with this place than I do. I really don't. I just work here."

"Okay, okay," Henry said. "I believe you. But what would be helpful is if you could give me the address for Evan Saltzman that you have on your computer. I'm only asking because it's possible that your boss was once someone named Ethan Saltz and having that address might help us locate him.

"If it helps," Henry added, "I will never reveal that you divulged this information. Right now I just want to find your boss and give him a chance to cooperate before he gets in very big trouble. You'd be doing him a favor."

Henry was watching Salah's eyes and could tell he didn't know what to do. "Maybe if you just excuse yourself for five minutes to use the bathroom," Henry said. "That would work as well."

"Okay," Salah said after a moment. "I actually do need to go and use the bathroom. What's your name again? Did you give me your card?"

"Oh, sorry," Henry said, handing him the fake card that identified him as Ted Lockwood. Salah left the room.

Henry moved fast, sitting down behind Salah's computer. He was staring at some kind of customer database with a number of fields—the customer's name, email address, physical address, place of business, methods of payment, a list of transactions. Salah had left the page for Evan Saltzman up and Henry photographed it with his phone. There was an address, but it was only a post office box in a place called Tohickon, Pennsylvania. He quickly looked at the amount of the most recent transaction—the refund—and saw that it was for $120,000.

Henry stood up just as Salah came back into the room. Salah's face was pale and damp along the hairline, like he'd splashed it with cold water.

Before leaving, Henry said, "Chris, there's no reason for you to believe everything I'm telling you, but you did the right thing this morning. Your boss is a bad man, and you should get away from him. Okay?"

"Am I in trouble?" Salah said.

"No, but you should get your résumé up to date."

Back in the car, Henry set his GPS for Tohickon, Pennsylvania.

CHAPTER 27

After Ethan had left, I used the bedpan, then reclined again on the cot, closed my eyes, and thought.

I'd gotten a good enough look at the chain that was keeping me secured. The cuff around my ankle was secured with a lock, and I wondered if Ethan kept the key to that lock on his person. If he did, it gave me a very slim possibility of escape. He wasn't scared of me, not physically scared, anyway; I'd learned that by how close he'd gotten to me when we'd had our conversation. So, if I could somehow procure a weapon it was possible that I could disable him while still shackled, then get the key and unlock the cuff. But I didn't have a weapon. And the chances were that the key was hanging somewhere in the house, out of reach.

I sat up and took a closer look at the cuff, wondering if there was any wiggle room that would allow me to somehow get my foot free. There wasn't. I could saw my foot off, but I didn't have a saw.

I lay back down, looking up at the water-damaged drop ceiling. I didn't think there was any way out of the situation, not a physical way. My best bet was to try to stay alive as long as possible in the hope that Henry Kimball might figure out where I was. And the way to stay alive was to keep Ethan's interest, keep him talking, keep him entertained. Once I'd made that decision, that my best hope was in delaying the inevitable, I relaxed a little and began to think of other things. I was worried about my parents, who would have reported me missing the night before. My mother would be panic-stricken, and my father would probably already be grieving. He'd told me once that every time I left the house he wondered if I'd return. It was because his own father had left his mother and him when he was young. He'd been a salesman, my grandfather, named Siegfried Kintner, and had left for a trip to the North of England and was never heard from again. "It explains everything about you," I'd said to my father once, when I'd been a freshman at Mather College. "Nothing explains everything about someone, Lil," he'd said.

I thought about my father and mother some more while waiting for Ethan to return. If these were my last hours on this earth, and they probably were, I wasn't planning on wasting them in terror or regret. And I wasn't in the worst possible position. I was alive and I'd found Ethan Saltz. That counted for something, at least temporarily.

Ethan returned at around noon, coming down the basement stairs, humming a tune I recognized as "Manic Monday" by the Bangles. He was carrying a paper bag with him, glanced in my direction, then set the bag on the bar. I was still lying on my back and he might have thought I was sleeping. I listened to him unwrap the bag and then I could smell food and I sat up.

"You're awake," he said.

"You brought lunch?"

"I have a meatball sub and an eggplant parm sub, and I have a ham and cheese."

"They all sound good," I said, "but if you're asking, I'll take the meatball."

He unfolded one of those old television tables and brought it over and put it in front of where I was sitting. As before, he'd gotten close enough to me that I could have touched him if I'd wanted to. I still couldn't imagine a scenario where I could harm him. He had about a hundred pounds on me, and there was nothing I could use for a weapon.

After setting up the table, he went and got the meatball sub and brought it over, putting a plastic bottle of Coke next to it. I resisted the urge to thank him and began to eat.

While I ate, Ethan sat quietly and watched me. It was unnerving, but I tried to ignore it. He'd changed his clothes since I'd last seen him, and he was dressed in soft tan corduroys, a checked shirt, and a blue blazer.

"Where are we?" I said, before taking my last bite of the sub.

"I told you already. A house I own under a different name."

"No, what town?"

"We are in the lovely burg of Tohickon in the state of Pennsylvania. Did you ever think you'd die in such a place?"

I shrugged. "I always thought I'd die in Shepaug, Connecticut, so I guess I'm all right with Tohickon. Where do you plan on dying?"

"Anywhere but here, I suppose," he said, laughing, looking a little confused, as though he were a child who hadn't grasped the basic concept of mortality yet.

"Surrounded by loved ones?" I said.

"As you know, I don't put too much weight on the concept of love."

"Have you ever loved anyone? Did you love your mother?"

"You're trying to needle me, which I understand. I didn't particularly love my mother, but I didn't hate her, either. She was just someone who gave birth to me. People think that connection—the maternal one—is so important, and yet it's so random. We don't get to pick who our parents are, any more than they get to pick their children. We'd all be better off going through this world without having high expectations for the people who share our blood. Don't you agree?"

I genuinely thought about it, then said, "Having high expectations for anyone is a mistake, but I do think family is important. It is to me, I suppose. What else is there, in the end? Our work and our family."

"The most important thing is legacy, leaving one's mark on this world. Leaving something in one's wake."

"I'll be dead then. What will I care?" I said.

He said, "It's nice to think about what people will write about me after I'm gone. I'll have killed a hundred people and gotten away with it, and everyone will be looking for the reason that I did it. Was it his parents? Did something go wrong in his childhood? Was it a sexual thing? And it's none of those."

"You kill people because you can," I said.

He smiled. "See, you get it."

"I've killed people, too," I said.

He tilted his head, still smiling. "Have you? You're not just telling me that because you think it's what I want to hear?"

"No, I'm telling you because it's the truth, and seeing as you're either going to kill me or I'm going to find some way to kill you, it doesn't matter if you know."

"Who have you killed?" he said.

"How old were you when you murdered your grandfather? I know you told me, but I've forgotten."

"I was eleven."

"I was fourteen when I first killed someone. His name was Chet, and he was one of my parents' summer guests, an artist."

"He was a pervert," Ethan said, not asking, and leaned in.

"He *was* a pervert," I said. "He hadn't done anything to me yet, but he was thinking about it. I killed him to protect myself."

"How did you get away with it?"

I told him the whole story, about luring Chet to the well and pushing him in, and how I'd packed up his things to make it look like he'd left our guesthouse. I told the story as truthfully as I could tell it.

"That's quite a story," Ethan said when I'd finished. "Now you're going to tell me how much you enjoyed killing him, right?"

"I didn't," I said. "It was a lot of work, and I'd rather have been reading, to be honest. There's a big difference between us. I've killed people because I don't mind killing. There's probably always been versions of me running throughout history. I'd be the one in the village who was tasked with drowning the bag of kittens when there were too many of them. Someone has to do it, so give the job to the person who isn't skittish. This is a bad example, because I'm not sure I could actually drown kittens, but killing Chet was not a problem for me. I didn't enjoy it, though. I've never enjoyed killing anyone."

"Who else have you killed?"

"I'm tired of talking," I said, hoping to end the conversation while he was still interested in talking with me. "I'm just tired, actually. Maybe I could lie down, and you could tell me about all the people you've killed."

"It's a long list."

"Tell me about some of them. Tell me about the people you killed trying to frame Alan Peralta."

He told me his stories, and I listened. I could feel the joy in his voice, not the joy that he had taken in killing people but the joy he was taking in telling me the details, telling me how clever he had been. I was particularly interested in what he told me about the murder of Nora Johnson down in Fort Myers, Florida, how he'd killed her right next to Alan Peralta.

After he'd spoken for a while, I said, "It seems clear to me that after you killed your grandfather you discovered that you liked it."

"Why do you assume that?"

"Because you've kept doing it, and you kill strangers, people who have done nothing to you, or, presumably, the world. It's obviously something you like."

He lowered his brows a little and I thought he was thinking about what I'd just said, as though it had never really occurred to him. "I do enjoy killing people," he said at last. "I'm not a psychopath, though. I don't love to see blood spurt from people and hear screams or things like that. I just like it as a game. It's hunting, I suppose."

"You don't think hunters get off on the act of killing?"

"Hunters are sick people. They're playing a game that is far too easy. When I kill someone, I'm compelled to do it in a way that will ensure I never get caught. Do you know how hard that is?"

"I do," I said, as I lay back down on top of the cot. I really was tired, but I was also thinking that it made sense to fade out of the conversation while I still had Ethan's interest.

"Killing is hard, but you know that."

"It doesn't make it an accomplishment," I said.

"You weren't proud of what you'd done to that pervert when you were fourteen?"

I thought about it. "I was happy, but no, I wasn't proud."

"You'd done something special."

"Not really. It was murder, and that's not particularly special, and it's not particularly rare, either. Not in the history of our species. Or any species."

"It is rare when it's done well."

"Getting away with murder doesn't make it special," I said. "Besides, it's clear that you eventually want to get caught in some way. That's why you've made your list."

"I think it will be of interest."

"Where did you put it?"

He didn't say anything immediately, and I turned my head slightly. "Do you think there's a chance I'm going to get out of here?"

"What do you mean?"

"You hesitated about telling me where you hid your list."

"I didn't want to hide it in too secure a place. I have a hollowed-out copy of a book in my office library at my house in Philadelphia. It's in there. Every name, date, and place. It will be found."

"What book did you choose?"

"*The Stories of John Cheever.*"

"So you are like a hunter, after all. You want heads on your wall eventually. You want people to know what you did."

He didn't say anything immediately, so I said, "There's nothing wrong with that."

"It is a kind of art, isn't it?"

I propped myself up on an elbow. "Killing?"

"Sure," he said. "Why not?"

"That sounds a little delusional," I said. "Art adds something to the world."

"What about all the great art there is about death? I'm sure you're a fan of Artemisia Gentileschi? *Judith Slaying Holofernes*?"

"But that actually is art," I said. "What you're doing, and what I did to Chet, that was just butchering, really. Getting away with it doesn't make it art. It might make you smart, or clever, but that's all it is."

Ethan was quiet, and I wondered if I'd gone too far, if he was going to get up and come over and slit my throat. I closed my eyes and accepted that possibility.

"We can't control other people's opinions," he said at last. "I suspect that when people know what I've done there will be varying takes on it." He sounded resigned, almost.

"I'm not sure the takes will be as varying as you think they are, but never mind. You're good at what you do, and you also enjoy it. I suppose that's the recipe for happiness as a human being."

"I do want to hear more about you, Lily," he said. "More about people you've killed."

"I'm tired," I said. "I'll tell you later."

"You're stalling for time. Do you think there's someone out there who might rescue you? Who have you told about me?"

"I haven't told anyone," I said. "But, yes, I'm stalling. I'm obviously a missing persons case at this point. Maybe someone saw you stalking me in Shepaug. Maybe someone here saw you take me from the trunk and bring me into the house. I don't know. Maybe you're about to get caught anyway, for something else you did. Stalling is my only option."

"Plus, you want to live as long as possible."

"I suppose I do. Live to see another food delivery, at least."

"I might be able to do better than a meatball sub," Ethan said, and in my peripheral vision I saw him stand and walk away from me.

CHAPTER 28

Tohickon, as far as Henry could tell, consisted of a post office, one school, one library, one gas station with a convenience store attached, one covered bridge, and one bar near it called the Covered Bridge Bar. He drove slowly down its streets and roads, past split-level houses and the occasional Victorian. The cars parked in front of these houses were American-made and a few years old, for the most part. Several houses had multiple cars in front of them, including old junkers on concrete blocks in front yards.

On the drive from Philadelphia, Henry, realizing he should have asked this earlier, called Chris Salah at the gallery.

"Chris, it's Ted Lockwood again. One more thing that I should have asked you. What kind of car does Charnock drive?"

"Oh, it's a beauty," Chris said. "A Jaguar. Vintage, I think, with two doors. He loves that car more than he loves his wife."

"What color is it?"

"It's green. A greeny-gray, I suppose. Or a gray-green. It's very sporty."

So as Henry drove slowly down the rutted roads of Tohickon, peering at houses and driveways, he was looking for gray-green Jaguars, even though what he was seeing was a lot of single-car garages. He imagined that if Ethan/Robert owned a house in this town, he might keep the Jaguar out of sight.

At just before noon, Henry parked in the town center across from the Covered Bridge Bar, hoping it would be open for lunch. He stared at the map of Tohickon he'd pulled up on his phone and thought he'd driven down just about every street in town. He was surprised, somehow, that no one had noticed and called the cops on him, but then again, it was a cold gray Saturday and Tohickon did feel like a ghost town.

He'd been putting off calling Lily's parents all morning but decided that he needed to do it now. He called the number Sharon had called him from the night before, and after two rings she picked up.

"Sharon, hi, it's Henry Kimball," he said. "Any news?"

"She's gone, Henry. The police have been through the woods and everything and there's no sign of her. David's beside himself. I just can't imagine where she would have gone without telling us first."

"So, the police have been helpful?"

"Well, they haven't found her, but they *are* looking. She hasn't gotten in touch with you?"

"She hasn't," Henry said.

"Okay," she said, and sighed. "I'll tell the police that. They asked if she had a boyfriend, and I told them about you."

"Oh," he said, about to add that he wasn't her boyfriend, but he didn't think it mattered. "I'll call you if I hear anything from her," he said. "And you'll do the same?"

"I will," she said.

After the phone call, Henry sat in the car. His bones felt empty, like they knew already that Lily was dead. He stayed in the car, not particularly hungry but keeping an eye on the bar across the street. He was out of options and decided it was time to start interviewing residents. At noon he saw a figure move in front of the plate-glass door, flipping a sign to say they were now open for business.

The inside was cheerier than he thought it would be. Wood-paneled walls, a horseshoe-shaped bar, and several booths with high backs and cushioned seats. He took a seat at the bar. Above the bottles was a faded painting of Tohickon's covered bridge. He looked around and saw that covered bridges, paintings of them anyway, and a few replicas, were the central design theme. An older woman with short gray hair asked him what he'd liked to drink.

"Do you have fresh coffee?" he said.

"I don't right now, hon, but if you're willing to wait ten minutes, I can make some."

He said he was and she disappeared through a swinging door. While she was gone, the front door opened and a lone man entered. He was large and had a florid face and sat three stools away from Henry, making puffing sounds as he settled onto his stool. When the bartender came back out, she spotted him and went immediately to the refrigerator under the bar and grabbed a bottle of Coors Light.

"How are you, Norman?" she said, uncapping the bottle and placing it down in front of him.

"Still feels like winter out there. I thought someone had said something about spring."

He sipped at his beer. The bartender said, "Juan made chili this morning if you're interested, so that might warm you up." She placed a lowball glass on the bar next to the Coors Light and added a shot of Jameson's to it.

"Ah, thank you, Mo," Norman said.

Mo disappeared through the swinging doors again and returned with Henry's cup of coffee, placing it in front of him. "You're a life-saver," he said, then asked if he could get a shot of Jameson's on the side as well.

"Do you need a menu?" Mo said, after pouring him his shot.

"Sure, I'll look at one."

Henry looked at the menu and ordered the chili. When Mo brought it five minutes later, he was ready with his cell phone out, the picture of Ethan Saltz.

"I'm actually in town looking for someone," he said to her. "I was hoping you could help."

"Sure," she said, and he held the phone out to her. She leaned in close, squinting.

"Yeah, I know him. He comes in here sometimes. But I don't know anything about him."

"When was the last time you saw him?" Henry said, surprised his voice sounded as calm as it did.

Mo frowned, her chin wrinkling. "Don't know exactly, but not recently. Like I said, it's not that I know him, but his face is familiar. He comes in here. Try Norman," she said, looking over at the man three stools down.

Norman had already been listening to the conversation, and when Henry turned to him, he held his hand out for the phone. Henry handed it over.

"Hmm," Norman said. "I think he told me his name was Brad Something. Nice guy. Hasn't been in here too recent, though, like Mo said." He handed the phone back, reaching his arm out very slowly as though it hurt him to move.

"Can I ask you some questions?" Henry said, moving his chili and coffee down and changing stools to be closer to him.

"Sure," Norman said. "But can I ask you why you're asking?"

"It's complicated, plus a little boring," Henry said. "I'm a private investigator and it's possible that the man in the picture, that Brad, has been involved in a financial scheme. By involved, it looks as though he's a victim and not a perpetrator. My client wants me to find him and it's turning out to be harder than I thought it would be."

"Well, you've come this far. He must have an address here in Tohickon."

"All my client knows is that he lives here, but, no, I don't have an address, and I'm having no luck with real estate records in locating him. You never knew his last name?"

"He introduced himself as Brad. Clearly that's not the name you have, or you wouldn't be grilling me about it."

Henry sipped his coffee, now laced with Irish whiskey. "I have limited information, that's for sure. You're the first lead I've gotten."

"I'm not going to be much help to you, I'm afraid. He's come in here for lunch before, just like you're doing now. And he's sat at the bar and the two of us talked, again, just like you and I are doing, and the only reason I remember his name was Brad was because he told it to me and I recalled thinking that he looked a little like Brad Pitt, you know, strong jaw, blue eyes. So the name stuck with me."

"Did he tell you anything about what he did or where he lived here in town?"

While the man thought, he moved his fingers on the surface of the bar like he was playing a piano. "Said he was an art collector and told me he had property here in town, but the way he said it made it sound like he didn't really live here."

"Okay," Henry said. "You've been helpful."

"What's your name again?"

"Ted Lockwood. Let me get you a card." He thumbed out another one of his fake private investigator cards. It was his last one.

"I'm Norman Hart."

"Let me buy you a drink, Norman," Henry said, catching Mo's eye.

Mo uncapped another bottle of beer and poured another short whiskey.

"If you were me, Norman," Henry said, "where would you go looking for this man's house here in Tohickon?"

"I suppose you could just knock on every door. There's only about three hundred houses in this whole town. But if you didn't want to do that, I suppose you could look for a fancy car out front of a house."

"Brad drove a fancy car?"

"Yeah, sorry I didn't mention that before. I saw it once parked in front of this bar. A Jaguar XJ and if I recall correctly, the year was 1976. It was a beaut. He told me how he only took it out for special occasions."

"It probably wouldn't be out in front of his house," Henry said. "Probably in a garage."

"Probably," Norman said. "Or under a tarp."

"Right," Henry said. Norman took a small sip of his whiskey

and then a small sip of his beer, then excused himself. He slid off his stool gracefully, like someone with a lot of practice. Henry's mind spun, excited to confirm that Saltz did live in this town, at least some of the time, but also thinking about what Norman had just said about protecting a car with a tarp. Driving around this morning, he'd seen so many different cars parked outside of houses, but it felt as though he'd seen a few that had been covered. He closed his eyes and replayed the drive, trying to shut out the Steely Dan song that was playing through the loudspeakers. And suddenly he remembered one of the covered cars, in front of a modest shingled house at the end of a quiet road. There were a couple of cars in front of it and one of them was under a black plastic tarp. For whatever reason, he'd just thought it was someone's project, probably a fixer-upper that had sat out the winter months, but what if it had been the Jaguar?

CHAPTER 29

Ethan had driven into Philadelphia in the Jaguar, not planning on seeing Rebecca just yet, but wanting to check in on the gallery and Chris. There were a few specific things he had to do at his desk—a belated call to an artist they would no longer be representing, a number of emails he hadn't answered—but mostly he needed a moment of calm. Kidnapping Lily Kintner and holding her at his Tohickon house felt like a triumph. But it was also risky. He needed to think about his next moves.

Chris was in the office when he walked in, and Ethan thought he must have been looking at porn or something on his computer, because he physically jumped when Ethan said hello.

"Everything okay, Chris?" he said.

"Yeah, yeah. Just didn't expect you and you scared the crap out of me."

"I'm not here long, but I'm finally going to pull the plug on Dennis Maxwell."

"Oh, thank fucking god. I've already had to talk to him twice this morning."

"I'll call him and let him know we're not moving forward with him. What else is going on around here?"

Chris made a weird show of turning his eyes to the ceiling as though thinking about it, then finally said how quiet it had been. He was lying, of course, and Ethan stared at him for a little longer than usual, just to make him uncomfortable, wondering exactly what he was hiding. It could be something harmless—Ethan knew, for instance, that Chris had been fucking one of the framers, a married guy who drove over every few weeks from

Delaware, and that they'd been doing it here in the gallery. But it could be something else.

"Has anyone come around looking for me?" Ethan said.

Again Chris made a show of thinking about it, then said that he didn't think so. He really was a terrible liar.

"Okay, fine," Ethan said. "Do you mind leaving the office while I call Maxwell?"

After Chris left and shut the door behind him, Ethan sat at his desk and thought for a moment. He knew that Lily was working hard at delaying the inevitable. He assumed it was just a natural instinct, the desire to stay alive as long as possible, and the hope that maybe someone would figure out where she was if enough time elapsed. But there was another possibility. Did she have a partner, someone who had helped her to figure out that he'd been responsible for the Alan Peralta murders? There was a chance, of course, that she did. But so what? Even if this other person knew the name Ethan Saltz there was no way that Ethan Saltz could be connected to Robert Charnock or to Brad Anderson. Still, he wondered. He knew he'd been careful, but even the most careful people make mistakes. And it wasn't as though he'd changed the way he looked or anything. There were a few photographs floating around on the internet of Ethan Saltz, although he'd made sure that Robert Charnock was never—or hardly ever—photographed in public.

He got up from his Herman Miller chair and left the office. There was a small kitchenette down the hall, and that was where he found Chris, making his chai tea.

"Hey, Chris," Ethan said. "I'm going to ask you again: Anyone been here looking for me?"

Chris's jaw dropped just a little and he took a deep breath and said, "Oh god, Robert. I'm so sorry. He told me not to tell you."

"Who told you?"

"It was this guy, this private investigator. He came around and told me that you're part of a financial scam or something. I told him nothing. I mean, there's nothing to tell him, right? And it seemed entirely possible that he had the wrong guy from the start, because he kept mentioning some other name."

"What other name?"

"Um, it was Evan Saltz. No, that's not right. Ethan Saltz."

"We have a client named Evan Saltzman," Ethan said, trying to keep his rage under control. "Was that who he was looking for?"

"No, no. The name was different."

"But you didn't tell him anything, did you?"

"No, of course not, Robert. Nothing important, anyway. I mean, I did say that the name of Ethan Saltz was familiar because we had a client with a similar name, but of course I didn't give him any information. I'm not stupid, Robert."

"What else did he ask?"

"That's it. It was no big deal, really, but he did say you were in trouble. Financial trouble."

Ethan took a deep breath. "Did he give you his name?"

"Yeah, yeah." Chris dug into the front pocket of his trousers and pulled out a card, handing it over to him. Ethan read it: *Ted Lockwood, Private Investigator*. Then a phone number and an email. No mailing address.

"What did he look like?"

"I don't know. A normal white guy. Thin. Messy hair. Looked like he hadn't slept for a couple of days."

"What was he wearing?"

"Pretty basic Levi's, I think. A light blue oxford shirt and a jacket that was probably a Harris tweed."

"Okay, Chris. If I find out you're holding out on me—"

"I'm not, Robert, I swear. He freaked me out, though. I mean, are we in trouble?" Chris was whispering. "Should I be worried?"

"No, don't worry. I think I know who this guy is, and he's just a pest. Don't worry at all."

Ethan imagined taking two steps across the linoleum and twisting Chris Salah's head so that he was facing the opposite direction, but then he told himself there'd be time to deal with Salah later. Right now he needed to get back to Tohickon. Before leaving, he told Chris to take the rest of the day off, and to not talk to any more people about gallery business.

He hit traffic leaving Philadelphia and tried to keep his rage in check. He'd been foolish keeping Lily alive as long as he had, and now there was someone else to worry about. A moving truck pulled out in front of him just as he was going to catch the tail end of a green light, and Ethan howled in his car. Martha Ratliff's face loomed in his mind. In some ways she was to blame for the shit show that was coming down on him now. Lily Kintner, too, but he'd be able to take care of her soon. If only he'd make it through this fucking light.

An hour later he parked outside of the Tohickon house. It wasn't dusk yet, but it felt like it, inky clouds blocking out the afternoon sun. For some reason, he hadn't quite figured out yet how exactly he was going to kill Lily Kintner. The easiest way would be to hit her again with a tranquilizer dart, and then he could just smother her with a pillow. He did know what he planned on doing with her body. Even though the house had a finished basement, one section of it had a dirt floor, a walled-off pantry through a door at the back of the basement. It was at most about ten-foot-by-ten-foot, unused shelving lining the walls. He'd already dug a grave, knowing one day that he might have use for it.

Sitting in his car for a little while longer, Ethan wondered why he'd waited this long to kill Lily. He wasn't squeamish about what he had do, but the truth was he wanted to spend a little more time with her, talk with her some more about killing people, about morality. He'd never met anyone like her before. Even if she was lying to him about her past, he still hadn't met anyone willing to lie about such things. And for one moment Ethan felt as though he knew what it might be like to be in love with someone. Not that he was in love with Lily. But he knew what the feeling was, an anticipation in seeing them again, in hearing their voice. A desire to prolong the time spent with them.

It was like a sudden, unpleasant glimpse into normal life. Was this how people lived? Waiting around for other people to provide feelings for them? He laughed out loud in his car, the sound of it almost startling him. Had he gone temporarily insane?

Fuck it, he thought, and made a decision to kill Lily Kintner with his hands. He was twice her size, and she was shackled to the floor. It would feel good to take her long slender throat and squeeze the life out of it.

He walked around to the back of the house and retrieved the key he hid under one of those fake rocks. He stepped into the house, feeling right away that something was a little off. The air was too still. It meant nothing, though; he'd had that kind of feeling before. But when he opened the door that led down the carpeted stairs to the basement, the feeling continued; the house was quiet, like there was no life in it. He walked down the stairs, hitting the switch along the way that lit up the fluorescent ceiling lights. As soon as he got down there, he saw that he had been right about there being something wrong. Lily was still on the cot, wrapped in her sheets, perfectly still. Her head was at an unnatural angle, and her mouth hung open. He moved halfway to her and saw the blood that lined her throat and pooled beneath her head.

CHAPTER 30

After Ethan Saltz had brought me lunch, then spoken at length about his accomplishments, all I had wanted to do was sleep. But he'd left me alone again, and I knew that I needed to at least explore every possibility of escape, however slim. I started with the cot that I was lying on. The frame was metal, and the musty mattress was filled with stuffing, no springs or anything like that. I slid down to the foot of the bed and stood up. I was still in the clothes that I'd been wearing when I walked into the Shepaug town center a hundred years ago. My shoes were still on my feet.

I took steps in every direction to see how far I could get. There was a framed print on the wall that was just out of my reach. It was a pop art illustration of a topless woman with short black hair and a black puma creeping around behind her. I could almost touch the edge of its white frame with a fingertip. Not that having access to the picture would be helpful. I could throw it at Saltz when he came back, but even if I managed to knock him out or hurt him, how would that help me?

What would be helpful was the nail that was probably holding up the print. I looked at the portion of the wall that I could reach. It was painted a deep maroon, heavily patched here and there where spackle had been used to cover up holes. I ran my hands along the surface, wondering if there were weak spots where I could punch through the plasterboard. Again, not sure how that would help me.

But my hand did detect a slight protrusion on the wall. I touched my finger to it and realized that it was a nail head, flush with the wall, that had been painted over. I scraped away at the paint and was able to uncover one edge, managing to slide a fingernail underneath it. I pulled at the nail head and my fingernail ripped. I shook my hand and tiny flecks of blood covered me and the wall. I put my finger in my mouth and with my other hand, searched my pockets. I was wearing jeans and there was a small pocket inside the larger one on the front right side. Inside was a single dime.

It took me about a minute, but using the dime I was finally able to extract the long thin nail from the wall. It was about an inch and a half and the tip wasn't exactly super-sharp, but it wasn't dull, either. I lay back down on the cot, no longer sleepy, my mind forming a plan. I took long deep breaths while experimenting with different ways of holding the nail. I put it between my index and middle fingers and closed my fist. I tried gripping the head using my thumb, and jabbed at my own thigh to see if I could get any purchase with the nail. I got some, but it wasn't great, so I used the nail to rip a strip away from the bedsheet, and looped the strip through my fingers, tightening it so that the fabric held my fingers together the way brass knuckles would. Then I slid the head of the nail between my fingers, making a fist and adjusting the nail so that the taut fabric held it in place. I jabbed at my thigh again, and the fabric made all the difference, the nail tip puncturing my jeans and pricking at my skin. I reached down and felt blood slowly sleeping into the denim.

I had my weapon. Now I needed a way to ensure that Saltz would get close enough to me so that I'd have a chance to use it.

I looked at my finger, still sleeping blood, then swiped it across my neck, probably leaving just a small streak. But if I was going to get Saltz to come close enough to me to find out if I was still alive, then I was going to need a lot more blood.

I thought about simply puncturing a small wound near my carotid artery. If I did it right, it would produce enough blood to make it look as though I'd cut my own throat and was lying dead on the cot. If I did it wrong, then I would actually be lying dead on the cot. I thought of cutting at my forearm, trying to hit one of the arteries, but even if it produced enough blood, what I really wanted to do was get that blood all over my neck area. I wanted Saltz to lean right over me, to look me in my eye. I wanted a shot at his carotid artery.

Then I thought of my ear. I had a fuzzy memory of a party my freshman year at Mather College when one of my three roommates—I think it was the goth version of Winona Ryder—got drunk and tried to pierce her own ear using one of the blades from a Swiss Army knife. She'd started to bleed, and it just hadn't stopped, so one of my other roommates, the one who looked like a preppy version of Winona Ryder (all three of my roommates oddly looked like Winona Ryder), had almost called an ambulance after the blood had completely soaked through several paper towels. We finally taped a tampon to my roommate's ear and eventually the bleeding stopped. My takeaway from that awful party had been that ears bleed a lot. I didn't know if that was a universal truth, or if it only applied to goth Winona Ryder, but it was time to find out.

I pulled down the lobe of my left ear with my left hand. I had never had my ears pierced, not being a fan of jewelry. I punched the tip of the nail through the lobe, pushing hard enough to break the skin and hurt my finger that was bracing the lobe from behind. Some blood trickled out, and I turned my whole body to the right so that it would run down the side of my neck. I needed the blood to be visible and I hoped it would look like I had somehow managed to slit my own throat. I felt the blood move across my skin, but there wasn't a lot of it, and it stopped before reaching the hollow of my throat. I held my ear again with my left hand, and this time after I pierced the skin with the nail I ripped at my ear. It hurt and tears pricked at my eyes, but I could feel the blood flowing more freely, and when I turned my head it rolled across my neck and began to drip onto the sheet under my head. After about a minute the blood slowed, so I reached up with my hand and pulled down my ear so the wound opened up more. My ear throbbed, but the feel of the warm blood tracing a line under my jaw and along my neck was strangely satisfying. I had made something happen.

When the wound had clotted, I licked my fingers and cleaned the blood from my ear. I wanted it to look like I had a fatal wound, not to look like I deliberately punctured my ear. I settled onto my back, turning my head slightly toward the stairwell, and covered my right hand, the one with the nail, half under part of the sheet. Then I waited.

It felt like two hours, but eventually I heard the creak of footsteps above me. I took several deep breaths, then listened to the sound of the basement door opening, the same footsteps now coming down the stairs, white light filling the basement. After blinking several times, I let my chin fall open, then stared blankly at the drop ceiling above me. I wanted to look dead. It worked, because I heard Saltz gasp, then race across the carpeted floor to get to me. He did exactly what I wanted him to do, leaning over me, studying me for signs of life.

I swung my fist and hit him in the temple. He reared back and slapped his hand to the bleeding wound. There was a slight smile on his face, as though he were pleased that I was fighting back. I hit him again, and this time it was perfect, punching him right up under his square jaw. When I pulled my hand away a small stream of blood sprayed out of the wound. The smile left Ethan Saltz's face. I thought he'd instantly try to stop the bleeding, but instead he wrapped his hands around my throat and started to squeeze. "Fucking bitch," he said as I watched the blood start to sheet down his neck and under his collar. I don't think he immediately realized that I'd punctured an artery, and by the time he pulled a hand away from my throat and grabbed at the wound, it was too late. His face was white, and he fell backward into a sitting position, one hand grasping at my shoulder to keep himself upright.

"You're going to die, Ethan," I said, my throat raspy.

Blood was coursing through his fingers, and he let go of me and fell to the floor, his head thumping against it. I sat up on the bed and we looked at each other. I'd already thought about this moment, thought about having a chance to say something to him, so I said it now.

"When I get out of here, Ethan, I'm going to go to your house and find your list of homicides and I'm going to burn it. No one will know what you did. No one."

Who knows if he heard me or comprehended what I was saying, but I like to think that he did.

CHAPTER 31

Just before dusk Henry drove through town one more time. He hadn't heard from Lily's mother, which meant that Lily hadn't been found, and even if she was somehow still alive, he didn't think she'd survive another night with Ethan Saltz or Robert Charnock, whatever name he was going by.

Still, he drove. There wasn't really any choice in the matter.

Earlier, after leaving the Covered Bridge Bar, he'd found the house where he thought he'd seen the car under the tarp, but maybe he'd remembered wrong, because there was only a Kia parked out front. Well, either he was wrong or someone was using the other car. It was getting dark, so he decided to take one more look at that particular house, slowing down along the street in front of the property. There were no streetlamps, but there was enough light left in the sky for Henry to see that there were now two vehicles out front. He parked, cutting the engine, then removed his snubnosed .38 revolver from the glove compartment. He got out of the car and slid the gun into his jacket pocket. When he got to the driveway he saw that one of the cars was definitely a vintage Jaguar. He removed the gun, told himself to breathe, and went to try the front door. He was scared, but the fear was more about the fate of Lily than the presence of Saltz. The door was locked.

He thought of ringing the bell or knocking but decided to look at the back of the house first. He went around the garage, along some crumbling paving stones. A motion-sensor light flicked on and Henry's heart seemed to stop for a moment. But he kept walking, turning the corner to see that one of the ground-floor windows was lit with interior light. He found the back door and tried the door-knob. It was unlocked.

Inside of the house he could hear nothing. He was in a back mudroom with open doors on either side. Peering through one door, he could make out what looked like a dining room. The other door led to a back hall. Henry took out his phone and hit the flashlight function. The first step he took down the now-illuminated hall produced a creak from the floorboard. He stopped moving, then heard a voice yell out, "Hello?"

"It's the police," he said in what he hoped was a confident voice.

"Down here," came the voice back, and he knew it was Lily.

He sped down the hallway. An open door led to a set of basement stairs, light coming from below. "Lily?" he shouted down.

"Henry, I'm down here. It's safe."

Still holding his gun in front of him, he descended into a finished basement flooded with harsh light. When he reached the bottom step, Lily said, "I'm over here."

He turned. She was sitting on a cot against the far wall. She was soaked in blood, half her face entirely coated. There was a man on the floor in front of her, also covered in blood, but he wasn't moving.

"Is he dead?" Henry said, still holding his gun.

"He is." Lily actually smiled. It looked ghoulish, that smile, something Henry would remember for the rest of his life.

He put the gun back in his jacket pocket and moved over to her, getting a better look at the man on the beige carpet. "Ethan Saltz?" he said.

"Yes. I can't believe you found us."

"He was going by the name of Robert Charnock," Henry said. "I think I found you too late."

"No," Lily said. "You were right on time." She kicked out her leg and he saw that she was chained at the ankle. "The key's not on him. I've checked. I thought I was going to starve to death down here while he rotted on the floor."

"Jesus," Henry said, more of an exhale than a word. And then he took the first real deep breath he'd taken since coming down the basement stairs, his nostrils filling with the smell of blood.

Lily, seeing Henry go pale, quickly said, "It's all okay now. Let's find the key to these cuffs and get out of here."

CHAPTER 32

Henry found the key hanging on a hook near the basement stairs. After I was unshackled, we sat together and made a plan. Then we searched for a place to put Saltz's body. There was a large pantry through a flimsy door in the basement. It was musty inside, with old shelving on the walls, and a dirt floor that looked like it had once been covered with cement that had given way to roots and frost heaves. There was a plastic tarp on the floor and when I moved it, I found that a grave had already been dug about three feet deep. On the shelves were bags of calcium oxide.

"That was for me, I guess," I said.

Seeing what was going to be my permanent resting place made my stomach turn. I told Henry I was going to go upstairs and use the bathroom. While I was up there I tried to be sick. The bathroom was cheaply outfitted but clean, and the medicine cabinet was full of products, soap and Q-tips and ibuprofen. I washed my face in the sink, then stripped off all my clothes and stepped into the shower and scrubbed my whole body clean. Then I dried off and wrapped the towel I used around me. I found a box of Band-Aids plus a tube of antibiotic cream and worked on my ear for a while. I took four ibuprofen, swallowing them with water directly from the tap.

In the kitchen I found a large garbage bag and put my clothes in it, then I went upstairs to the second floor. The room where it looked as though Ethan Saltz occasionally slept had a similar feel to the downstairs bathroom. Cheap furnishings but neat. The single bed was made and there were a few paperback novels on the bedside table. Old stuff. A V. C. Andrews book. Stephen King's *It*. Underneath the books was a copy of *New York* magazine. I flipped through it and found an article with Saltz's byline. It was called "A Teenage Guru in Terlingua, Texas." I suspected there were other relics from Saltz's past throughout this house, but I wasn't particularly interested in finding them.

I looked through his closet and found a pair of old skinny jeans plus a flannel shirt, and pulled them on. They were too big for me, but they'd do.

I returned to the basement and found that Henry had already dragged Saltz's body into the hole. He saw me in my new outfit, holding the garbage bag containing my clothes, and said, "Shower feel good?"

"You have no idea."

We added my clothes to the grave, plus the sheets from the cot and the shackles that had crusted blood on them, then covered everything with the quicklime. I found a bottle of bleach and we cleaned up the rest of the basement as best we could. On a worktable I found the bag I'd taken with me when I'd gone into the Shepaug town center. In it was the granola my mother liked, plus my wallet and house keys.

"We should really cement over this floor, and that way he'll never be found," Henry said.

"I'm not too worried about it," I said. "He'll be found eventually, but I don't think it will be for a long time. And when they find him, I don't think they'll make a connection with either Ethan Saltz or with Robert Charnock. Maybe they will, but I don't think it will matter much at that point. And there'll never be a connection to either of us."

"It'll be a mystery," Henry said.

We did put the tarp back over the floor and both of us stood and looked at it for a moment. "Any last words?" Henry said.

"Good riddance to bad rubbish."

Henry said, "At least he dug his own grave for us."

"That's true." Neither of us immediately moved, and I said, "Got a limerick for the occasion?"

Henry thought for a moment then said, "There once was a killer named Ethan, who murdered without a good reason. Now he's dead in a hole, both the man and his soul, having excreted his final excretion."

I didn't say anything right away, and Henry said, "The excretion is the blood."

"No, I got it. I liked it. You do have a real talent."

Henry smiled, but when I took his hand in mine I could feel that it was trembling.

Before leaving, we went through the entire house, wiping any spots where we might have left prints. Then we locked the house behind us, and Henry said, "We should drive the Jaguar back to Philadelphia and park it. When they start looking for Charnock they'll also be looking for his car. Can you drive a manual?"

I told him I could and followed him back to Philadelphia. Henry kept to the exact speed limit the whole way. It was just before dawn, the sky beginning to fill with streaks of pale orange light, and there were not a lot of cars on the road. We left the Jaguar about a quarter mile from the gallery, wiped clean and unlocked. I threw the keys in a dumpster.

After getting back in Henry's car, I said, "There's one last thing I have to do."

"What's that?"

"Ethan Saltz made a list of everyone he killed. He kept it in a fake book in his library and he told me which book. I need to get that list."

"Why?"

"He kept that list in the hopes that someone would find it after he died. He wanted to be famous, to be known as one of the most prolific serial killers in history. That was his real dream."

"So why do you need to get it first?"

"Because I promised him I'd burn it, make sure that no one ever knew his name."

"You promised him that?"

"It was when he was dying," I said.

Henry paused, then said, "Do you think it matters?"

"What?"

"Do you think it matters if you keep that promise, I mean. He's dead now. Maybe it's enough that he died thinking he'd never be remembered."

"No, it matters," I said. "I know it's risky and stupid, but I want to get that book. I made a promise."

"Okay," Henry said.

We found a twenty-four-hour diner and got ourselves big breakfasts, then Henry left me there alone, and I found a newspaper on the diner counter, bringing it back to my booth to read. He was gone for a little over an hour, and when he came back he told me that he'd seen Rebecca, Ethan's wife, leave the brownstone, and that he'd used one of his picks to unlock the low-entry door that had been built into the side of the steps just below street level.

"Do you think you tripped an alarm?"

"I waited twenty minutes and no police arrived, so no. But when you go in there I wouldn't linger."

I got a to-go bag of sandwiches from the diner, figuring it couldn't hurt to look like a food delivery person, and went straight to Saltz's house and through the door that had probably, once upon a time, been a servants' entrance. I emerged into a kitchen with a stone floor and a butcher-block table and shouted hello into the house just to make sure I was the only one there. No one shouted back.

Moving quickly, I went up three sets of stairs and found Ethan's study, happy that it wasn't locked. One entire wall was a built-in bookshelf and I began to scan the spines, then realized that the books were strictly alphabetized by author. I found the Cheever book, recognizable by its red spine, and opened it up, finding the small cutout where Saltz had made a hiding space. Inside was a sheet of paper, folded up, and what looked like an old metal toy soldier. I left the soldier and took the list.

Henry drove me back to Shepaug. Along the way we stopped at a shopping complex that had a Marshalls, where I bought underwear, a pair of jeans, and a cotton sweater. We threw Saltz's clothes in another dumpster.

Back in the car, maybe knowing that we were only two towns away from my parents' house, Henry didn't immediately start the engine. He turned and said, "What are you going to tell your parents?"

"I haven't exactly figured it out yet, but I think the easiest thing to tell them is that I ran off to meet someone, that it was a mistake, and that you came and rescued me. If I make it about a romance, somehow, they'll ask fewer questions."

"They've involved the police."

"I know. We'll just tell them it was all a big mistake. It'll be a mess, but it will pass."

"And what are you going to do with the list? Are you going to burn it?"

"I won't burn it, no, but I'll make sure no one else ever sees it."

"Wouldn't it be better if it did end up with the police? It could help close the files on some cases, and maybe it would console some grieving families."

"I've thought of that," I said, "but I don't want Ethan Saltz to win. He was truly evil, just a mistake of nature, I think. The people who got killed by him might as well have been struck by lightning. Does that make sense?"

"I guess so."

"And it's not my job to do the police's work for them."

"I don't know," he said. "Right now I'm just glad you managed to kill him before he killed you."

"I keep thinking that, too, but if I'm honest, I was ready to die. It would have been worth it."

"What do you mean?"

"Like I said, he was evil. If I'd died trying to stop him, then it still would have been the right thing to do."

"You think so?" Henry said.

"I do."

Before pulling out of the shopping complex, Henry asked to look at the list. I'd already read through it myself and handed it over.

"He numbered it," he said.

"Yes, he did."

He was quiet for a moment while he read, then gave it back, saying, "I think someone's missing."

"Josie Nixon's name, the woman who died in Shepaug."

"Right. Maybe she was actually a suicide."

"Maybe," I said.

ALAN

F all was usually Alan's least busy time of year. Schools and universities had just started their new semesters and professional development was on the back burner. But there was an annual technology conference in Ann Arbor, Michigan, during the third weekend of October that he'd attended before, and when he'd been sent an invitation to be an exhibitor again, he'd decided to attend. It would be the first conference he'd been to since Martha, his wife, had passed.

He arranged to have his wares shipped to the conference center and hotel where ArborTech was being held, then had flown in a day early to set up. It felt surreal to be working again, back in the saddle as though nothing had really changed. He'd spent the whole summer dealing with the wreckage left behind by his wife's death. He'd endured numerous police interviews, some of which made Alan feel as though he were somehow a suspect in the killing, despite the fact that he'd been in Saratoga Springs when the incident had taken place. He'd turned down several requests for press interviews, although he'd naturally followed the story himself. It was the second home-invasion death within a year in Portsmouth, the first happening on the other side of town, an elderly woman living alone whose house had, unlike Alan and Martha's, been robbed. Down deep, Alan knew that what happened to his own wife had nothing to do with what had happened to Jean Leonard in the Colonial Pines Neighborhood.

People had told Alan not to make any big life decisions until a year after the death, but he knew he couldn't stay in the same house in which Martha had died so violently. He'd put it on the market at a very competitive price and sold it within days, moving into a furnished town house south of Portland in the town of Hampton. He'd left Gilbert behind with a cat-loving neighbor, feeling a little guilty, but Gilbert had belonged to Martha, not him.

And he'd moved on with his life.

After setting up his booth in the exhibitors' hall, Alan left the conference center and hotel to take a walk. He now remembered why he liked this particular conference. It was held downtown but adjacent to a large city park. It was a cold day, and unlike in New England, it seemed as though all the trees in Michigan were already bare. The park was covered with desiccated leaves the color of rust and the low sky was an ominous gray. Alan, after walking for less than half an hour, turned around and headed back to the warmth of the hotel.

His brief marriage to Martha now seemed like a distant memory. He'd been alone for a long time and then he wasn't and now he was alone again. It had always been an experiment, his marriage, a way to test out a different kind of life. His first marriage had been a disaster. His mother had warned him at the time, pulling him aside a month before the wedding to tell him that Angelina had the mark of a whore. He hadn't listened to her then, but she'd been right, of course, Angelina leaving after he laid down the law about how she should act in their bedroom. She'd given him ideas, Angelina. Lots of women had, but he didn't expect that from a wife.

The truth was he'd always had bad thoughts. But he had good thoughts as well, plenty of those, and he told himself that the good thoughts evened out the bad thoughts. That was why he'd decided that he could marry again, because Martha only gave him good thoughts. He loved her, and wanted to protect her, and he even wanted to make love to her, to touch her physically. Sometimes she made him say bad things into her ear, but mostly it was fine. The good evened out the bad.

When he was on the road, he was a different man. He knew

that, but convinced himself that the man on the road had nothing to do with the man who was married to Martha Ratliff and lived in a nice house in New Hampshire. It was like that ad campaign for Las Vegas—*What happens in Vegas stays in Vegas*—but his Vegas was all the time he spent away from home. It worked for a while, the Vegas motto. On the road he let himself feel hungry, he let the feelings build up and build up, and then he would find a woman. He always found one, sooner or later, because the world was full of dirty little whores. All you had to do was go looking for them. Sometimes you didn't even have to look. They'd come and find you.

That was what had happened with Josie Nixon. He didn't like to think about her too much, but he had to, sometimes, because what happened with her had changed his life forever. There was *before* Josie Nixon, and there was *after* Josie Nixon, and there was no way to get back to the *before*.

He had spotted her right away during registration, at the conference at Shepaug University. She was wearing a blood-red dress that showed a lot of cleavage. He guessed that the word for her was gothic, but there was also something literary about her look, like she had come straight from Edgar Allan Poe's sex dreams. Her makeup was dark against very pale skin. There were tattoos on her exposed calves.

They met the next night when he spotted her alone on a couch. He'd seen her earlier, actually, weaving her way from the bar, a glass of red wine in her hand. He could tell by the way she was walking that she was drunk. Then he lost track of her, wondering if she'd gone out to eat somewhere in the small Connecticut town, or if maybe she was already spreading her legs for some man. He was about to leave when he spotted her on one of the couches that lined the walls of the hall where the conference was being held. He sat down next to her, the cheap plastic cushion making a sound like a groan. He told her the story he used on his trips, how he was married but it was passionless, and she told him how she was happily married but that she had sex with other people. She made it sound like a normal thing to do.

It was funny, thinking back to that time, and remembering that on the night he went to Josie's room, he almost hadn't gone. She'd invited him, told him she had some things to do first and for him to show up at midnight. Told him to knock three times on the door. If the conference had been held in a city, then maybe Alan would have gone out onto the streets to look for someone else—girls leaving bars, girls selling themselves for drug money—but the conference was at a rural campus. Where was Alan supposed to go? So, at midnight he knocked on Josie Nixon's door just as she'd told him to. She'd opened the door and there she was, stark-naked. She had tattoos over her entire body (*Mark of the whore*, his mother's voice said in his head) and one nipple was pierced. Her smile was so big that he was a little afraid of her teeth. He should have turned around and left, but he didn't.

Afterward, she told him that she'd had fun even though he hadn't really performed properly. She told him she liked what he did with his hands. And then she said, hesitating before she said it, "I suspect that your problem is that you're scared of sexually confident women. Most men are, you know."

He laughed as though she'd said something funny, said "probably."

"Don't worry about it," she said.

"What are you scared of?" he asked, just wanting to change the subject.

"I'm not scared of anything," she said, then laughed, and added, "No, that's such a lie. I'm terrified of heights. I don't even like being this high up in this dorm room."

"You know this room has a balcony?"

"Like that wasn't the first fucking thing I noticed when I got here."

"Let's step out there," he said.

"Are you crazy?"

"It's a beautiful night. I was out on my balcony earlier and you can see all the stars. We'll go for half a minute. You'll be conquering your fears, and then afterward maybe I'll try conquering my fears of sexually confident women." He worried that he'd said those last three words with a little too much sarcasm and anger, but she didn't seem to notice. The rest of what happened was a disjointed blur. Eventually she agreed to step out on the balcony. When they were out there, his arms around her waist, she closed her eyes, spreading out her arms to feel the humid night air. Alan didn't know for sure if he'd brought her out there to throw over the side or if he decided to do it at the last minute. All he knew was that he lifted her and then she was tumbling over the edge of the balcony, a strange, pinched scream in her throat.

After that night, the world went topsy-turvy. He tried to forget what he'd done, but it kept coming back to him in the waking hours of nighttime. Sometimes when he thought about it he was sick to his stomach. And sometimes it made him harder than he'd been since he was a teenager. It evened out.

In Florida he'd gotten drunk at another hotel bar and wound up in a car in the parking lot next to a woman, unzipping his fly, telling him he was a bad boy (*he was, he was*). And the next thing he knew she was struggling, flailing out with her arms, and someone in the backseat had something around her neck. He watched the whole thing happen. He thought he did, anyway. It was another confusing moment, too much alcohol in his bloodstream, confused about what time it was, voices in his head. Maybe it had never happened at all. No, he didn't think that. It happened. And after the girl was dead, the man in the back seat said, "Easy, there, friend. You better run now." He remembered it well, that other voice. And mostly he believed it was real. It was only sometimes that he thought maybe he'd been the one who strangled her.

All Alan really knew was that he had somehow manifested her

death. He might not have been the one choking her, but he'd made it happen.

He'd brought death into his world and now it was eating everything up.

He knew these thoughts were crazy. He knew that. But what other explanation could there be? There was before Josie Nixon and after Josie Nixon, and there was no going back to the before. When he found out that Martha had been killed in their own bedroom, he hadn't even been surprised. It confirmed everything he'd already known. A monster had risen up the night he threw Josie Nixon off that balcony. And that monster was in charge.

Back in his hotel room in Ann Arbor, he lay down on top of the covers and kept thinking about it, thinking about how death had come into his life and changed everything. Maybe he shouldn't have come on this trip. Maybe it was too soon. At the town house in Hampton he hadn't had so many of these thoughts.

But the following day Alan put on his suit pants and suit jacket and went down and manned his booth. The morning was slow, a trickle of teachers and administrators glancing toward his table, not wanting to commit and really look at what he had, but by lunch there was a big crowd and he sold around five hundred dollars' worth of merchandise. The remainder of the day flew by, Alan's mind free of all the junk that he'd been thinking about the night before.

That night he felt even better. He walked to a brewpub and had a decent dinner, inadvertently sitting next to a table of attendees from the same conference, two men and two women. One of the women was wearing a skirt that came to mid-thigh, and when she slid back into her booth after returning from the bathroom her skirt had slid up and Alan could see her white dimpled thigh. She wasn't that pretty, weak chin, limp hair, probably a lifetime nerd who now taught computer science at some regional tech school, but the way she kept crossing and uncrossing her legs made Alan think she was most likely up for it, and he might just be . . .

Suddenly she was tugging down her skirt and looking over at him accusingly and their eyes met and Alan turned away, feeling a red flush move up his neck. He paid up and left the brewpub, wandering for a while, looking for a different kind of bar, maybe one where the women weren't so stuck-up. He eventually did find a college bar, sat at a small booth to the back, drinking stouts and watching the college girls. Those girls were definitely up for it, practically begging for it, but not one of them even looked his way.

Back at the conference hotel he thought of getting one last beer at the bar, but as he was walking across the lobby carpet he stumbled a little and had to stop. "You okay?" a woman asked, and took hold of his arm.

"Yeah, yeah," he said.

He made it up to the seventh floor to his room but couldn't find his key card anywhere. So he went all the way back down to the lobby to get a new one. By the time he was finally in his hotel room, his mind was fuzzy and the room was gently spinning. He took his shoes off, but that was all he removed before climbing onto his bed and falling into a hole of sleep.

The voices—or maybe it was only one voice—didn't wake him up, but the hand on his face did. At first it was tapping gently, and he thought it might be Martha telling him he'd overslept, or Gilbert wanting to be fed, but then it felt as though he'd been slapped. Lightly, but still a slap. His eyes opened.

She was straddling him on the bed, a pale woman in a tight dark winter hat. "Hi, Alan," she said.

"Who are you?" His voice sounded gummy in his own ears.

"You don't know me. I was a friend of your wife's from a long time ago."

His eyes were closing again, and the woman held him by his cheeks and shook his head until he said, "How did you . . . ?"

"I just need to ask you a few questions, okay, Alan?"

"Okay," he said, suddenly happy to answer questions. It was a dream, obviously, what was happening, and he wasn't scared of dreams. He was relaxed, floating.

"Do you remember Josie Nixon?" the woman said. She was pale, all right, and her breath, so close to his, didn't smell of anything. There was something familiar about her, but only a little. Maybe he'd dreamt of her before.

"Are you a ghost?" Alan said.

"If you'd like," she said, and Alan was pleased that she said that. It was a friendly dream he was having. "I'm a ghost that wants to know about Josie Nixon."

"I didn't mean to hurt her," Alan said.

"But you did, you did hurt her."

"I threw her off a balcony."

"Why did you do that? Do you remember?"

He did remember, but the words weren't moving very well from his head to his mouth. Eventually he said, "I don't know."

"That's okay," the ghost said. "We all have our reasons."

"Why are you here?" Alan said.

"I'm here to kill you."

He knew her words should be scary, but somehow he wasn't frightened when she said them. Maybe because it was all a dream. Or maybe because he wasn't scared of death. Maybe he hadn't been scared of death for a while now.

"How are you going to do it?" he said.

"That's up to you. You do know there's a balcony in this hotel room, don't you?"

"It was the first thing I saw," Alan said. And now the words were coming out of his mouth without having to think about them first. They were flowing.

The ghost helped him off the bed—it was easier than he thought it would be—and she brought him out to the balcony.

Alan could hear the wind but couldn't really feel it. "So many stars," he said.

The ghost helped him over the balcony railing—it wasn't easy—but he lowered himself down onto the narrow lip of concrete just on the other side of the rail. Now he could feel the wind. It was cold, but it was also soft. She touched his shoulder, but he turned around and said, "No, I don't need your help."

"Are you sure?"

"I'm a grown man. I can do this on my own."

It was the first time he saw her smile, her teeth like little moons. And then, without any help from her, he stepped into the quiet, yielding air.

ACKNOWLEDGMENTS

Angus Cargill, Mireya Chiriboga, Caspian Dennis, Danielle Dieterich, Emily Fisher, Kaitlin Harri, Patricia Highsmith, Jennifer Gunter King, Stephen King, Jenny Lewis, Jessica Lyons, Libby Marshall, Tara McEvoy, Robert Riordan, Anne Sexton, Josh Smith, Nat Sobel, Virginia Stanley, Liate Stehlik, Keith Stillman, Sandy Violette, Lexie von Zedlitz, Judith Weber, Jessica Williams, Phoebe Williams, and Charlene Sawyer.